BAD CHEMISTRY

Richard Lowell

Bad Chemistry

Richard Lowell

Quarky Media

Boulder Colorado

Bad Chemistry

Published by Quarky Media, PO Box 3332, Boulder, CO
80307

ISBN: 978-0-9973131-1-6 (ebook)
ISBN: 978-0-9973131-0-9 (print)

For Lesley who helps and inspires me.

To - Carly

Richard Lowell Smith

Prologue

The man is excited about living out one of his fantasies. He's in the office of a large barn and the window he's looking out has just the view he wants since he can see the porch of the house and also the path leading up to it. He's waiting for his housekeeper/mistress to come down the path. He took her shoes from her but he figures she'll still be coming.

What fun this will be!

It's six o'clock but he doesn't know when she'll come so he decides to stay the whole evening.

Another hour goes by and he sees her coming down the path. He says to himself, "The little bitch is wearing my boots!"

She enters the house and the man has to decide how long to wait before he goes in.

He has a large fish-cleaning knife in a leather case on his belt and he has a dart gun used for paralyzing animals. He paid a lot of money for the dart gun on the Internet. He feels the handle of the knife and chuckles. He sharpened it himself so he knows it's sharp enough to shave with. He can't wait to see the look on their faces when he enters.

It's time.

He leaves the barn and strides to the house. The door is never locked. It's his rule.

He tiptoes down the hall and stops outside a bedroom, giddy with anticipation.

He bursts in. "Did you really think you could get away with this?"

The young woman and the young man are locked in a naked embrace.

The young man's jaw drops. "Oh boss, I can expla--"

A paralyzing dart hits him before he can finish his sentence.

The man takes out his knife and the young woman screams and runs for the door but the man catches her and drags her back to the bed.

"Please, *Señor*, we are in love!"

She screams.

There's a lot of blood.

Chapter 1

Loren Sharp had a problem. He had a problem because his old friend and boss Ted "Silk" Benson had a problem. Silk had called and told him to come over to his office.

Loren, a widower, was a Senior Research Chemist in the Agricultural Chemicals Section of the Organic Chemicals Division of Marchem Industries and had been there for almost twenty years. He had joined Marchem just after getting his Ph.D. in chemistry from the University of Wisconsin. He was forty-six, of average height and had dark brown hair peppered with gray.

Loren walked over from his laboratory through a tunnel connecting the research center and the administration building. The tunnel was painted a sickly yellow and no matter how often they fixed the roof, there were always readily apparent watermarks on the walls. Long ago management had murals painted on the walls but apparently somebody didn't like them. So before one of the stockholders meetings they were painted over. Strangely, crickets liked the tunnels. He wondered how they expected to attract lady crickets in the tunnels and how such small insects could make so much noise.

At Silk's office he greeted his secretary. "Hi Rosie,

you called?" She was a strawberry blonde. She was not very attractive but always very well groomed and had a vivacious personality. She dressed young for her age and had a nice if somewhat sexy wardrobe. Today she had on a red suit with a white silk blouse.

For a brief moment Loren remembered the time when he and Rose had been close. She and Loren were in the same building for five years and dated a bit after Loren's wife, Gwen, died. When Rose was transferred to the administration building things cooled off. But he thought she still had warm feelings for him.

"How are the kids, Loren?" asked Rose. He had two adult children, a daughter and a son.

He smiled at her. "Ann is still in graduate school in physics. She'll graduate soon. Bill is having a hard time adjusting to his mother's death."

"Is he working?"

"Not yet," he said. "He may go back to college."

Silk exited his office and said, "I need to talk to you, Loren." He seemed irritated. He was tall and thin. He wore wire frame glasses and his brown hair was straight and parted in the middle

Loren and Silk entered Silk's office together. A sickening, sweet odor pervaded the office and Loren decided his cologne or aftershave was to blame.

Silk sat down at his desk and Loren sat across from him. Loren had been in his office before but not in a while. Not much had changed, same desk, credenza, couch, Picasso prints and pictures of wife, son and daughter. The office had a nice window with a view of a grassy hill. The furniture was modern in style and functional. Silk had a new computer, however, and a puzzle-like screen saver was in operation.

Almost as puzzling as Silk. What was this about?

Silk wore a pin stripe vest with no coat, a light blue shirt and a flowered tie. His pinstriped suit coat was hanging on a coat rack in the corner.

It was quite a change from earlier days when he wore jeans and a lab coat. Back then everybody knew Benson was headed for bigger things. His presentations to management were smooth as silk. He knew all the buzz-words. If his research left something to be desired, he made it sound like Nobel stuff.

Loren had given him his nickname "Silk" after one of his especially smooth presentations by saying, "Wow. Ted, that was smooth as silk." Everybody picked up on it and Benson didn't seem to mind. In fact, he seemed to like it.

"Hi, Silk," Loren said. "How's it going?" The two men had shared a laboratory early in their careers. It was clear from Silk's expression that he no longer thought that the nickname was appropriate.

"Fine. How's the family?"

"As well as can be expected."

Benson didn't waste any more time. It was clear he had something on his mind. "Look Loren, I have a problem." There was a pause.

It had been a long time since Benson had asked for his help. "And you think I can help?"

"I've been told you're friendly with Wolfgang Reitz."

Loren was surprised. "I had lunch with him once in a while and we talked, but I wouldn't say we were friends." He didn't think Wolfgang could be a problem since he'd always gotten along with him.

"Do you think you could talk to him?"

"I suppose. About what?"

Benson handed him a paper. "Read it."

Dr. Benson:

I do not believe that you are aware that I am the true inventor of Martox. I can assure you that this is true. Furthermore, I wish to inform you that the manufacturing process that I have developed is flawed and if there is an attempt to use it, not only will it not work, but it presents a grave danger to anyone in the vicinity.

Only I have the key to this situation and will only reveal the solution to it if I am given the recognition, personal and monetary, which I deserve. This is not an idle threat.

Sincerely yours,

Wolfgang Reitz, Ph. D.

Loren finished reading and gave Benson an incredulous look. "Do you take this seriously?"

Benson almost shouted, "You know what the man is like. Do you?"

"Well, I never thought of Wolfy as a kidder. I thought of him as a serious scientist."

"You call him Wolfy?"

Loren said, "Well, it's a name he picked up when he first got here. Joe Ferguson started it. Wolfgang, Wolfy, seemed to like it. I guess it made it seem like he fit in. For an émigré German it made him more comfortable. "

"Did he help develop the Martox process?" said Benson. "Doesn't Joe Ferguson have the patent?" His face showed confusion.

"As far as I recall Wolfy may have made a

contribution," Loren said. "He definitely knows the process. But it's been repeated hundreds of times with no problems."

Benson pounded his desk. "Then what the hell is he talking about?" His face turned very red. His eyes bugged out of his head.

Loren shrugged. He couldn't believe there was a problem with the process. "I have no idea."

"I want you to go see him."

He wasn't sure he liked Ted Benson anymore. "God damn it. I was hired to do research for this company not to chase after some nutty German. Why me?"

"I've checked around and you seem to be the one who knows him best."

He shook his head. "I only had lunch with him a few times and we only talked occasionally."

"Lor," Benson put out his hands, palms up. "You know how important Martox is to the corporation. If we don't commercialize this product we're in big trouble."

Loren smiled. "Not to mention your career."

Benson nodded. "Okay, that's true." His voice seemed to be pleading, "I want you to do this. I won't forget it. I'll make it up to you."

"Okay, okay. But I don't even know where he lives."

"I've talked to personnel. He moved after he retired." Benson handed him a copy of the letter and a piece of paper with Wolfgang's address.

He took the paper and said, "I don't know how to handle this." He was very unhappy with this assignment.

Benson smiled rather weakly. "Do the best you can. A lot is riding on this."

Loren shook his head. "You owe me one. But I'll do

the best I can," he said as he left the office.

He was upset as he walked back through the tunnel. The whole Wolfy situation was very unusual. Grave danger? He had never heard of such a problem.

He decided he better go see Wolfgang.

Soon.

Loren couldn't get his mind on anything but his future talk with Wolfgang so he left work at three thirty p.m.

Wolfgang had moved from Webster Groves, a St. Louis suburb, out west to Eureka. It was usually a thirty-minute drive from Newton and Loren had hoped to beat the traffic but there was an accident on Highway 44 and things were slow.

As Loren sat in traffic, he thought about Wolfgang. On his first day Ted Benson had escorted him around the building. In Loren's lab Benson introduced Wolfgang and the two men shook hands.

"It's nice to meet you," Wolfgang said. "My English is not very good yet. It will improve I hope."

"Wolfgang is an expert on phosphorus chemistry," Benson said. "He should fit into our work quite well." Wolfgang moved into a laboratory three doors down the hall from Loren's lab.

A few days later Loren went into the instrument room to run an infrared spectrum.

There was only one IR spectrometer and Wolfgang was using it. "I'll be done in a few minutes," he said.

When the scan was finished, Loren started his scan, "I don't get much information from IR, but I run one anyway."

Wolfgang said, "I can get a lot from IR. Maybe I can

help you interpret your results. It's one of my specialties."
Loren did find Wolfgang very helpful.

One day Loren was eating lunch alone in the company
cafeteria when Wolfgang came up with his tray and asked if
he could join him. After that they had lunch together two or
three times a month. Loren found him to be an interesting
person.

Back on the highway, thankfully, the weather was
warm and dry for early April. Loren had promised his
friend Gloria that he would be over at six o'clock. He hated
to be late. In fact he often arrived early to functions.

The hotshot drivers were going in and out of traffic
trying to gain some advantage. The Eureka exit was coming
up so he tried to inch over to the right. He made it but was
barely missed by a pickup in a big hurry to get home for the
cocktail hour. He slowed and got off.

Wolfgang's new house was only half a mile off the
freeway and he made it by four fifteen. White stucco. It sort
of fit Wolfgang. Loren could see the corner of a big fence
around the back. Also fit. He parked right in front of the
house and rang the bell. It took three rings but was finally
answered by Ilse, Wolfgang's wife.

"Ya, what do you want?" she said.

"Ilse, don't you recognize me?" he said. He'd met
her at a few parties quite a long time ago. Wolfgang had
taken her along to events when they had first arrived from
Germany but then he started coming alone and then quit
coming.

"Ya, Loren Sharp. What do you want?"

"Is Wolfgang available?"

"He is in his laboratory. He does not like to be
bothered."

"Would you ask him if he would see me?"

"Just go in back and ask him yourself. I am not his servant." Ilse escorted Loren through the house and set him free in the back yard.

A six-foot fence topped with barbed wire surrounded the yard. The fence was mostly covered with ivy or Clematis. It looked like the plan was to eventually cover the whole fence. A one-story cinder block building connected the sections of fence. The yard would be a lush garden of roses and other beautiful flowers but it was not yet in bloom. He thought it seemed very incongruous to mix flowers with barbed wire.

The door to the building had a sign, *Wolfen Chemical Co. NO ADMITTANCE*. He decided to knock anyway.

After three knocks with long silences between them Wolfgang opened the door and squinted at the sunlight. His face was contorted as though he were mad. He was a tall thin man with white hair and his most prominent features were his bushy eyebrows and his bulbous nose.

"Ya, who is it?" he said angrily.

"Loren Sharp."

Wolfgang smiled. "Loren! How nice to see you. Come in."

Loren entered and his jaw dropped. The room was a chemistry laboratory that had all the equipment necessary to do modern chemical research, fume hoods, nuclear magnetic resonance, gas liquid chromatography, infrared, the works. It contained maybe three hundred thousand dollars' worth of equipment. There was also a desk piled high with journals and papers.

"Wolfy, how did you manage all of this?"

"I spent most of my retirement money equipping this."

"I'm impressed. What are you doing here?"

Wolfy's mood and manner suddenly changed. "Why do you want to know?"

Loren shrugged. "Just conversation."

"Why are you here?" Wolfy asked.

"I wanted to see you and I thought maybe you could shed some light on this." Loren showed him a copy of the letter he'd sent to Benson.

He took on a threatening look. "So you are here spying on me. I might haf known. Go back and tell Benson I am serious and he better do as I say."

Loren shook his head. "Come on, you're not serious."

"I am very serious and I think you should leave now."

"What do you hope to gain by this, Wolfy?"

"Get out, Loren!"

Loren decided that his anger was real and there was no point in continuing the conversation. "Okay. I don't know what you think you can gain by this but I am leaving."

"Go. Go now!"

Loren left through the house that now seemed, for all intents, empty.

He thought, Wow, that was not what I expected. I thought he'd be cordial. He's gone off the deep end.

The traffic was slow but moving. Loren tried to drive carefully. Gee, he thought, I hope I can get to Gloria's before six. He was looking forward to seeing her.

Chapter 2

Traffic was not as bad as Loren had feared so he arrived at Gloria's front door at five fifty p.m. She lived in a midtown St. Louis condo. Not bad but not upscale. He rang the bell and she opened the door.

"Loren, you always arrive early," she said, smiling. "Some people think that's rude."

"Well, I know, but the traffic was not too bad," he said, smiling back. "I could go and sit in my car for a while if you are not ready."

She laughed. "No, no come in." She was blonde, average height and wore no makeup. She was quite attractive but she preferred to project a businesslike image.

Her living room was an office. It had a desk piled high with papers, a metal file cabinet and a computer. There were also some comfortable chairs and a sofa.

They walked through the living room to the kitchen and sat down at the kitchen table. In contrast to the living room/office, the kitchen was very neat and tidy.

He'd known Gloria Stevens for about five years, since before his wife died.

Gloria, a divorcee, had been a patent attorney at Marchem and had written some of Loren's patent applications. He liked her from the moment he met her. She made him laugh and she laughed at his jokes. He had to invite her to meet his wife Gwen. Gwen had liked her too and they'd started to double date.

Two years ago Gloria decided to start a private practice that appeared to be doing okay. He lost track of her for a while until she showed up at Gwen's funeral. After that it seemed only natural that he start seeing her. Were they friends or lovers? It was not clear.

"What kind of day did you have?" he asked.

She smiled. "A good day. Two new clients."

He was pleased. "Great. What kind of cases?"

"A trust and a divorce."

"I didn't know you did divorces." He was surprised.

"I just started. After all, I'm experienced," Gloria said, laughing. "How about a glass of wine?"

"Oh, I brought some. I forgot it in my car. I'll get it." He prided himself on his knowledge of wines. He had roomed with a French student in college who was an expert. Michel was always bringing wine, which he shared with Loren, into the fraternity house. It could have gotten them in trouble with the school authorities but they were never caught. After graduation he'd kept up his interest in wines and preferred French wines. He went to his car and brought in a nice bordeaux that he had laid down several years earlier.

He opened it dramatically. He poured out two glasses and they both sniffed and sipped.

"Very good wine, Thank you," Gloria said. "What did you do today?"

He shook his head, "Very unusual day. Silk Benson called me to his office."

"What did he want?" she asked.

"Well, he had a problem. Do you remember Wolfgang Reitz?"

"Yes, I had some contacts with him."

He recounted his experiences with Benson and Wolfgang.

She shook her head. "Martox is very important to the company. Silk must have been climbing the walls."

"Yes, I'd say so."

"Do you take this seriously? Could something be wrong with the process?"

"Wolfgang is not a kidder," he said.

"But, that process has been repeated hundreds of times. Right? You told me so."

"True.".

"Well, what do you think?"

Loren shrugged, "I honestly don't know."

"Of course this is extortion."

"We can hardly have him arrested. If what he says is true there is a lot to lose."

"Keep me informed," she said.

He nodded. "Of course."

She changed the subject. "What's new with Ann Lauren?"

He shrugged and said, "You know she got her degree?"
She nodded.

"Bill and I went out to her graduation and we took her and a bunch of her friends out to dinner. It was fun."

Gloria smiled. "You told me."

"Other than that, nothing."

"I'm sorry to hear it," she said. "I hope she gets a break soon."

Bad Chemistry

Loren's daughter Ann Lauren had just been granted a Ph.D. in physics after spending several years working very hard. Now she had been looking for an academic job and nothing doing. The government cancellation of the superconducting supercollider a while back didn't help. America was no longer the leader in high energy physics. He was upset about it. He thought maybe she should try industry.

"Let's eat," she said. She could be a gourmet cook when she wanted to be but seldom bothered anymore. This night they had pepperoni pizza but it was homemade and quite good. No dessert. Too many calories.

After dinner she popped some popcorn and they watched a movie on HBO. It was nine o'clock when the movie ended.

"I guess Bill will be home by now," Loren said.

"Oh yes, Bill. What's happening with him?"

"He's still struggling."

"You should tell that boy, man, to get a job."

"He's still getting over his mother's death."

"When will he be over it? It's been over a year."

He shrugged. That was a good question. "I don't know. I have to go." He didn't like discussing Bill's situation.

"Okay. Let me know what is happening with Wolfgang and the threat."

"Okay," he said. "Bye." Loren was always confused when he left Gloria. He wanted to kiss her but he thought she might not like it and it would ruin their friendship.

He drove home feeling quite unsettled. It was usually so when he had been with Gloria.

Bill was not home. He was worried about him. He had a hard time getting to sleep

Chapter 3

Detective Lieutenant Douglas Sanderson didn't like Captain Joe O'Brien. Supposedly opposites attract. Not this time. They were both members of the Police Force and O'Brien was the boss, but Sanderson had connections.

O'Brien had called Sanderson to his office and he got right to the point, "Sanderson, you do not fit my image of a cop." The office was very plain with just a desk, three chairs and a file cabinet.

"How so?" asked Doug.

"Those tailored suits and the Porsche do not create the right impression. People could think you are on the take."

"Well, I am who I am. Do you have issues with my work?"

"No, you do a good job, but we need to be above suspicion."

"I am above suspicion. And I solve more murders than any other cop in town."

O'Brien shook his head. "I can see this is getting nowhere." Joe O'Brien was a classic cop. His father was a cop and so was his grandfather. He was of medium height and stocky with male pattern baldness. Not handsome but not ugly either. He started as a beat cop and rose to captain over twenty-five years on the force. He was now fifty. He had no ambitions or prospects of rising further.

Douglas Sanderson's late father was a prominent and wealthy attorney. He was active in politics and knew a lot of people in government. He never ran for public office himself, preferring to be king maker rather than king. He had a profound influence on the career of the present mayor of the city.

Doug was interested in the law from an early age. He was president of a junior police auxiliary when he was a teen and he tried a year of law school but found it too tame. He zipped through the police academy and joined the force at the tender age of twenty two. He rose rapidly through the ranks both from his skill and through his father's influence. There was a lot of resentment aimed at him in the force but he actually deserved every promotion he got.

O'Brien knew he was an insightful and ingenious police officer but he refused to acknowledge it. Was he jealous?

With his father's death, Doug split an estate worth many millions with his sister who was married to a dentist and lived in San Jose. He didn't have to work but he loved police work.

"Do you think you could tell me what you are currently working on?" said O'Brien sarcastically.

Doug grinned. "I usually take my Aunt Mavis' car for its emission control test and when I asked her recently, she said she didn't need it done because she had the paper. Her friend had given it to her. Her friend's maid had gotten it somewhere."

"Your Aunt Mavis?" O'Brien shook his head, "This is police business?"

"Yes," he said. "She had mentioned, while sitting under the hair dryer at the beauty parlor, she didn't like the hassle of getting an emission test for her car so she had her nephew do it for her. The friend said she never did that anymore because she could get her an approved form without a test. I told her that's illegal and she better not do it. I've been looking into it"

O'Brien shook his head some more, "That's interesting but do you think you could find time do some of the unit's official business?"

Doug nodded. "Of course. I'm always ready to do that."

"I'm glad to hear it. I want you to investigate a suspicious death. A chemist out in Eureka was found dead on the floor of his lab. "

O'Brien handed Doug a piece of paper, "Here's the address. There are a couple of uniforms on the scene."

Doug nodded, "Okay, I'll check it out."

The address O'Brien gave Doug was in Eureka, a few miles down I-44 from St. Louis. *So O'Brien doesn't like my car. That's too bad. I like it very much.*

A pickup truck suddenly cut in front of the Porsche, causing him to decelerate. If another car had been following closely behind him, there would have been a collision. He took a mental note of the license plate number of the pickup. He thought he just might look up the driver. Maybe the driver had some outstanding tickets or summonses and he would love to make him pay.

Doug reached the Eureka exit and left the highway. He had no trouble finding the house. He'd looked it up before he had left.

A squad car was parked in front with a uniformed policeman standing next to it. The uniform was a man named Mike Unruh who knew and liked him. Doug generally got along better with the rank and file than he did with the bosses.

"Hello, lieutenant, long time no see," said Mike.

"Hi, Mike. I haven't gotten out this way in quite a while. What have we got here?"

"Follow me," Mike said. He led Doug through a fence gate at the side of the house into a back yard that seemed like a miniature botanical garden with many rose bushes and other plants. It would really be beautiful when all the plants were in bloom.

A sign on the door of a large garage read: *Wolfen Chemical Co. NO ADMITTANCE.* Yellow police tape honeycombed the door: *Crime Scene. Authorized personnel only.* Mike opened the door, took down the tape and the two men entered the garage.

Lying curled up on the floor was the body of an elderly gentleman. The face and hands had a strange bluish color. The body was dressed casually in jeans and a work shirt. Doug had seen his share of dead bodies but never had seen this kind of skin coloration. It didn't seem to indicate an accident. He felt a twinge of pity when he wondered if the victim had suffered.

Mike said, "He's Wolfgang Reitz."

"What do we know about him?" Doug asked.

"Some kind of scientist," Mike said.

Doug was familiar with laboratory layouts from many visits to the forensic lab. "Hmm, seems like a pretty complete chemical lab. Any hazardous chemicals found near the body?"

Mike shrugged. "We haven't moved anything."

So not an accident. "Who found the body?" Doug asked.

"The wife, Ilse. She said he didn't come in for dinner so she went out to check on him and found him like this."

"I have to talk to her," said Doug.

Mike shook his head. "She said she was going to take a sedative and go to bed so I guess you will have to wait till another time."

Not good. But if she was already asleep, there was nothing he could do. "Okay, did she say anything else?"

"She said he was visited late this afternoon by a Loren Sharp, a colleague at Marchem Company," said Mike.

"Was this Reitz alive when Sharp left?"

Mike shrugged again. "Not sure."

"I'll have to talk to him," Doug said. "I assume you called for the coroner and CSI."

"Sure, they should be here any minute."

"I won't wait," Doug said. "Tell them to send me their report."

As it was after eight p.m. Doug headed for home. He decided he would visit Sharp the next morning. He was intrigued to visit the Marchem research laboratories. He'd been in the department's forensic labs before but never a commercial lab until today.

Chapter 4

Loren was up at six thirty a.m. as usual. He got to the lab at seven thirty and already had a voice mail message from Benson. "Come over as soon as you get in."

Loren had a cup of coffee and walked over to Benson's office.

Benson was standing in the door to his office. The two men entered.

"Well, fill me in," said Benson.

"He threw me out," Loren said.

"What do you mean?" Benson's hand was shaking.

Loren shrugged and recounted his visit with Wolfgang.

"You must have found out something," pleaded Benson. "You know how important this is. He said there was grave danger. You don't think he could have sabotaged the plant, do you?"

"I don't know," Loren said. "But I think Wolfgang really thinks he is the true inventor of Martox."

"It's not true is it?" Benson asked. "Joe Ferguson holds the patent, doesn't he?"

"From what I know Wolfgang has a good case."

"My God, what a mess. Anything else?"

"You've heard all I know."

Benson paused, seemingly gathering his thoughts. "All right, but I'll get back to you with our next move," he said. "We need to know for sure if the process and the plant are okay. It's supposed to go online any day now."

Loren knew they needed to be sure. The last thing anyone wanted was an industrial accident. "You may need to delay the plant start up."

"There's millions of dollars on the line," Benson said.

"Lives may be on the line," Loren said. "Let me know what else I can do to help."

Benson nodded.

Loren spent the time walking to his lab mulling over the conversation with Benson. It was certainly a perplexing situation. Was there a problem with the process or not? If so, how could it have remained undetected for so long? He wished he wasn't involved in it.

He loved doing scientific research, so much so, that sometimes he was gone from his family too much. After his wife died he spent even more time in the lab. He was eager to get back to it.

But when he got back to his lab, Richard "Andy" Anderson, his lab assistant, was excited. "There's a policeman in the lobby asking for you," he said quickly.

What now? "A policeman? What does he want?" Loren asked.

"I have no idea. You better get over there."

Loren hurried down to the lobby and found a well-dressed, good-looking man chatting with the security guard that sat at the front counter. Did the police find out about Wolfy's threat?

The man extended a hand. "Dr. Sharp? I'm Doug

Sanderson. I'm with the police department."

Loren shook Doug's hand. "What can I help you with?"

Doug motioned Loren over to the sofa and they sat down. The lobby had several comfortable chairs, a sofa and low tables.

"I understand you paid a visit to Wolfgang Reitz yesterday," Doug said.

Loren nodded his head. "Yes, that's true."

"May I ask why?"

Loren didn't think that the situation with Wolfgang Reitz should become public knowledge. He couldn't tell what Sanderson knew already. He decided to let Ted Benson make the decision whether to answer Sanderson's questions.

"I think you better ask our director why I was there. Why do you want to know?" said Loren.

"Reitz was found dead last night."

Loren's mouth dropped open. "What? How?" He was shocked. "That's horrible." Oh, no. Now how would they find out about the grave danger and the possible explosion?

"You seem surprised. The autopsy is being performed as we speak, but it appears he was poisoned."

"Poor Wolfy. How? What happened?"

"We have not determined the circumstances. The investigation is still preliminary. When did you leave Dr. Reitz?"

"I think it was between four and five p.m."

"Was he alive when you left?"

"Of course!" The cop couldn't think he'd killed Wolfy!

"What kind of a mood was Dr. Reitz in?"

Loren thought for a while and pulled on his ear. Finally

he said, "He was quite irritable. He seemed to be in a bad mood."

"Did he say what was bothering him?"

"No, he just asked me to leave. Am I a suspect?"

"No, we know he was alive when you left."

"How do you know that?" asked Loren. "Why did you ask me if he was alive when I left?"

Doug shrugged. "We talked to Dr. Reitz's wife first thing this morning. In fact, officers are still questioning her. She said you left about four thirty p.m. There was mail in the lab and we checked with the post office and they said mail was delivered about five o'clock p.m. Mrs. Reitz says her husband always brought in the mail."

"Makes sense."

Doug shifted around in his chair and changed the subject, "What does Kane and Able mean to you?"

Loren pulled on his ear again. "Cain and Abel? Like from the bible? The guy who killed his brother?"

"No." Doug spelled out the names.

"Why do you ask?" Loren did know of a Kane and an Ableson, former Marchem employees.

"Dr. Reitz had a notation on his calendar to that effect at five thirty."

Loren had bad memories of Kane and Able. They almost ran the company into the ground. "It may be a reference to Earl Kane and Sidney Ableson," he said slowly. "They were referred to as Kane and Able."

"Who are they?"

"I never liked them. They were two top corporate executives at Marchem. Kane was Director of Environmental Affairs and Ableson was his assistant for the Ag group. They were not good executives. They left the company under rather strange circumstances."

"Why strange?"

"Here today, gone tomorrow. There were a lot of rumors."

Doug nodded. "What kind of rumors?"

Loren wondered how he should respond. Finally, he said, "Kickbacks, lots of under the table stuff. Nothing was ever proven."

"Do you know the connection to Reitz?"

"They all worked here," Loren said. "And actually, I think Ableson grew roses and kept some of them in the company greenhouses. Reitz did the same. Ableson would come over and they would go to the greenhouses and talk roses. I think Wolfgang even went over to Ableson's house on a few occasions."

"Do you know why Reitz would be contacting them now?"

Loren shook his head. "I haven't the foggiest."

"Where are these Kane and Able guys now?"

"No idea."

"If you think of anything else, here's my card," Doug said. "Call me anytime. How do I get to your directors office? What's his name, Benson?"

"Ted Benson. Take the elevator to the second floor, turn left to B building, go to the second floor and go all the way to the back. His name is on the door. Here, I'll get you pointed in the right direction." Loren walked him to the tunnel doors and passed him through.

"Thanks, maybe I'll be talking to you again," Doug said.

Loren nodded as the detective walked away.

He was having trouble believing all this. He pulled on

his ear. It was beginning to hurt. He called Benson.

Chapter 5

Doug made the trek to B-building and a receptionist met him at the end of the tunnel and escorted him to Benson's office. Benson was waiting for him.

"Please sit down," said Benson. "It's not every day a policeman visits me. What can I do for you?"

Doug took a seat and said, "Wolfgang Reitz was found dead last night."

Benson's face contorted. "Dead? How? What happened?"

"He was found dead on the floor of his lab. We suspect poisoning,"

"I'm sorry to hear that," he said. "But what has it got to do with me?"

"Loren Sharp visited Reitz the day he died but he said you'd tell me the reason."

"Loren? What did he tell you? Is he a suspect?"

"No," Doug said. "We know Reitz was alive when Sharp left. Do you have a reason to believe Sharp was involved?"

"No, I was just curious."

"The reason I'm here is I want to know why he went to

see Dr. Reitz," Doug said.

"That's confidential," said Benson.

"Nothing is confidential in a possible murder investigation. I can make it difficult for you," Doug said in an officious tone.

"Do you make a habit of browbeating people?" Benson's face reddened. Suspicious.

"When necessary. How about it?"

"This is confidential and I'm showing you this under protest."

Benson took the Reitz letter from his desk and gave it to Doug who read it.

Doug asked, "What does it mean?"

"It means that Reitz was trying to blackmail us."

Doug moved to the edge of his chair. "Please explain."

"Martox is a new insecticide which we have developed and is effective against a variety of insects, even some which are resistant to current materials. It has little or no human toxicity and is expected to be very profitable."

"So how is Reitz involved?" Doug asked.

"Apparently he thinks he is the inventor and he has not been recognized and compensated for the invention of Martox."

"Can that be true?"

"Everyone recognizes Joe Ferguson as the inventor. He was granted the patent."

"Then what is Reitz talking about?" said Doug.

"I don't know," said Benson, losing eye contact.

"What's this grave danger? Could it be a bomb?

"I don't know."

Doug stared at him for a few moments. "Should we call the bomb squad?"

"No," Benson said. "Hazardous chemicals might be involved. We're handling it."

"Blackmailers usually ask for money. What does he want?"

"I don't know." He didn't know much.

Doug continued his questions. "Do you know two men named Kane and Ableson?"

Benson's mouth dropped open. "Maybe. Why?"

"They have a connection to Reitz."

"What kind of connection?" Benson asked.

"I'm asking the questions, here," Doug said. "Tell me about Kane and Ableson. Withholding information in a murder investigation will cause trouble for you."

Benson grimaced. "I really don't know what happened, why they left."

"Who does?"

"The only ones who knew were Kane, Ableson and George Donaldson. But you won't get anything from Donaldson."

"Why not?"

"He's dead."

Suspicious. "Murder?" Doug asked.

"No. He was our CEO at the time and was listening to a presentation at one of our plants shortly after they left. He got up to make a comment and dropped over. Dead before he hit the floor the doctors said."

"All right, Dr. Benson. Thank you for your cooperation. You will probably be hearing from me again." Marchem was probably involved somehow in Reitz's murder.

Doug was very tired when he got home. He just

wanted to take a shower and put on his pajamas, robe and slippers. He wanted to have a beer, watch some baseball and go to bed.

But his phone rang. It was his Aunt Mavis and she was near hysteria. "Douglas! My friend Catalina Perez has been killed! Run over by a car!"

"I'm very sorry to hear that, Mavis. But you have to try to calm down. Take a few deep breaths."

She paused and Doug could hear several deep breaths. "All right, I feel better," she said. She was a widow; her wealthy husband had died two years ago. She was Doug's father's sister.

He said, "I'll be right over. Try to stay calm." She was like a second mother to him and he loved her dearly. His parents were very busy people, often traveling and leaving young Doug with his aunt and uncle. They became very fond of Doug and he of them. They had no children of their own.

He quickly changed to a sweat suit and running shoes and got the Porsche out of the garage under his condo. His condo was in a very new place in Clayton, an upscale inner suburb of St. Louis.

His aunt lived in a condo about half a mile from his and he broke the speed limit going over to her place. Being a policeman has some advantages.

She opened her door after one ring of the doorbell. "Oh, Douglas, I feel so bad. She was such a nice lady. We saw each other every week. We played bridge together. We had a lot in common and had lots of mutual friends." Mavis was a noted beauty in her youth and now at seventy was still a handsome woman. Her white, perfectly coifed hair was striking.

Doug and Mavis sat down in her living room. Doug smiled and said, "Are you feeling better?" The room was tastefully furnished. The furniture looked obviously expensive with lots of substantial brown leather and mahogany. Doug remembered most of it from Mavis' and Uncle Carl's house but she had added a tasteful flowered armchair. He wondered if Uncle Carl would have approved. Mavis moved to the apartment shortly after Carl died.

"Yes," she said. "You being here helps a lot."

Above the fireplace in a gold leafed frame was a portrait of Mavis' late husband. It looked down on the room like some honored advisor. She glanced at the portrait often before she spoke. It was like she was asking it for advice. Carl had been a lawyer and he had joined Doug's father's law firm early in his career. He eventually formed his own law firm and was very successful.

"Tell me what happened," Doug said gently.

"Cathy, actually her name is Catalina but she liked Cathy, was crossing the street after shopping at Stone's supermarket here in Clayton. A car smashed right into her!"

"I'm sorry." Doug used his most soothing voice. "So, it was an accident?"

"I'm not sure," she said. "Can you check? Poor Cathy, she didn't deserve this."

"Yes," he said. "There should be a police report. What's her last name again?"

"Perez," Mavis said. "I just heard about it from her son. He called me."

"What's the son like? I will have to talk with him. I assume he knows some details."

"I don't know him very well. Cathy doted on him. His name is Robert. I think he is an accountant at the Marchem

Company. I can't believe Cathy had any enemies. It had to be an accident, right?"

More Marchem? Odd. "I'll check everything out. Can you give me the son's phone number and address? Did he live with Ms. Perez?"

"I'll get them for you. Yes, Robert lived with Cathy, Catalina." Mavis got up, wrote the numbers on a piece of note paper and gave the paper to Doug.

"Mavis," he said, "you better have some warm milk and go to bed."

She said, "Yes I will."

He said goodbye and left. He decided he should see Robert Perez soon. He also wanted to see a police report. His cop instinct was telling him Ms. Perez's death might be something other than an accident.

Chapter 6

Loren was called into an emergency staff meeting by Karen Olivo. She was the chemistry department secretary. Many thought the place would collapse without her.

The research group was assembled and waiting for Benson in a large conference room with a large, plastic-topped table and metal unpadded chairs. Loren noted the presence of Paul Revere, Chin (C.W.) Wong, Abe Jones, Ollie Lamb, Joe Ferguson, Peter Rose and John Taylor. As far as Loren knew, these were the Ph.D. chemists in the research department who knew Wolfgang Reitz.

"What's Benson want?" Revere asked. He was a tall, youngish, slim blond who took a lot of teasing about his name and was always threatening to have it legally changed but never did.

"Let him tell you," said Loren.

Benson made his entrance ten minutes late. He was always late to meetings with underlings but never with superiors. Loren thought he was trying to make a statement.

Benson sat at the head of the table as he always did. He looked around and said, "Glad you could all come.

We've got a serious problem. He informed the group about Wolfgang's death and about the letter he sent. An incredulous look spread around the table.

"That's too bad about Wolfgang," Lamb said. "But what do you mean explode?"

Revere said, "Nooo, it can't be."

Ferguson said, "What a bunch of bullshit."

Benson raised his hand. "Look, what I'm telling you is true. Wolfgang's dead. A policeman spoke to both Loren and I this morning about it. As for the explosion, I have the letter. You can read it."

"I still don't believe it," Lamb said.

"You better believe it because it is true. Do any of you know anything that could help in this situation?"

There was a deafening silence in the room.

"Anything at all might be helpful," said Benson.

No one spoke.

Benson abruptly got up, said, "If you think of anything call me. Loren will you send out some kind of notice on this situation before the rumors start flying?" and left the room. Loren thought it was an odd request but said nothing.

The room was buzzing after Benson left but Loren got up and left and the others followed. In the hall, after the meeting, Ferguson stopped Loren.

He said, "What is this bullshit about Wolfgang being the inventor of Martox? Everyone knows I hold the patent."

Loren was upset about the whole situation. "Look Joe, what everyone knows is that Wolfgang suggested the compound at the seminar he gave on his work. Just because you rushed back to your lab and made the compound and rushed in a patent disclosure doesn't mean you are the true inventor. So don't give me that stuff. I know the truth."

Bad Chemistry

Ferguson stalked off saying, "Fuck you, Loren."

Old man Markham must be spinning in his grave. Johnathan Markham founded Markham Chemical. He had an idea of scientists as men who shared information and always did the right thing. He forgot they were human beings.

He was a paint salesman who found out there was a shortage of carbolic acid because of the war in Europe where it was used as an antiseptic. He amassed a fortune by making it in a rented garage and selling it to the U.S. government. His efforts eventually grew into the Marchem Corporation.

Loren went back to his lab and typed up an email that dealt with the death of Wolfgang Reitz. It said the police were still investigating. After a lot of thought, he didn't include anything about the letter to Benson.

When he took the notice to the Xerox machine to make a paper copy, he found Debbie Johnson using the machine. She was a looker, twenty-three years old, blonde, blue eyes and stacked. She had been at Marchem for six months after receiving a Master's degree in chemistry from the University of Minnesota

He said, "Hello, Debbie. How long will you be?

She said, "I'm just about done." From what Loren could tell, she was having a hard time adjusting to a new job and a new town.

"What are you doing for dinner?" he asked her, trying to be nice. Gloria would probably like her, a bright young woman.

She said, "I don't think I should date people from my place of employment."

Good grief. She was half his age. "It wouldn't be a date," he said. "I meant you could join me and my, uh, friend, Gloria. I just thought you might be a little lonely since you are relatively new in town."

"Joking." She laughed. "I was just kidding you, Dr. Sharp. I will be glad to go to dinner with you guys."

How was that a joke? "I've changed my mind. Maybe some other time," he said.

"Anytime," she said and left.

Loren made his copy and put it up on the bulletin board.

When he went back to the lab and said to Andy, "That Debbie is kind of dippy. I don't understand young people nowadays."

"Abe Jones says she's a very good chemist," Andy said.

Loren shrugged and left for the day.

When he got home about four o'clock he heard the television running in the family room. He went in and found his son Bill asleep on the couch. Loren turned off the television but let him sleep.

Loren read for a while and then started cooking dinner. His specialty was spaghetti with cheese and bacon sauce, pasta carbonara. Along with some salad it would make a good dinner. When the sauce was simmering he awakened Bill.

Bill was six feet tall, slender and had a bushy head of brown hair. He had a few acne scars he was self-conscious about but they were not very visible. He was twenty-one but looked younger. Most people thought he was a good-looking boy.

Bad Chemistry

Since his mother's death he'd been very moody. He loved his mother very much and had trouble getting over her death. He hadn't worked or studied since she died. Some people thought he was using her death as an excuse. Loren wasn't sure what to think.

"Where were you last night?" he asked. Bill hadn't made it home.

Bill was still sleepy and took his time to reply. "I was over at Nick's. We were playing video games and it got late so I decided to stay over."

Loren never liked Nick. He was really a disrespectful kid. "I know you're an adult but I would appreciate it if you would call when you are going to stay out all night."

"I knew you were over at Gloria's so I didn't bother to call."

"You could have left a message," Loren said.

"Okay, Okay. I'll do it next time." Bill was getting angry. "As you said, I'm an adult."

Loren didn't want to fight. "Let's eat."

They ate quietly at the kitchen table.

When they finished, they stacked the dishes in the dishwasher together.

Bill very rarely did things like that. While they were working he said, "You know, Dad, I think we are growing apart. I think we should do some things together. How about if I come over to the lab, have lunch and you can show me the new stuff like you used to?"

Loren was surprised and delighted. "Sure, meet me in the lobby about eleven thirty."

"I'll be there," Bill said.

They watched television together and later had some nachos. Loren was feeling good.

Richard Lowell

Before bed he checked his email and had a message from his daughter Ann Lauren:

Dear Pop,

I got an offer of an interview trip to The University of Wisconsin! I'm really excited. They're doing work in my field. Only downer is they have no women on their faculty. We will see.

Hope you are doing well.

Love,

Ann

Loren went to bed a happy man.

Chapter 7

Loren was still a happy man when he drove to the lab in the morning. He played several marches in his car on the way to work. He had the reputation of usually being calm and collected, but maybe his love of marches indicated an inner aggressiveness. By the end of "Pomp and Circumstance," "Stars and Stripes Forever" and "Colonel Bogey," he was turning into the parking lot.

At that point the problems of yesterday hit him. He hoped that he could have a morning of uninterrupted research.

It was not to be. When he got to his desk he found a note from Karen. It said Detective Sanderson was waiting for him in the lobby.

Loren said, "Shit," to no one in particular. When he got to the lobby he found the detective sitting on a comfortable sofa reading some papers.

He stood and said, "Nice to see you again, Dr. Sharp."

"Please call me Loren."

He replied, "Okay, then please call me Doug."

Loren took a seat opposite him.

"I have been thinking about the Reitz case, Loren, and I think there was foul play involved," Doug said.

"What makes you say that?"

"I have been talking to Mrs. Reitz and people here at Marchem and I think we can eliminate suicide. He had a number of appointments scheduled that I don't think he would have made if he were planning suicide. In talking to you and others, Reitz was said to be an expert in handling chemicals and it does not seem logical that he would have such a serious accident. If suicide and an accident are out of the picture, it must be a homicide."

"That sounds reasonable to me," said Loren.

Doug then said, "I would like you to go with me out to Reitz's lab and see if we can find any evidence of foul play. I don't have the scientific expertise to make judgments in this case."

"Why me?"

"You have been there before and maybe you would see some changes from when you were there."

"I really don't want to get involved. I have other things to do. Why don't you get one of your forensic guys to go?"

"They do mostly lab work and are not really familiar with a research lab. Besides, they're busy and I would have to go through channels to get one to be assigned. It could take days."

Loren was not pleased. "I guess it is my civic duty, huh? Okay, I can leave now but I have to be back by eleven. My son is coming to lunch."

"Shouldn't be a problem." Doug had an unmarked, recent Crown Victoria parked in the visitors' lot. Loren got in the passenger side and Doug drove.

Loren made conversation. "You married?"

"Divorced."

"I'm sorry," said Loren.

"Don't be. The parting was amicable. She just couldn't take being married to a policeman. The hours, risks and loneliness were too much for her. Lots of policemen have troubled marriages. I gave her a generous settlement and didn't contest the divorce. She lives in Denver. I still see her from time to time."

Loren thought he and Doug had several similarities. Although Loren was forty six, had more gray in his hair, was a little shorter and had a little paunch, there was a physical resemblance between the two men. Neither of them was in a serious relationship. And, they both seemed to enjoy research. In Loren's case it was chemical research and in Doug's case it was solving crimes, but many of the principles seemed the same.

Doug said, "The traffic is light today."

After that statement the men were silent the rest of the way to Reitz's house. They arrived in good time and parked in the street in front. They entered the back yard through the gate in the fence. Doug had gotten a key. Mrs. Reitz had given the police permission to enter the lab when they needed.

The roses in the garden were beginning to bloom. They were beautiful, reds, pinks and a splendid Peace variety among others. Some other varieties of flowers were mixed in. In stark contrast to the flowers, a yellow crime scene tape covered the door to the laboratory and a large lock was on the door.

Doug lingered in the yard a few moments. "These flowers are spectacular. Somebody has a green thumb."

Loren smiled. "Actually it was Wolfy. He loved roses. It was a hobby."

"Very impressive."

"Did you put that lock on the door?" said Loren.

"No, that was on Reitz's desk along with the key. The crime scene people put it on the door. It is the only thing that has been moved. Apparently Reitz was afraid of someone searching his lab and double locked the door when he was not in the lab. I thought it would be a good idea to keep the place locked up, so I had them put it on."

They entered the lab after Doug unlocked the door.

Doug asked Loren to describe what the things in the lab were used for.

Loren pointed to the hoods on the right side and said. "A fume hood is a cabinet-like structure with glass doors and connected to a ventilator. The purpose is to prevent toxic or noxious gases from making contact with the worker."

The desk was covered with various books and papers. A chemistry journal was open on the desktop and several books were stacked up. A white lab coat was hanging on a hook on the wall. The left side of the lab had a nuclear magnetic resonance instrument that was not new but looked quite serviceable.

Loren said, "The NMR measures the number and environment of the hydrogen atoms in a substance. It is an aid for determining the composition. The chromatography units are used to separate the components of a mixture."

In the middle of the room was a bench on which had been placed assorted chemicals and equipment. On the floor in front of the far hood was a chalk outline of a body, no doubt where Reitz's body had been found. Loren teared up a little when he saw it.

"Can I show you some photos of the body?" Doug asked.

"I guess so," Loren said.

Doug showed him some photos.

"He was blue?" Loren asked. "You didn't mention that, did you?"

"What does it mean?" Doug asked. "Our lab guys are still running tests."

"It means Wolfy died from cyanide poisoning," Loren said. "And that's very suspicious. Wolfy was an expert in dealing with cyanide." He looked up at Doug. "I think you're right. I think he was murdered." He shook his head. Poor Wolfy.

"Thanks," Doug said. "It's a good thing I brought you over here."

In the far hood was a silver cylinder about three feet tall and with skull and crossbones on it and caution, hydrogen cyanide in large letters.

"Look," Loren pointed at the cylinder. "Is that the murder weapon?"

"Maybe?" Doug said. "Study the scene and see if you can find anything which looks out of the usual. How does a cyanide cylinder work?"

"See that tubing attached to the top of the cylinder?" Loren said. "Hydrogen cyanide is a liquid when under pressure in a closed vessel. The material boils below room temperature. The tubing is attached to a nitrogen outlet and when you open the valve on top of the cylinder and pressurize with nitrogen the liquid cyanide will flow through the tubing on the outlet."

Doug asked, "Is the cylinder empty?"

Loren picked up a beaker, filled it with ice so the HCN would not flash and went to the far hood. He put the tubing from the cylinder outlet in a beaker in the ice, turned on the valve and the nitrogen. A colorless liquid flowed through the outlet tubing. Loren turned off the valves and left the ice mixture in the hood.

"We'll let that evaporate," Loren said. "Pretty obvious that the cylinder is not empty."

"How fast would the cyanide work?" Doug asked. "Would Reitz have time to turn off the cylinder if he realized he was being poisoned?"

"Possibly but not likely," Loren said. "People who work with hydrogen cyanide have a saying: When you work with hydrogen cyanide, if you're alive you're okay. That's because death is very fast when you inhale a fatal dose. It's also very hard to handle."

"How so?" Doug started taking notes.

"Besides being very toxic, it polymerizes if not stabilized by the addition of acid. Sometimes the polymerization is explosive. The polymer is a black gunk that tends to plug up tubes and valves. Once I was using a small transfer cylinder and when I opened the valve nothing came out. When I started to take off the valve, so I could refill it, it started to hiss. It wasn't empty. I quickly tossed it into the hood and let it vent for a while. After I was sure it was empty I took off the valve and it was plugged with the black gunk."

He smiled a little. "Actually, some scientists studying what they call creation chemistry believe the black gunk was a precursor to amino acids that eventually led to life on the earth. Imagine, a deadly poison leading to life. How ironic. I think some terrorists even experimented with hydrogen cyanide for a while. They killed some dogs but I guess they found it too hard to come by and handle. "

Doug shook his head. "How does it kill?"

"Are you asking what the mode of action is?"

"I guess so."

"As you probably know, hemoglobin transports oxygen throughout the body," Loren said. "The body needs oxygen to perform its metabolic functions. The cyanide ion attaches to hemoglobin more strongly than oxygen so the hemoglobin loses its ability transport oxygen. The cyanide can actually knock oxygen off the hemoglobin molecule. The person thus dies from lack of oxygen. There are other poison gases that function in the same way. For example, carbon monoxide and hydrogen sulfide, which is the smell of rotten eggs, although they require a higher dose than cyanide. "

Doug seemed interested. "I have read some World War One stories that talk about poison gas. I think they mention chlorine, phosgene and mustard gas. How do they work?"

"Chlorine is a very reactive, corrosive material which attacks the lining of the lungs," Loren said. "Eventually the lungs will fill up with liquid and the person dies. Fortunately chlorine is so unpleasant that people would leave the scene before lethal exposure. The advantage of phosgene as a war gas is that it can be breathed since it is not too unpleasant. I haven't smelled it but I have heard that it has the odor of new-mown hay. Once in the lungs it reacts with moisture to form hydrochloric acid that attacks the lining of the lungs. Mustard gas is a liquid irritant that attacks the skin and incapacitates the victim."

"What about nerve gas?"

"Nerve gas is not a gas at all but a liquid. It is applied as an aerosol and attacks the nervous system. The victim can no longer breathe. I guess any highly reactive volatile chemical, such as methyl isocyanate for example, the bad actor in the Bhopal tragedy, could be called a poison gas. Then there is the subject of tear gases that are called lachrymators." He paused. "But I guess I'm telling you more than you wanted to know. I'm sorry. I always loved to teach."

Doug shook his head. "No, it's very interesting. Maybe someday I will have use for the information. Who knows? I think all knowledge is useful. At least I probably am a whiz at trivia."

"Another thing that seems strange is there is no apparatus in the hood," Loren pointed. "If Wolfy was doing an experiment he would have had some kind of reactor set up to add the cyanide to. As you see the hood is empty except for the cylinder. Another thing, the body didn't have on a lab coat, right?"

"No lab coat."

"Wolfy always wore a lab coat when he was working in the lab. And I don't see any butyl nitrite ampoules around."

What are they?" asked Doug.

"An antidote for cyanide if you sniff it in time. Wolfy always kept them handy when he worked with cyanide."

Doug was nodding his head. "Looks like we have a murder."

"Seems so," said Loren.

"It's good you came with me. Loren. You've been really helpful. I wouldn't have been able to make all those observations."

Doug motioned Loren over to the desk and showed him Reitz's calendar, "You see, Kane and Able five o'clock."

"Yes." Loren nodded. "I wonder what business Wolfy

had with them. Do you think they were here?"

"I don't know. Mrs. Reitz said she was preparing dinner and did not see the back yard from around four thirty to six. I think I will have to speak to those gentlemen."

Loren said, "Good luck," and started toward the door. "I have to get back."

Traffic was light and they got back to the lab at ten thirty. Doug let Loren out after thanking him again and roared off.

Loren shook his head and wondered what was going to happen next. He went in the building to wait for his son.

Chapter 8

Doug drove over to the Clayton Police station, identified himself, and asked the duty officer if he could see the officer in charge of the Perez case. The duty officer told him where to go.

Doug went to Sergeant Grant's desk. He gave the man his card. "Hi there, Sergeant Grant. I was wondering what you could tell me about the Perez case."

Grant pushed back from his desk. "I was just working on the report." He pointed. "Basically, this Perez woman was run down in the street. There were two witnesses, a man waiting for a bus across the street and a woman just exiting the supermarket. They both said it was a dark SUV, either black or dark blue that came around the corner and never slowed down. It slammed into Ms. Perez and threw her up in the air. She landed on the hood of the SUV and slid off. The SUV left the scene without even slowing down. She was dead at the scene."

Doug asked, "Did they think it was deliberate?" Not slowing down was suspicious.

"They didn't say," said Grant.

"Is there anything else you can tell me about the case?"

asked Doug.

"No, we are working on it."

"Please keep me informed," said Doug. He was beginning to think Ms. Perez's death was a murder. At least, it was certainly a hit and run.

"Why are you interested?' said Grant.

"It's personal. The deceased was a friend of my aunt.

Grant scratched his head. Doug could tell he thought it didn't seem to be in his jurisdiction. Doug thanked him and left.

When he returned to his car he took out his cell phone and dialed the phone number Mavis had given him for the Perez residence.

After several rings an agitated voice answered. "Hi. This is Bobby."

"My name is Doug Sanderson. I'm with the police. I'd like to talk with you about your mother's death."

There was a lengthy pause and then Bobby said, "Gee, I'm kind of busy right now. The police already questioned me."

Suspicious. Why wouldn't he want justice for his mom? "It will only take a few minutes."

Well okay, come over but I can only give you a few minutes."

Since Doug was only a few blocks away he said, "I'll be right over."

The Perez place was a high rise in the high rent district. Doug found a parking place on the street. He looked for the Perez apartment number on the list. It was on the top floor. He called Bobby on the house phone and was given a code to punch in to open the elevator. He took the elevator up and got out at a plush hallway. There was only one apartment so he rang the bell. A disheveled young man wearing a running suit opened the door. He had dark curly hair and was quite good-looking.

He squinted at Doug like the light hurt his eyes. "Yes?"

"Hello, Bobby. I'm Doug Sanderson,"

He motioned Doug in. "I only have a few minutes."

They took seats in the living room and Doug looked around at the somewhat overdone room. It had a fifties look about it, with some wood and some upholstered furniture that was obviously expensive. There were a number of nice paintings on the walls. He couldn't tell if they were originals. The view out of the large window was impressive.

"Beautiful place," Doug said. "Your mother must have been wealthy."

"My father's money. He died two years ago." He glanced at a closed door off the living room.

"Are you the only heir?"

"Yes, but I fail to see what that has to do with my mother's death. It's really none of your business."

Doug changed the subject. "I understand you work at Marchem."

Bobby shook his head. "Again, I don't see what that has to do with mother's death."

"I just met some people at Marchem. Dr. Loren Sharp for one. He's in research. Do you know him?" His instincts were telling him to keep the kid talking.

"No. I don't know any of the research people. Can we get to why you are here?"

"All right. Do you know of any reason someone would hurt your mother?"

"No. Everyone loved my mother. She loved everybody

back."

"Do you know anything about a counterfeit auto emission report?"

The blood drained from Bobby's face. Bingo. He composed himself with some difficulty. "No I don't. Why do you ask?"

"Your mother talked to my aunt about it."

"Your aunt? Who's your aunt?"

"Mavis Gage."

"I know Mavis. I guess she was a good friend to my mother but I really don't know why you're here. I can't help you. I've told you everything I know." Not about the maid's involvement.

"I'd like to talk to your maid," Doug said.

"It's her day off. Why do you want to talk to her?"

"I think she may have some helpful information. She's the one who gave my aunt the fake inspection report."

"I can't believe she knows anything about that. She's a very retiring person." Bobby kept looking at the closed bedroom door like he expected someone to enter the room. Does Bobby have a woman in the other room? Or is the maid?

Doug stood. "Is someone else here? I'd like to talk to her."

Bobby jumped up. "Uh, no. I'm the only one here." He glanced at the door again. Yeah, right.

But the rules of evidence were strict. "Can I go in this room?" He took a step towards the closed door.

"No!" Bobby said.

Doug gave Bobby his card and said, "I'll be going. If you think of something you want to tell me, you can call my cell. And please have your maid call me."

Bobby nodded and Doug left.

Doug doubted that Bobby would have his maid call. He decided that Bobby knew more than he was telling. He should see more of Roberto Perez.

Chapter 9

Loren met Bill in the lobby.

Bill had shown up at the research center right on time. That was not one of his usual characteristics. Maybe be was starting to shape up.

The cafeteria was a short walk through the tunnel. It was early so there were not many people in the cafeteria and they easily found seats. Bill got a cheeseburger and Loren, feeling fatherly, joined him but worried about the cholesterol.

Bill was friendly and spoke optimistically about the future. It was refreshing and they even discussed him going back to college.

After lunch they toured the research center. Loren showed him the new computers in the library, and storeroom, and the new instruments in the physical science center.

The glass blowers gave him a demonstration, making him a little glass horse.

"Just like when I was a kid," Bill said. He seemed touched.

Loren was definitely touched. He remembered bringing

Bill and Ann here when they were little and how the two of them had been thrilled with their tiny glass animals. "Thanks, guys," he said. "I appreciate it."

Bill and Loren went to his lab and he discussed his recent research.

Bill seemed impressed. At about two o'clock he said he had to get going so Loren took him down to the lobby and he signed out. Loren smiled as he watched his son leave. He seems better. Maybe he's turned the corner.

Loren was feeling so good he decided to take Gloria out to dinner. He called her and she agreed. He spent the rest of the afternoon working on the computer.

After work, Gloria was ready despite the fact that Loren was ten minutes early. She just smiled and shook her head a little as she let him inside.

"Where would you like to go?" he asked.

"How about Georgio's?" she said, being agreeable. She knew he liked the place.

"Good idea. I haven't been there in a while."

The restaurant was about two miles away and traffic was bad, so there was plenty of time for conversation. In the car, Gloria said, "I was at the supermarket today and they had this big display of organically grown apples. What is that organic stuff all about?" She knew he liked to expound.

"In my opinion it's a merchandising ploy based on fear tactics," he said, just getting warmed up. "Fear sells in politics and in the marketplace. The merchants have scared some people into thinking there's something wrong with the food they've been buying, so buy theirs--which is safe. They're not specific about what's wrong with the food they've been buying. It's part of the fear of chemicals that's popular now." He paused to take a breath. "Actually everything is chemical. You are chemicals."

Gloria chuckled. "Yes. I've heard that argument before but they're really talking about man-made chemicals. You're prejudiced because you make a living out of chemicals."

"True. But I try to be open-minded. Life would be pretty grim without man-made chemicals."

"What do you mean?"

"There would be no drugs, like antibiotics, no gas for your car, no plastics, your food would spoil, and on and on."

"I see what you mean, but I still think that some pesticides can be harmful."

"Probably, especially if they are not used correctly. But let's talk pesticides, not chemicals. There are plenty of toxic materials out there that are so-called natural. Organic farmers don't like chemical fertilizers so they use natural fertilizers. That's manure. Almost every month a salmonella outbreak seems to occur that's mostly a result of using manure. Actually I think it's a good idea to wash all produce, organic or not.

"I suppose that's true. I still think you are prejudiced."

He decided not to argue. "Perhaps."

She grinned. "What about the bioengineered foods?" She knew that would set him off.

He was about to expound on one of his favorite topics but they finally arrived at the restaurant. They entered and asked for a table for two.

The restaurant host said, "Did you have a reservation?"

"No, we don't," said Loren.

"It will be a one hour wait, sir," the host said.

Gloria shrugged and nodded.

Loren gave his name and they went to wait in the bar. "This isn't so bad," he said. "Good company. Nice refreshments. What can I get you to drink?"

They spent an hour in the bar drinking Margaritas. Finally they got a table in the back and were feeling mellow. Loren ordered a bottle of wine.

They sipped the wine. "Delicious," he said.

The waiter came and they ordered.

Gloria stared at Loren. "Why did you ask me to dinner so suddenly?"

"Well, I had a successful time with Bill today," he said. "He seemed to be shaping up and I felt like celebrating."

She stared harder at him. "I thought you might have something important to tell me."

He shook his head. "No, I don't. Why?"

"Never mind," she said and took a sip of wine. After a few moments, she said, "That's nice that Bill's doing better."

They had a pleasant evening chatting, eating and drinking. Loren paid the bill and they left the restaurant.

Loren probably shouldn't have driven but he said he felt fine. The trip to Gloria's was uneventful. She didn't say a word.

"Do you want to come in?" she asked, as he turned off the car.

"Just for a minute." He liked to go in with her because he didn't like her going into a dark condo. He liked protecting her.

She fumbled for her keys but got in successfully.

When the lights were on and her coat was off, Loren said, "I should be leaving." He realized he hadn't thought of Wolfy all evening. "Thanks for a nice evening."

But Gloria was tearing up. "Loren, do you realize I'm a woman? Do you find me attractive?"

"Of course I do, to both questions," he said. Why was she asking this now?

"I just wondered. Good night then." She opened the front door.

Loren left, confused. What did she want from him? Should he have stayed? But she asked him to go. He was upset, with all kinds of questions.

When he got home and went to bed he had trouble sleeping.

He kept thinking about Gloria.

Chapter 10

Doug was waiting for Loren when he came into work the next morning.

For his part, Loren seemed preoccupied. He also didn't seem happy to see Doug. "I didn't expect to see you again so soon."

"I wanted to ask you how I could get in touch with Kane and Ableson," Doug said.

"I suppose you need to talk to somebody in personnel," Loren said. "Hey, Carter, do you have an internal phone book Detective Sanderson could use?"

"Yes." The desk man put a phone book on the counter.

"I think you will find what you want in there," Loren said.

Doug picked up the book and began to study it.

"Is that it?" Loren asked.

"Just a minute," Doug said.

Loren sat down on one of the couches, sighing.

Doug used the lobby phone; an internal line might make people more cooperative. He was shifted to several people until a rude woman told him they were not allowed to give out addresses of retirees. He said it was a police matter and he could get a court order. She put her boss on the phone and he grudgingly told Doug to wait. Several minutes later the boss came back on the line.

Doug was getting impatient.

The boss said, "The only address we have is: *in care of Charles Shapiro, Attorney at Law, 123 Morton Street, Suite 220, Denver, Colorado.*"

He wrote it down. "For both men?"

"Yes."

Odd. "Thanks." He hung up. If worst came to worst, he might have to go out to Colorado.

He turned back to Loren, who appeared preoccupied again. "Can I talk to some of their coworkers?"

"Yeah," Loren said. "I can take you down to the waste treatment group. This way."

They walked down a floor to an office with *WASTE TREATMENT AND REDUCTION* on the door.

They went inside. "Can you ask Bowman and Jensen meet us in the conference room?" Loren asked the secretary.

She said, "Sure thing."

Soon, four of them were all gathered around the conference room table.

"Doug," Loren said, "this is John Bowman, a microbiologist and Mike Jensen, an incineration expert." They nodded at their names. They were both pretty nondescript middle-aged white guys.

"This is Detective Doug Sanderson," Loren continued. "He's investigating Reitz's death. He wants some background on Earl Kane and Sidney Ableson.

"We worked together," Bowman said. "I travelled with

Kane to many vendors and plants. We spent a lot of time on airplanes and in restaurants and bars. He usually was secretive and had a very combative, competitive nature, but when he had a drink or two he would open up.

"I had the same kind of experiences with him," said Jensen.

"What about Ableson?" Doug asked.

Bowman shrugged. "He was Kane's lackey."

"Basically," Jensen said. "He thinks Kane's a great guy. I think they met at the University of Chicago Business School."

"From what you say, I don't get why Kane was so successful," Doug said.

"Damn good question," Bowman said.

"He must have something on one of the higher ups," Jensen said, and they both laughed like it was an old joke.

"A lot of somethings," Bowman said.

Loren added, "I think I did hear some friend of Kane's dad, who was some kind of colonel, got him the job, and Kane got Ableson the job."

"Is that it?" Doug asked, starting to get annoyed.

Bowman raised his shoulders. "Just a bunch of drunken bragging."

"Tell me," Doug said.

Bowman and Jensen gave each other a long look.

Bowman cleared his throat. "Kane thought waste management offered many opportunities for wheeling and dealing so he contrived to get into that department," he said. "A few choice maneuvers made him assistant to the head of the department. He got Ableson to follow the director who he thought might be cheating on his wife. Sure enough, the pictures taken showed beyond a doubt that the director was, in fact, seeing his secretary in compromising circumstances. Kane offered the director two choices. Resign and recommend him as his replacement or his wife would see the pictures. The director suddenly developed health problems and had to retire."

"He told you all this?" said Doug.

"When he was drinking," said Jensen. "Not great at holding his liquor."

Bowman continued, "I heard later Kane couldn't believe it was so easy. He grew bolder. He started slowly with some minor kickbacks from waste haulers and moved on to some creative accounting practices in his department. He finally had his own secret business going within Marchem. He was very proud of himself because his father finally approved of him. But his house of cards eventually collapsed and he was forced out of the company."

"Thank God." Loren was shaking his head.

"Why isn't this guy in jail?" Doug asked.

"Dunno," Jensen said.

"Damn good question," Bowman said again.

Ted Benson had left Doug a lot of voicemails. He'd also asked Doug to stop by on his way out of Marchem. But he didn't have any helpful information for the detective. He just wanted to know what Doug had figured out. Unfortunately, it wasn't much.

Chapter 11

Loren had a productive morning of research after the detective left. He'd managed to put worrying about Gloria and murder and possible explosions out of his mind. This, despite the fact that Benson kept emailing him with updates about their investigation into the Martox manufacturing process.

He felt he was going to be successful with his current project and was pleased. Lunch was at the food cart.

Carter from the lobby was ahead of him in line. He said, "Did your son find his jacket?"

"What jacket?" Loren asked.

"Oh, didn't you know? Yesterday your son came back in and said he left his jacket and could he go and get it. I thought it would be all right."

Loren grunted an answer. He wolfed down his yogurt and cookie. What Bill was up to? He had a bad feeling about it decided he had better find out. He decided retrace their steps.

First he went to the library where he asked the librarian if she saw a young man hanging around yesterday.

She said, "You mean your son? Yes, I saw him up in the textbook area. I thought you were still with him."

"How long did he stay?"

"I don't know. I went back to my office."

Mighty strange. Bill was not very interested in chemistry although he had taken a semester of it.

Next stop was the storeroom. "Did you see my son yesterday afternoon after we were here together?"

The attendant said, "Yes. I saw a young guy looking at the bulletin board in the back. I didn't think it was unusual."

Loren did. The surplus chemical storage room was the only thing in the back and was a separate room that was used to store chemicals which were not used up. The chemists could come down and see if a chemical they needed was in the collection and could check it out. It saved the corporation some money.

"Thanks," He said. He pointed to the back, meaning, could he go back there?

The attendant nodded.

Loren went into the chemical storage room.

A computer was provided in the room and the chemists recorded the surplus chemicals they brought in and took out. They entered their name and location every time they did either. About a thousand chemicals or more in variously sized containers lined the shelves in alphabetical order. Some of the chemicals had been in the storage room for years and some of the containers were leaking. Some of the chemicals could be dangerous. Many were toxic and some had a fire or explosion risk. It reminded him of the chemical storage room at the university he attended and probably most college and high school chemical storerooms. This place needs a thorough cleaning.

He pulled on his ear, at a loss as to where to start

looking until he noticed there were circles free of dust on the shelves. Ah ha.

He systematically looked in the computer registry for chemicals that should be in the area of the dust-free circles. The first five had withdrawal notations but the sixth was not entered.

"My God," Loren said to himself. "Barbituric acid. The kid is going to try to make speed."

He went to the lobby and asked Carter if he saw Bill leave, hoping he was wrong and Bill hadn't left with any chemicals.

But Carter said he didn't think he saw him leave. He must have left by another exit.

Loren was devastated. Bill's new leaf was apparently a ploy to steal chemicals.

Shit! How was he going to handle this? It was a difficult situation.

Chapter 12

Doug never received a call from the Perez's maid. He wasn't surprised and decided to call her. He assumed she would be at the Perez residence.

"This is the Perez residence," she said, "This is Maria." Bingo.

"My name is Douglas Sanderson. I'm with the police department. I would like to ask you a few questions about Ms. Perez's death.

She said haltingly, "I'm sorry, I don't know anything about that." Her voice quivered.

"Maria, I would like to come over and talk to you."

"No. No. I have to clean the apartment. I'm too busy."

He ignored her protests. "I'll be right over."

He took out the Porsche and sped over to the Perez residence. It was a nice day and he put the top down, got to the apartment house in ten minutes and found a metered spot right in front. He remembered the code for the elevator and took it up to the apartment. He rang the bell several times but there was no answer. Finally he banged on the door. After a few minutes the door was cracked open,

"Yes?" Maria asked.

"It's Doug Sanderson from the police. I called." He flashed his badge.

"I told you I was too busy."

He didn't like to do it but he decided some intimidation was required, "This is a murder investigation and not cooperating with the police is a crime. Do you want to come down to the police department?"

She opened the door and, without a word, followed Doug into the living room. She was a small woman wearing the traditional maid's uniform of black dress and white apron. She was in her late twenties or early thirties and wore her hair in a bun at the back of her head. She was rather pretty in a traditional Spanish way. He sat on the couch and motioned her to sit.

He started with some innocuous questions. "Is Roberto, Bobby, here?"

She shook her head.

"What's your last name Maria?"

"Martinez."

"How long have you worked for Ms. Perez?" he asked.

"About two years."

Her hands were shaking and she was obviously uncomfortable so he took his time and let her calm down. "I guess Roberto is going to keep you on after his mother's death?"

"Yes. He has said so."

"Quite a tragedy, Ms. Perez's death."

Maria nodded her head. "Yes. She was a very kind woman. Strict, but kind and fair."

"Is there anything you can tell me about her death? Any enemies or anyone who would hurt her?"

"No, of course not." She shook her head. "Who would want to hurt her?"

"Do you know anything about a fake emissions test certificate she gave to Mrs. Gage?"

The blood left her face and she went rigid. "No, no, I don't know anything about that."

He reluctantly decided it was time for some more intimidation. "Maria, I think you're lying. If you don't tell the truth I will have to arrest you and take you down to the police station."

She started to cry. "No, no I can't tell you about the certificate. My boyfriend says he will kill me if I tell anybody."

He leaned forward. "Who's your boyfriend?"

"I can't tell you. He will kill me." She started to cry in earnest.

"If you tell me the truth we can protect you."

Maria just kept sobbing.

Doug decided he had gotten all he could get out of Maria. This boyfriend was a good lead.

There were other ways to get the information. He handed her his handkerchief, "Dry your eyes and calm down, Maria. I'll be going now. I'm sorry if I upset you. I hope you'll be feeling better soon."

Doug went back to headquarters and got on his computer. He had gotten Maria's phone number from Aunt Mavis. A friend found for him that a particular number was often called from Maria's number. The number was for a house in University City owned by one Carlos Valdez. He decided Carlos had to be the boyfriend so he called the number.

A voicemail message clicked on. "Merchant Services Incorporated is not available right now. Please leave a message." He hung up.

He tried again several times and decided that Carlos was screening his calls and would probably never pick up from an unknown caller unless a message was left.

He had another thought. Maybe it would be better to observe Valdez for a while without his knowing it. He figured he would need help but he knew O'Brien would not authorize a stakeout unless he got pressure from the chief. He decided there was enough animosity between him and O'Brien so he decided not to use his leverage. It looked like a job for his old buddy Charles "Charlie Chan" Wong.

Charlie was a private detective who Doug had used a few times to get information that he couldn't get from regular sources mainly because of cost. He still had his office phone number in his little black book so he dialed it. He got voicemail.

"You have reached Cathay Investigations. Please leave a message at the beep or call my cell phone." It then gave the cell phone number. Doug dialed it.

"Hello, Charlie speaking."

"Charlie, it's Doug Sanderson."

"Well Doug, nice to hear from you. Is this business or pleasure?"

"It's always a pleasure to talk to you, Charlie, but this is business."

"What's up?"

"I want you to tail a guy."

"That sounds like it is within my competencies. I'm on surveillance right now, but for you I can start tomorrow. What's he done?"

"I'd like to come to your office to discuss it."

"I gave up my office and I'm working from my house. It's more convenient and cheaper. I can see you tomorrow at my house."

"What time?"

"Make it seven-thirty a.m. I have to go out about eight o'clock. You remember where my house is don't you?"

Seven thirty was a little early for Doug but he said, "Yes, I'll see you then."

"Great. See you then."

Doug had investigated Charlie's background when they first met and had gotten to know him pretty well over the years. As a boy, Charlie was fascinated by old Charlie Chan movies even though the actor playing Charlie Chan wasn't even Chinese. Charlie Wong thought that Charlie Chan was a genius the way he solved the fictional crimes with great skill. He wanted to be just like Charlie Chan. Lacking both the funds and the inclination to go to college, he enrolled in the police academy as soon as he finished high school and was old enough. He graduated with honors and immediately joined the force. That's when Doug got to know and like him. He spent five years as a patrolman and decided promotions were coming too slowly so he decided to start his own private detective agency. He made a living tailing spouses and finding missing persons as well as some miscellaneous cases that interested him.

Doug didn't like getting up at six thirty a.m. but he thought it was important to see Charlie as soon as possible. He had a bagel and coffee, put on a navy jogging suit and rolled out in the Porsche. He'd been at Charlie's a couple times for Super Bowl parties so he knew the way. Charlie was a big football fan. The house was in Olivette and had been Charlie's parents' house. Both his parents were dead.

It didn't take Doug long to get to the house and he parked in front. Charlie answered the door at once. He had on a tan polo shirt with brown casual slacks and brown loafers. He was five feet seven with dark brown hair and brown eyes. He wasn't bad-looking.

"Hey, Doug! How nice to see you," Charlie said.

"Same here, Charlie."

"Come in."

The living room looked the same way it had looked for the Super Bowl parties. Apparently Charlie wasn't much for interior décor. They walked into one of the bedrooms that obviously functioned as an office. There was no bed. Charlie motioned to Doug to sit down in a side chair across from the big desk in the room. There were several pictures of Charlie in various poses with past clients on the walls along with his framed private detective license. Charlie took up residence in a big desk chair behind the desk and lit up a cigarette.

"What can I do for you, Doug?"

"I want you to tail a guy."

"So you said. I can do that, but why don't you use your own police help?"

"Captain O'Brien and I are not getting along right now. He wouldn't cooperate unless I had some evidence. Also, I may have to go out of town soon." He was quickly running out of leads in the Reitz murder.

"Okay. I'll start tomorrow." One of his advantages was his ability to blend into the background. Very rarely or ever had he been made when tailing someone.

Doug gave him a paper with Valdez's address. "His

name is Carlos Valdez. He lives in U City."

"Practically my own neighborhood," Charlie said. "What's he done? Is he dangerous?"

"He could be. So watch your back," Doug said. "He might be part of a counterfeiting ring. He might have run a woman down in the street. I don't know for sure if he's done anything illegal but I'm counting on you to help me find out."

"Do you have a description? Sounds like he's Hispanic."

"Probably, but I've never met him," Doug said.

"What kind of car does he drive?"

"I don't know but I can find out from motor vehicles."

"Never mind. I can handle that. What do you want to know, specifically, about this guy?" asked Charlie.

"I just want to know where he goes and who he sees."

Charlie looked at his calendar. "I can start tomorrow." I figure you're not using police funds for this so for you, I will only charge a hundred and fifty dollars a day."

"That's your usual fee."

Charlie grinned. "Yeah, but with your money, I could charge more."

Doug shook his head and smiled. "Thanks, pal. You're all heart. Okay, you're hired."

"I'll give you a report when I get something interesting. Do you want email or phone or cell?"

"Make it email. I may be in Denver on another case. If you get something big you can call my cell phone."

Charlie smiled, "You've got it. Same old email address?"

"Yes, same address and same cell phone. Be talking to you." Doug left.

Back at the precinct, Doug looked up Kane's lawyer Shapiro's phone number and dialed the number on his cell phone. Shapiro's secretary answered and said Mr. Shapiro was not in the office. He tried to get some information from the secretary as to when he might reach him but she was not cooperative. Over the course of the morning, he tried several more times and finally reached Shapiro.

"Hi, Mr. Shapiro, this is detective Doug Sanderson in St. Louis."

"Hello. What can I do for you?" Shapiro sounded wary.

"I'm trying to contact an Earl Kane and a Sidney Ableson. Do you have their contact information?"

"I'm unable to divulge any information about possible clients."

"This is police business. Can you tell me anything about them?"

"No."

"Are you their lawyer?"

"I'm unable to divulge--"

"Yeah, yeah," Doug said. "Can you at least tell me if they're in Colorado?"

"I'm unable--"

"Yeah, thanks a lot." Doug hung up. That lawyer was very cagey. In his experience, cagey lawyers had something to hide. The exchange made him very curious and enforced the idea that he had to talk to Shapiro further and get in contact with Kane and Ableson.

Chapter 13

Loren was very worried because Bill didn't come home at all and didn't answer his phone. He didn't know how else to get a hold of him. Did he try to make speed? Where? Did something go wrong? Was he hurt?

He arrived at the lab late after a restless night and again found a note that Doug was waiting for him in the lobby. After picking up two doughnuts and two coffees at the cart, he went to the lobby and greeted the detective. Loren was beginning to like him. Maybe he could help with Bill.

"Hi Doug. You are getting to be an everyday affair," Loren said. "Have a doughnut and some coffee."

"Thanks. I didn't have breakfast." Doug took the coffee and doughnut.

Loren spoke with his mouth full of doughnut. "What brings you out today?"

"I've been trying to get in touch with Kane and Ableson. I've been in contact with their lawyer in Denver but he said he couldn't help me. I've decided to go to out there and speak to him in person." He paused. "I want you to go with me."

"What? Why on earth would I do that and why would

you want me to?" Loren shook his head vigorously. "No."

Doug said, "You've helped me a lot already. I feel I have limitations with this case. I don't have enough scientific background for a thorough investigation. Also, you know the two men."

Loren gulped his coffee. "I know them only to say hello when passing in the hall."

"That's better than I know them. I want you to go as a scientific advisor. Of course, your expenses will be covered. We will get you officially made a police consultant and we can deputize you."

"No thanks, I'm not a detective. I have plenty to do here. My son could be in trouble. No way."

"You were very helpful on our visit to Reitz's lab. It should only take a few days."

"No, it's not going to happen," Loren said, shaking his head some more.

Doug reached for the lobby phone and dialed. He asked for Dr. Benson and then said, "Dr. Benson, this is detective Sanderson. I have Loren Sharp here and I would like you to speak to him about the matter we discussed." He handed the phone to Loren."

Benson said, "Loren, I think it would be very helpful if you would accompany Sanderson. You may be able to get some information that would help with the Martox process problem. We have to get to the bottom of this Martox thing. And, of course, we should help find Reitz's killer if we can. I'm asking you to go. I'll make it up to you,"

"This is two you owe me," Loren said and hung up.

He turned to Doug. "So you talked to Ted Benson. It's obviously a put-up job. But this is a really bad time for me. My son Bill's in trouble. I'm not sure I can leave."

"What's up?"

Loren debated what to say. Now that it came down to it, he wasn't sure he wanted to tell a cop his son might be manufacturing drugs. "He's, uh, missing."

"How long?"

"He didn't come home last night."

Doug pulled out his cell. "How old is he? What was he wearing?"

"He's twenty-one."

The detective stared at him.

"I can tell you think I'm being stupid," Loren said. "But I know something's wrong. Do you have kids?"

Doug put his phone away. "No."

"Okay," Loren said, sighing. "I guess I'm going." He'd have to get Gloria or someone to find Bill. "When do we leave? I can't be gone long."

Doug handed him a plane ticket.

"God, you already had a ticket. You must have been confident I would go."

"Well it saves time. The ticket could be refunded. Benson told me Marchem would pay your expenses.

"Oh, you've been talking to him a lot."

"Yes, he seems pretty anxious about the Martox situation."

"I know."

We fly out at five. I'll pick you up at three-thirty here in the lobby."

"Today? God, you move fast."

"Police procedure," said Doug with a smile.

Loren went home. There was still no sign of Bill. He tried his cell again and it went straight to voicemail again.

He didn't know what else to do.

He decided to call Gloria. Considering their last awkward conversation, he wasn't looking forward to it. What if she didn't even answer?

But she answered right away. "Loren? What's up? It's not like you to call me in the middle of the day."

"I know this is an imposition, but I have to go out of town on business. Is there any chance you could check on Bill?" Loren traveled quite a bit for his job, setting up plants and the like.

"Bill?" she asked. "Why does he need to be checked on?"

"I'm, uh, just worried about him. He didn't come home last night, and I can't get a hold of him."

"Okay," she said slowly. "I'm very busy, but I will check on him if you want me to."

"Thank you," he said. "I really appreciate it." He wasn't sure what else to say. "I have to go."

"Bye." They hung up. Apparently, they could both avoid talking about their last awkward conversation. Loren still didn't know what she wanted from him. He wasn't sure himself what he wanted. He knew he cared about her. And now he knew he could count on her in a pinch.

Since he didn't get much sleep the night before, he tried to take a nap. He surprised himself and managed to sleep for a while. When his alarm went off, he threw some clothes and toiletries in his roll-aboard. He wolfed down a sandwich and drove back to the lab.

He sent email out to several of his colleagues about his coming absence and went down to the lobby. He was early so he read a copy of the Marchem annual report. He had not read the report lately and was pleased to see the company was doing so well. At exactly three-thirty Doug's car pulled up to the lobby entrance.

Loren got in and Doug drove directly to the airport. They parked in long-range parking, got their luggage out of the trunk and walked to the ticket counter. After checking in, going through security, and finding the gate they had about a half hour to wait. Loren was in a sour mood. He was not happy about the trip. Where was Bill?

Chapter 14

At the airport, Loren wasn't happy. Doug seemed to realize it and he kept the conversation at a minimum. The plane was on time and they boarded. They sat together but Loren pulled out a copy of Chemical and Engineering News and started reading.

"Do you travel much, Loren?" Doug asked.

"I go to New Orleans often for my work and I used to go to Colorado when my kids were going to college there. That's about it now. I used to travel a lot with my wife. We had some amazing trips, Europe, Bermuda." He paused. "You seem to have a lot of money. May I ask how you have so much on a policeman's salary?"

"My father had a successful law firm and made a lot of money. When he died, I got half of it." Doug shrugged.

"Some of your methods seem unorthodox. Or is it standard operating procedure for a St. Louis cop to take off for Denver at the drop of a hat?"

"I also inherited my father's influence. Lots of people in high places owed him favors, including our current Mayor. I sometimes take advantage of that. My captain gives me a pretty long leash as long as it doesn't cost him any money," Doug said. "Money can level the playing field. But I only use it against the bad guys."

Loren didn't really want to talk, so he went back to his magazine.

The plane was on time getting in, but it was raining in Denver. They went to the rental car agency and picked up a car and drove to the Radisson. When they were checked in, Doug said he was going to call his ex-wife. Loren said he was tired and would watch some television and go to bed. They agreed to meet in a restaurant for breakfast at seven-thirty a.m. Loren and Doug went to their rooms.

Both men were on time for breakfast and Loren was in a somewhat better mood. He'd talked to Gloria and while she hadn't talked directly to Bill, she'd seen his car in Loren's driveway.

They both ordered breakfast.

Doug said, "I just read in the morning paper about melamine being found in Chinese milk. How could that happen?"

"Good question," Loren said, warming to the topic. "It turns out the melamine molecule contains a lot of nitrogen in a small amount of weight. Protein is assayed essentially by analyzing for nitrogen and applying a factor. The more protein, the higher quality of the milk and the higher the price. However melamine, which is usually used to make plastic dinnerware and such, is slightly toxic."

"So some genius with a little knowledge was being clever," said Doug.

"And greedy."

"A little knowledge and a little greed make for a dangerous situation.

"That's for sure," said Loren. "So, you said you're still in contact with your ex-wife? How's that work?"

"We call or email once in a while. When I'm in Colorado I try to see her."

Loren sensed that Doug was still very interested in his ex-wife. "What's she like?"

He pulled out a picture. "She's an artist. Very talented but rather emotional. I miss her."

"I miss my late wife, too," Loren said. "Is she beautiful?"

"My wife or yours?" Doug was being playful.

"I was speaking of yours but mine was too," Loren said.

"Yes, as you can see she's very attractive." Doug showed him the picture. "The picture doesn't do her justice."

"She's very beautiful."

Doug said, "Thanks. But, let's get this show on the road. I'll call Shapiro. We should go try to see him." He took out his cell phone and walked away, leaving Loren at the table.

Loren had to pay the bill. This did not help his mood. Even though he was being reimbursed it was a bother.

Doug came back to the table. "So, I thought I'd go see Shapiro on my own. You don't mind, do you?"

"No way," Loren said. "I didn't fly all the way out here to do nothing."

"Suit yourself."

Doug drove them over to Shapiro's office building. There was no parking and finally he parked in a no parking zone. The office was in an impressive new glass sided building. They looked at the building directory and took the elevator to Shapiro's third floor office. The door said, *Charles E. Shapiro and George W. Ross. Attorneys at Law.*

The outer office was plush. The paintings on the walls must have been good copies, they would be worth several hundred thousand dollars if real. The secretary at the desk was also plush. She was tall, slim, blonde and very pretty. She was very well dressed.

Loren looked around and was impressed. Doug also seemed impressed.

"Can I help you?" she said.

"We would like to see Mr. Shapiro," said Doug.

"What's your name?"

"We're with the police." Doug flashed his badge fast enough so she couldn't see it was not the Denver police. "I'm detective Douglas Sanderson and this is our consultant, Dr. Loren Sharp."

Loren nodded when his name was mentioned. He wasn't exactly with the police. It must be more of Doug's unorthodox methods.

The secretary informed Shapiro by intercom that the police wished to see him.

Shapiro said he was busy and that the police would have to wait.

They settled down in the waiting area with old *Field and Stream* magazines and after a half an hour Shapiro's door opened.

"Ah, Mr. Sanderson, I believe we've spoken on the phone." Shapiro was tall and quite thin, clean-shaven but with a full head of bushy hair with only a trace of gray. He was perhaps forty-five but could be older.

"Yes," Doug said. "And this is my colleague Dr. Sharp."

"Nice to meet you," Loren said, politely.

Shapiro gestured them into his office. Whatever he was working on that required keeping them waiting was not evident. The office was tastefully done in woods, glass and brass. A large portrait hung behind Shapiro's large desk. Shapiro noticed Doug staring at the portrait.

"That is Sir Edward Coke, the father of English jurisprudence," Shapiro said. "The portrait belonged to my father. I thought it was a nice touch." Loren thought it was a little stuffy.

But Doug said, "Yes, it is. A touch of class." They all sat down.

"I think you know why we're here," Doug said. "We need to get in touch with Earl Kane and Sidney Ableson."

"Mr. Kane has not given me a free-hand as far as whom I give out their phone number or address. It falls under attorney-client privilege. Of course, if you make it worth it for me, I might cooperate.

"How would I do that?" Doug asked.

"I have a charitable foundation. If you would like to contribute to it, I would be very pleased. Most contributions are at least four figures.

Wow, this guy was a crook.

But Doug smiled. "That sounds like a bribe."

"Call it what you will."

Doug took a small recorder from his jacket pocket and said, "Perhaps the Bar would like to hear that exchange." Loren was surprised. And irritated. Why hadn't Doug told him what he was going to do?

Shapiro shook his head. "I should have known better. Okay. But you will only get Kane's answering machine.

"I only have an old address and a phone number. When I

want to get in touch with Kane or Ableson I call the phone number and leave a message. I state my business and if Kane wants to discuss it he'll call me back. The address is for a ranch in northeast Colorado. I've seldom been there. I sometimes send him documents. I have the impression they don't like visitors."

Doug looked interested. "What kind of business are they in?"

"Some kind of cattle business from what I understand."

"Why all the secrecy?" Doug asked.

"It's actually none of your business but I believe that they are doing some kind of secret research."

Loren perked up. "What kind of research?"

"I'm not at liberty to say." Shapiro gave Doug a piece of paper that had the phone number and address on it.

"I guess that concludes our business." Doug got up to leave and Loren followed.

"I guess so," said Shapiro as he waved goodbye.

Doug said, "Thank you for your help," as they left.

"Yeah, thanks," Loren said.

"Any time," said Shapiro with a forced smile.

When they got back to the car Doug popped the locks.

"Next time you're going to blackmail someone I'd like to be in on the plan," Loren said, frowning, getting in.

"I didn't know he'd say or do something incriminating."

"Yeah, right," Loren said.

"Okay, I had d strong suspicion," Doug said.

"The mysterious research sounds interesting," Loren said. "Too bad he didn't tell us anything else about it."

"I'm right with you, there." Doug took out the Colorado map he obtained at the car rental agency. The address Shapiro had written down was just Thompson, CO. He found it on the map up toward the northeast corner of the state. It apparently was the county seat.

He pointed. "Looks like we might be taking a trip tomorrow."

"That sounds good," said Loren, who wanted to get the whole trip over with.

"I'm going to call Kane after lunch and see what happens," Doug said. "If Kane doesn't call back, we should go out to the ranch."

"How far is the place?"

"About a hundred and forty miles northeast."

Loren frowned. "When would we go?"

"I'll call soon and I'll give him the rest of the day to respond. If he doesn't, we'll go out there in the morning."

"Okay." The sooner they went to this ranch, the sooner they could get home.

Doug nodded. "Listen, my ex-wife, Mona, has invited us to dinner tonight. I hope you will come. She wants to meet you."

"Meet me? Why?"

"She says she's never met a scientist. Come along. You'll like her."

Loren was feeling bored after his uneventful day so he agreed to go.

Chapter 15

Doug drove the two of them to Mona's. She lived in a small but nice house in Aurora near the old Stapleton airport. He drove like he was in a hurry to get there.

Mona opened the door before they knocked as if she had been waiting for them. Doug and she embraced as though they were still married. Obviously there were still some feelings left.

She was a beautiful woman with dark brown, almost-black hair, a clear complexion, a sensual mouth and the greenest eyes Doug had ever seen. Although she had on a smock and baggy pants, her figure was the equal of any Hollywood star.

Loren seemed very impressed with her.

"Come in, come in, I've been waiting for you," she said. "You must be Dr. Sharp."

Loren seemed almost tongue-tied but he smiled. "Please call me Loren."

"Okay, I'm Mona." She laughed. The men joined in.

They went into the back of the house to an airy room with large windows. There was an extensive shelf with colored glass in it on one end of the room and a big worktable in the center that had tools and equipment on it. Near one of the windows was a sofa and two comfortable chairs with a cocktail table in between and several large plants were arranged on stands near the windows. The scene behind the windows showed a good view of the mountains.

"I think this is the most pleasant room in the house," she said. "Please sit down."

Doug waved his hand, at her work. "Mona is an art glass artist."

"Oh, I wondered what all this stuff was for," said Loren.

Mona shook her head. "I probably would be classified as a craftsman rather than an artist."

Doug said, "Don't be modest, Mona." He turned to Loren. "She has exhibited in several museums and her pieces sell for small fortunes."

"Wow," Loren said. "Very impressive."

"Oh, cut it out, Doug," said Mona. "What brings you guys to Colorado?"

Doug told her about the suspected murder of Wolfgang Reitz and the names of Kane and Ableson on his calendar for around the time he died.

"A case," Mona said. "I might have guessed." But she smiled. "Well, that all sounds suspicious but not much to go on.

"Well, perhaps, but it had to be checked out," said Doug. "Their secretive behavior makes me more suspicious." My cop intuition is telling me there's something here.

"And Loren, you are advising Douglas on scientific aspects?" she asked.

He chuckled. "That's what Doug told me. I also know

the men." Loren couldn't seem to take his eyes off Mona.

Doug couldn't blame him. She was as charming as ever. He was glad they came.

"What are you guys drinking?" she asked. "I made some margaritas."

Doug and Loren both said they would like a margarita. Mona left and returned with three good sized drinks.

The drinks were delicious. Doug smacked his lips. "Nice, Mona. Thanks."

"Yes, delicious," Loren said.

"Is there anything I can do to help your investigation?" Mona asked.

"Not unless you know about cyanide poisoning, the Martox manufacturing process or these guys Kane and Ableson," Loren said. He seemed preoccupied.

"No, thanks, Mona," Doug said. "We've got it covered."

"Let's eat," she said.

They went into the dining room and sat down. The room was filled with glass art. Sculptures and glass-topped boxes with lights inside were all around the room. The window had a stunning art glass panel with perhaps a thousand pieces. All of the pieces were beautiful. The table was decorated with a number of glass statuettes, candleholders and vases. The vases all had roses in them. Loren seemed very impressed.

Doug said, "Beautiful. I see you have been a busy girl."

"Yes. I have really been into my work since I moved to Colorado." She smiled and then went into the kitchen and returned with a hot casserole. She put it on the table and took off the cover. It was some kind of Mexican dish.

The simplicity of the food was in contrast with the elegant setting but the food smelled wonderful and Doug very hungry.

"Go for it guys. It's my own recipe," she said.

Doug and Loren both took large helpings.

"Delicious," Loren said.

Doug also found it to be delicious. It had just the right amount of spice. "Yeah. This is great."

Mona opened a bottle of Australian wine, shiraz.

Loren said, "This is very good." He took note of the label.

A simple green salad completed the meal.

The conversation turned to Colorado, art glass, the investigation, Loren's job and the Denver Broncos. They had a friendly discussion.

There was no dessert but after dinner drinks were offered. Loren had some cognac with his coffee and the others only had coffee.

After dinner they returned to the studio and Mona showed them a number of her projects.

Loren said, "Wow, Mona. You're very talented."

Doug nodded. "Definitely." He was very attentive but didn't say much. He really missed her.

Around ten o'clock Doug decided they should be going back to the hotel. Perhaps Kane had called and they wanted to get an early start in the morning.

She hugged them both when they left and gave them both a dazzling smile.

On the way back to the hotel Loren was very complimentary about her. "She is certainly a charming woman."

"Umm," said Doug. What was she up to?

Loren asked, "Didn't you enjoy the evening?"

"Yes, I did, but I was trying to find out where Mona's at these days."

"What do you mean?"

"She may have been too charming. Mona's a bit of a predator. She collects scalps. At least she was. From the way she came on to you, probably she still is."

"What do you mean?"

"She makes men fall in love with her and then dumps them. She gets a kick out of it. Some kind of ego thing."

"That's not your divorce talking, is it?" Loren asked.

Was it? Doug didn't answer.

By the time they got back to the hotel Kane still hadn't called.

"What time in the morning?" Loren asked.

"How about meeting for breakfast at eight o'clock?"

"Okay, see you in the morning."

They went up to their rooms.

Doug couldn't get to sleep. There was too much going on. There was too much to figure out.

Chapter 16

Loren didn't sleep well but he showed up on time at the restaurant.

Doug was not there.

He got a table for two and ordered coffee. By eight fifteen a.m. he'd had two cups of coffee and some toast. Doug still hadn't shown up yet.

He told the waitress he'd be back and went to the house phone. He called Doug's room but he didn't answer. Just as he hung up he saw Doug come in the front door of the hotel and went over to meet him.

He was agitated. "Where have you been?"

Doug seemed flustered, too. "I was out checking the car. We have a long trip today." He was wearing the same clothes he had on the evening before, and looked disheveled. Strange for such a meticulous man.

"I have a table in the restaurant," Loren said.

"Good, I'm starved."

They went into the restaurant and ordered. They each had bacon, eggs and toast. Loren never ate like that at home but somehow it was okay when traveling.

Doug said, "We better pack some things in case we

have to stay overnight."

Loren wasn't happy. "Okay. But I hope we don't have to stay over."

Doug signed the bill and they went to their rooms to freshen up and pack a few things before hitting the road. They met back in the lobby and Doug had changed his clothes. Loren was dying to ask what was going on but decided to be discreet.

Doug drove and they started up US 25. Traffic was very bad until they turned off on US 76 and then it slimmed down. After about twenty minutes the countryside turned from urban to prairie.

"Are we still in Colorado or did we somehow cross to Kansas?" asked Loren, grinning.

"It isn't what you think of when you think of Colorado, is it?" Doug said.

They drove through miles of scrub and suddenly Doug pulled over to the side of the road, yawning. "Can you drive for a while?"

"Okay," Loren said. "But I don't exactly know where we're going."

"You'll be fine. When you get to Sterling wake me up," said Doug.

They exchanged places and Loren drove to Sterling while Doug slept. He pulled into a hamburger place's parking lot and awakened Doug.

Doug stretched and looked around. "How about a burger?"

"Sure," Loren said, even though it was only ten-thirty. They went into the burger place and both ordered two cheeseburgers with fries and a coke. Since it was an odd hour, the place was almost empty so the food came up fast.

The employees seemed bored.

The two men sat down at one of the bolted-down tables.

"Is it much further?" asked Loren.

"About thirty miles," said Doug. "But no more freeway."

"What are we going to do when we get to Thompson?"

I thought we would go to the post office first and see if they can give us directions to the Kane and Ableson ranch. If they can't or won't, I think we would visit the county sheriff to see if he can help us."

"Sounds like a decent plan," Loren said. "What if we strike out?"

Doug shrugged. "We'll think of something else."

The men went back to the car and left town. Doug turned onto a single lane road and drove in silence until they arrived in Thompson, which was not a big town. It boasted two taverns, three restaurants, three churches, a motel, a post office, a red brick city hall that functioned as the county seat and several small businesses including a general store.

"We better check in to the motel before we leave town for the ranch," said Doug.

Loren wasn't happy. He thought they might be leaving this evening. "Are we staying over?" He needed to get back to Bill. And what about Wolfy's threat to the new Martox plant?

"Probably," Doug said. "At least we will have rooms if we need to."

Loren said nothing. They drove over to the Garden Motel and entered the office.

"We need a couple of rooms for the night," Doug said.

The desk clerk was about seventeen and dressed in jeans and a cowboy shirt. He had an unpleasant look on his pimply face. Loren decided he didn't like to be interrupted while looking at his girlie magazine.

"Only got one room," he said in a snarling way. That was hard to believe in this small town.

"One or two beds?" Doug asked.

"Two."

"Well, Loren, I guess we're room- mates," Doug said.

"Swell," said Loren in a voice that indicated he didn't think it was.

Doug signed in and gave the boy his Amex.

"We don't take that," said the clerk. "Visa, MasterCard or cash in advance."

Loren gave the boy his Visa, the boy ran it and the men left.

"He sure was an unpleasant youngster," Doug said.

"I don't think he likes his job," Loren said.

"Evidently not."

They got in the car and drove over to the post office, parking in front. There were no other cars. Inside, the place was a rather typical rural post office, small with a partition, a counter and an entry to the back. They told the counter clerk they wanted to see the postmaster. The clerk shouted "Valeria!"

The postmaster came from the back. She was a Hispanic woman of rather ample proportions.

"What do you want?" she said in an unpleasant voice. Apparently she did not like to be disturbed. Why was everyone in this town so grumpy?

Doug flashed his badge fast enough that she couldn't determine what was on it. "I'm from the police department and I'm trying to locate a local resident."

"It's not our policy to give out addresses of our clients," Valeria said.

Loren smiled, trying to turn on the charm. "You'd really help us out. We'd appreciate it."

Her expression seemed to be softening.

"This is a police matter," said Doug.

And then she was all business again. "Then you'd better go see the sheriff," she said.

"All right, but we may be back," Doug said.

Loren and Doug got back in the car and drove over to city hall and parked. In the front hall the building directory said: *SHERIFF 104.*

Room 104 was just down the hall and there was a sign: *Peter J. Swieki, SHERIFF.* The door stood open and the sheriff was sitting at his desk cleaning a large revolver.

"Sheriff Swieki?" asked Doug.

"That's Swi-eki, partner, but you can just call me Pete" said the sheriff, putting down the revolver. "What can I do for you gentlemen?" He was a big man with lots of red hair and a beard to match. His most prominent features were his nose and his waistline. He wore blue jeans and a blue shirt with a badge pinned on it. He had a very large silver buckle on his belt but he also had on red suspenders.

Doug said, "I'm a police detective. I'm looking for two local residents named Kane and Ableson. I got their address from their lawyer but he wasn't specific. He just gave the post office, here."

"I don't recognize you," the sheriff said. "Where're you from?"

"St. Louis," Doug said.

Swieki whistled. "You're outta your jurisdiction."

"It's regarding a m--" Doug said.

Loren interrupted. "It's a serious matter, regarding his lawyer. We'd appreciate any help you could give us."

"Well..." Sheriff Swieki looked uncomfortable, shifting in his chair. "I've met Mr. Kane but never met Ableson or been out to their place. Kane told me he was doing secret cattle breeding experiments and didn't want any strangers snooping around."

"Experiments?" Loren asked. "What kind of cattle breeding experiments?" Since when did these guys know anything about cattle?

Swieki said, "Don't know exactly, but Kane said they'd revolutionize cattle breeding and it was worth a lot of money.

"Do you know the way to his ranch?" asked Doug.

The sheriff was rapidly getting more uncomfortable. "Yeah. I do. But I don't know if I should tell you. Mr. Kane wouldn't like it. He told me not to help any strangers find his place."

"As I told you, we come with a confidential message from his lawyer," Loren said. "I'm sure he'd want to see us."

"I think I'll call him and see if he wants to see you guys," Swieki said.

Doug put on a menacing face. "That won't be necessary. As I said, we come from his lawyer. We'd like to get out there before dark and we're not very familiar with this area. I don't think Kane would like it if you delayed us."

"Okay, but I don't like it," said the sheriff. He drew a simple map and gave it to Doug. He was reaching for his phone as the two men left his office.

They drove about five miles on blacktop and turned onto a gravel road, driving for about three miles. They came upon a sign said: *K&A RANCH. AUTHORISED PERSONNEL ONLY.* Doug turned in and drove another three miles until they came to a ten foot chain link fence. The gate was closed.

"What do we do now?" said Loren.

Doug shook his head. "Not much we can do. I don't see a bell or anything." He blew the car horn in frustration. There was no reply.

"I guess we need a plan B." At this point Loren was intrigued.

Doug did a U turn and headed back the way they came. They'd gone about a half mile when they met a truck going toward the ranch. He pulled another U turn and cautiously followed it. It was white and unmarked except for green lettering on the cab that couldn't be read from behind. He pulled over and the two men got out and cautiously walked up to where they could see it.

The trucker briefly stopped before the gate and the gate slid open. The driver went through the gate and disappeared up the road. The gate slid shut.

"Radio-controlled gate," Loren said, pulling on his ear.

"No doubt," Doug said. "Authorized personnel only. This seems to be quite an operation. We're going to have to find out what's going on here. It looks very suspicious." They got back in the car and started back to Thompson.

"Why all the secrecy?" Loren was getting into it. He loved a good puzzle. "I can't believe Earl Kane's doing cattle breeding research. He doesn't have a scientific bone in his body. He's an operator, a politician. Maybe Ableson, but not Kane. No way, I don't believe it. What are we going to do? We need to figure this out."

"I have an idea," Doug said.

"What?"

"I'll tell you when I get it arranged."

The men drove in silence the rest of the way back to the motel and moved into their room. It was two pm.

"Let's have some lunch," Doug said.

"Yeah. I can use some. This traveling makes me hungry."

There was a diner next to the motel. It looked clean if not luxurious so the men went in. They both ordered burgers which turned out to be big and good. Doug had iced tea and Loren a Coors.

"That trip was a waste of time," Loren said.

Doug shook his head. "No. We got the lay of the land. We can develop a plan."

"So, what's the plan?"

"I'm going to try to arrange it this afternoon."

"Arrange what?"

"Blocked by land, go by air."

What did that mean? "Let me know what we're going to do as soon as you can." Loren stood up. "I need to make a phone call." He needed to find out what was going on at home.

Chapter 17

Doug went to the motel room and tried looking some stuff up on his cell phone but there was no local service. He called Mona on the phone in his room. "Hi, Mona," he said. "How are you?"

"Doug? I'm pretty good, considering." He could hear the smile in her voice. "I thought you guys were out in the country investigating. What's up?"

"I know this is an imposition, but can you look up helicopter services in the Denver area?"

"Why can't you do it?"

"No service."

"Sure. Just a sec." After a few moments she gave him five numbers. They exchanged a few more pleasantries and hung up.

On the landline, Doug called the first one and was told they only did local Denver charters. The second and third numbers yielded the same result but the fourth said he had a buddy in the business in Sterling and he gave him the phone number. He dialed the number and after several rings the phone was answered,

"VN Flying service. Vern speaking."

"I need to rent a helicopter," said Doug.

"You've called the right place. I assume you want a pilot too."

"That's correct," Doug said. "I want to fly over a ranch near Thompson."

"Sounds good. My fee is two hundred dollars per hour for legal jobs and four hundred dollars for illegal."

Doug laughed. "This is a legal job. At least I think it is. Can you come at dusk and land in the field behind the Garden Motel?'

"Yep." The two men finalized the arrangements.

Loren showed up at the room. "I need to use the landline."

"Help yourself." Doug gestured at the phone.

Loren dialed. "Gloria?"

"Loren?" Doug didn't have any trouble hearing Gloria's side of the conversation.

"How's Bill?" Loren asked.

"I haven't been able to get him on the phone," she said. "I finally went over to your house and let myself in. Bill wasn't there but he was--judging by the pile of dirty dishes and his messy bedroom."

"That's something, I guess." Loren sighed. "Was my note still there on the refrigerator?"

"No, I didn't see any note."

"Okay, please keep checking on him."

"I will, but why are you so worried about him? He's been alone before."

Loren looked at Doug. "I'll tell you when I see you."

"When are you coming home?"

"Right now I couldn't say. We're having trouble

contacting the men we came out here to see." He paused. "You haven't heard from Benson, have you? Any news? Or maybe he's looking for me?"

"No. Why?"

"I'll tell you later."

"Someday you will have to tell me what this is all about. I miss you."

"Me too. See you soon. I hope. Thanks for all your help. I appreciate it." They hung up.

Loren leaned back on one of the beds, getting comfortable.

"Everything all right at home?" Doug asked.

"You mean besides one of my colleagues getting murdered, but not before he threatened to blow up one of our plants?"

"Yeah, besides that."

Loren didn't immediately answer. "I'm not sure," he finally said.

Doug told Loren about the helicopter.

Loren frowned "This sounds a little extreme and maybe illegal. I didn't bargain for this when I agreed to come here with you."

"Don't you want to get to the bottom of this?"

"Sure, but what has all this got to do with Wolfy's murder? And I don't see how it could have anything to do with the Martox plant."

"We won't know till we talk to Kane."

"Okay, but I don't like it," said Loren.

The two men relaxed on the beds for a few moments.

Finally, Loren said, "I don't want to just sit here. If Kane is doing some kind of research, he might have had a lot of equipment mailed here. I think I'll go talk to that postmistress Valeria again." He sat up. "I can check the feed store in town, too, to see if Kane's been buying food or supplies for livestock."

"Good thinking." Doug was impressed. "I guess if you're going to do that, I can take another crack at the sheriff. He knows more than he's saying. Meet back here before sunset."

When the two men met up again at the motel, neither was happy.

"Everyone in town seems to know something they're not saying," Loren said.

"Yeah, the sheriff wasn't talking, either," Doug said. Odd, for law enforcement to be so uncooperative.

"It's almost like they're afraid," Loren said.

"Maybe," Doug said. "But we should go." They walked out to the field together.

As requested, Vernon Newton landed his helicopter in the field right before dusk. The chopper looked flyable but just barely. It seemed to be some kind of surplus military type. The pilot kept the rotors going at reduced speed while waving at Doug and Loren to get in.

The two men ran out and jumped in.

"Ah, which of you is Sanderson? I'm Vern Newton. Call me Vern." He was a small man but very muscular. He wore fatigues and, even though the sun was going down, sunglasses. A crew cut and drooping mustache completed his image.

Doug identified himself and told Vern to fly to the northeast.

"Roger," Vern said.

"So VN Air Service stands for Vern Newton," Loren

said.

"Some days it does and some days it stands for Viet Nam."

"I take it you are a veteran," Doug said.

"Four years flying in Nam," Vern said.

There were few landmarks on the ground, just rolling scrub but Doug thought that if they flew to the northeast they would eventually come to the ranch. Sure enough, after a short flight, the fence came into view. Doug told Vern to gain altitude so there would be as little noise as possible. The first thing they saw in the setting sun was a featureless area half as big as a football field.

"If that isn't a camouflage net I'll be surprised. I saw plenty of them in Nam," Vern said.

"I wonder what they're hiding," Doug said.

"It doesn't look like research to me," Loren said.

A short distance from the net was a one-story cinderblock building with no windows and several vents on the roof. What appeared to be a loading dock was on one end with several steel drums stacked up.

"Do you have any binoculars, Vern?" Doug asked.

Vern pointed at a compartment

Doug found some GI binoculars and tried to read the labels on the drums but it was growing too dark. The chopper banked and headed northeast. A barn-like building came into view with a paddock attached.

"I don't think that could hold very many cows," Loren said.

There was an older house about thirty yards from the barn. A Jeep-like vehicle was parked in front of the house.

The chopper headed east and found a rather unimposing ranch house with an attached garage. Two utility vehicles were parked outside.

"Looks like living quarters," Doug said. "There doesn't seem to be anything else to see. Let's get out of here."

The helicopter banked and headed back to Thompson.

There was little talk on the way back to Thompson. Doug didn't want to involve Vern in their investigation and Loren was also being discrete. The sun was down when they arrived back at the motel but there was sufficient light from the town so a good landing could be made in the same field they took off from. Doug gave Vern two hundred and fifty dollars and Vern said if they needed his services again he would be happy to oblige and he took off.

Doug and Loren agreed to go out to dinner and went back to their room to clean up.

Sheriff Swieki knocked on their door while Loren was in the shower.

Doug quickly finished dressing and opened the door.

"What is all this about a helicopter flying around here?" the sheriff said. "We have a quiet town and we don't like to be disturbed." It was obvious he was angry. "What are you up to?"

"Sightseeing," Doug said.

"We don't have many sights around here to see."

"So we found out."

Doug's flippant attitude seemed to make the sheriff angrier, "If you were bothering Mr. Kane, you'll be sorry. You better be careful about what you do around here. You could get in a lot of trouble. I think you should leave town. And soon."

Doug shrugged. "Whatever you say, sheriff."

The sheriff stalked off and Doug closed the door.

A little later he and Loren went to the diner and

ordered burgers and Coors. "The sheriff stopped by while you were in the shower."

"What did he want?" Loren took a sip of his beer.

"He seemed pissed we're investigating Kane."

"That's interesting," Loren said. "And, considering he's the sheriff, a little frightening. What do we do next?"

"It's clear, because of all the secrecy and warnings, that something illegal's being done at that ranch." Doug sipped his own beer.

"Do you really think it's related to Wolfy's murder or the threat against the Martox plant?"

"Maybe. I think we have to find out."

Loren nodded. "I agree. But, how are we going to do that? We can't get in to see what is really going on."

"I think we'll pay Mr. Kane a midnight visit."

"You mean sneak in? Trespass?"

"I guess you could say that."

"I don't know," Loren said. "This is getting a little deep for me. We have no legal grounds for doing that. I don't see how it has anything to do with Wolfy's murder or the plant. We're out in the middle of nowhere."

"It's our only lead and my gut's telling me there's something important here. I'm going in but you don't have to. If you prefer to wait here, that's okay." He paused. "You know the men. What do you think they're up to?"

Loren tugged on his earlobe. "Given his history at Marchem I think it's possible he's doing some kind of illegal waste dumping. Frankly, he gave me the creeps. He might be involved in something even worse."

"See? That's good information," Doug said. "You could be even more helpful. Let your conscience be your guide. "

"What if we're caught? Surely, they heard the helicopter and will be especially alert."

Doug tried to calm him down. "I should think Kane would throw us out or maybe call the sheriff. A fine would be the worst punishment and that doesn't bother me." He knew that wasn't true. His gut was telling him Kane was a dangerous man and his reaction to their trespass could be deadly. But he needed backup and Loren was the only guy here.

"Well, okay, but it's your responsibility," Loren said eventually.

They paid and left the diner.

They went to their room to plan and then Doug went over to the general store. He bought a coil of polypropylene clothesline and a replacement hoe handle.

Around eleven pm the two men set out in the rental car. It was very dark since the moon was behind heavy clouds and there were no streetlights.

As they drove through the dark, Loren said, "Do you really think what we're doing is a good idea?"

Doug said, "We already decided. Relax, I'm a cop. I know what I'm doing."

Loren stared at the side of the road and moved back as if he'd seen something there in the dark.

"You need to get a grip, Loren." He jerked the wheel and the car swerved back toward the center of the road.

Loren gasped.

"Your jumpiness is making me jumpy. Try to calm down. It's hard enough driving on this strange road in the dark."

"Well, excuse me, if I--" he started to say angrily, but seemed to reconsider. "Sorry."

"Look on the bright side. The darkness will make our entry easier," said Doug without a lot of conviction. They drove on.

Finally, Doug said, "The mileage says we're within a mile of the gate."

"Was I just me, or did that trip seem like it took at least three hours?"

"No. It wasn't just you." Doug pulled off the road, stopped and turned off the headlights. "We walk from here."

"How do we get over the fence?"

"I don't know if you noticed but the chain link fence ends about a hundred yards down on both sides and then there is only five foot high barbed wire," whispered Doug.

"How do we get over the barbed wire?" Loren was also whispering.

"You'll see." Doug got out of the car and got the clothesline and hoe handle out of the trunk. He cut a piece from the clothesline about twelve feet long and threw the rest back in the trunk.

The men set off diagonally cross country, not on the road. It was totally dark and they ran into small hills and gullies and a lot of brush. It was pretty tough going. After stumbling along for about a mile and a half they finally came to the barbed wire. They were away from the inhabited part of the ranch but a light on the back of the cinderblock building gave just enough light to make out the fence.

Doug took the piece of polypropylene clothesline, looped it over the wire and pulled the end out from under the bottom wire. He tied a knot in the rope, tied in the hoe handle and twisted the handle. The wire pulled together leaving a good size gap under the fence and he pushed the handle into the ground.

"Your gate, sir," Doug said, bowing to Loren.

Loren went first under the fence and Doug followed.

"We're in. What now?" Loren asked.

"We'll follow the fence down toward the building, keeping as far from the light as possible."

They started walking toward the building keeping low and close to the fence. A door opened in the back of the building and a man came out and lit a cigarette. Doug and Loren got down on the ground and observed.

"My God, that's Arnold Novack," Loren said.

"Who's he?"

"He was a chemist at Marchem. He retired last year and I heard he moved to Colorado. What's going on here?" More Marchem?

Loren and Doug stayed down on the ground until the man put the cigarette out in a tray by the door and went back in.

Doug whispered, "Let's go to the camouflage net. Stay on the side away from the building. No more talking."

They slowly edged their way up to the area covered by the camouflage net. It covered a large pit. Fifty-five gallon drums were piled three high in the pit.

"What is that smell?" Doug whispered.

"Chlorinated hydrocarbons," Loren whispered. "Some of these drums must be leaking."

They stared into the pit. "Some of the drums are fiber packs used for packaging powders."

"Are we in danger here?" Doug asked. Fresh dirt covered the front end of the pit for about thirty yards, the back end was slanted up and heavy-duty forklift and an

113

earthmover were parked at the top. He pinched his nose and shook his head.

Loren nodded. "Not sure, but, probably."

Doug motioned to Loren to follow him and he started around the pit. They went to the corner of the pit toward the building and headed toward the loading dock. If someone came out of the building now they were in trouble. They kneeled by the side of the dock and Doug pointed to the drums.

Loren quietly read the labels. "Acetone, ether, diethyl maleate and urea." He looked at Doug and silently mouthed the word drugs.

Doug nodded, wishing he had an infrared camera and motioned to start back to where they came in. They had all they wanted.

They started past the pit and were met by a man pointing an automatic weapon at them as they came around the building. They both stopped abruptly.

"Hold it right there, boys," the man said. "Looks like you're doing some trespassing."

Just as he said it the moon peeked out from the clouds and showed over the man's right shoulder. The man had a full head of blond hair and was dressed in khakis and a tan shirt. Doug didn't think mentioning he was a cop would help them any.

After glaring at Doug, Loren said, "We don't mean you any harm. Why don't you just let us go?"

In response, the blond motioned with his weapon that Loren and Doug should walk to the side of the building away from the pit. Parked there was an open utility vehicle with another man dressed similarly but with a reproduction of a confederate forage cap on his head.

The blond man said, "Get in the back seat, Tom. You two get in the front." He pointed at Loren and said, "You drive. Tom and I will have our weapons pointed at the back of your heads. Any funny business and you're dead."

"You don't need to kill us. We're cooperating." Loren took the wheel and the blond man told him to just follow the road. Loren started the vehicle and started down the road.

Doug stared at Loren. He seemed calm. It was as if his fear of being caught was worse than being caught, and now that it had happened he felt better.

The road went northwest for about a half a mile and came to the inhabited part of the ranch. Loren was told to park in front of the ranch house.

"Okay, we go in," the blond man said. "You stay, Tom."

Doug and Loren got out of the vehicle and started up the stairs with the automatic weapon pointed at their backs. This wasn't an ideal situation.

They entered the ranch house. Loren made a noise of surprise. Despite the plain exterior, the inside of the ranch house was as elegant as any expensive New York law firm's office. A big oriental carpet covered the floor of the entry and there was elegant antique furniture around the walls. A crystal chandelier hung from the ceiling.

"I guess crime pays," he muttered.

"Shh," Doug said. The last thing they wanted to do was piss off people pointing guns at them.

Chapter 18

Loren couldn't believe he let himself get in this situation. But now that the suspense of *will they get caught* was over he actually felt a little bit better. What in the world was Novack doing here? Would he help them?

On the other hand, what was going on here with all those chemicals was undoubtedly not good. They needed to be stopped.

The blond man told them to move on down the hall. Loren's old knee injury was aching, all that sneaking around in the dark hadn't done it any favors. They came to an open door to an ample and sumptuous office.

Sitting behind the desk was a man with dark hair graying around the temples. Kane. He looked older than the Kane he remembered. He would have been handsome except for his eyes that were small and beady. Pig eyes.

The man behind the desk had on a navy blue sports coat with a light gray golf shirt and, no doubt, was Earl Kane. On the top was a desk set, a calendar holder, pens and a clock. Loren wondered if they were solid gold. Behind the desk was a painting of a nude that could have been an original Renoir. Several pieces of overstuffed furniture were spread around the room but none were in front of the desk. An ornate clock ticked on a credenza behind the desk. A silver pistol was prominent on the desktop.

Loren and Doug entered the room but the blond man stayed at the door, weapon pointed in Doug's direction. Loren stayed back while Doug went and stood in front of the desk.

The blond man said, "I found these two nosing around our project."

Kane looked at Loren. "Sharp! What are you doing here?"

Loren shifted his feet. "I wonder that myself."

"We've been expecting somebody," Kane said. "We don't get many helicopter flyovers."

Loren gave Doug a look that combined disgust and I told you so.

"I suppose you're the Sanderson who's been calling me," said Kane.

Doug stepped closer to the desk. "Yes, I have been trying to talk to you about a case I'm working on. I'm with the police." Doug seemed to be trying to act as though he just wanted to interview Kane about his connection with Reitz.

Loren knew that now that they'd seen that pit of chemicals, they were in serious trouble.

"Really?" Kane asked. "What is it you want?"

"We suspect Wolfgang Reitz, who I believe you know, has been murdered." Doug gamely forged ahead. "He had your name and Mr. Ableson's name on his calendar for about the time of his death. Is there anything you can tell us about this?"

"Reitz!" Kane exclaimed, shaking his head. "That fool. He called me and said he wanted me to finance a patent suit against Marchem to get the Martox patent awarded to him. He got my answering machine and I didn't call him back. Not my type of activity. I don't trust lawyers."

That explains it. Poor Wolfy.

"So you weren't in St. Louis?" Doug asked.

"No," Kane said.

"But Reitz did call you," Doug said.

"Yes, he did," Kane said. "I don't know why he thought I would help him."

"Do you know anything about the Martox process?" Loren asked.

"What?" Kane said. "Why would I?

Loren was edging toward the door. "I guess Wolfgang thought Ableson would be receptive. Reitz and Ableson were both rose lovers and spoke many times."

"Oh yes, good old Sidney." Kane chuckled. Loren was getting a bad feeling.

"Where is Ableson?" said Doug.

Kane smiled humorlessly and said, "He left."

Did he leave?

"Where did he go?" said Doug.

"Gosh, I'm not sure." Kane held up his hands, palms up.

Damn. Was he even still alive?

"I guess that clears things up," Doug said. "We'll be going then. Thank you for your time." Loren hadn't known Doug was such an optimist.

Kane laughed some more. "After what you've seen do you think you're getting off this ranch alive?"

"What do you mean?" Doug asked.

Loren knew what he meant.

"What I mean is don't try to tell me you are not aware of what our little operation is all about. If you don't know, Sharp certainly does."

Illegal dumping of hazardous materials.

"It's really none of our business," Loren said. "You could let us go." Had he seen Ann and Bill for the last time? Would they be all right without him? Had he seen Gloria for the last time? He was filled with a rush of feeling for her. He would never get a chance to tell her he loved her.

"This is not my jurisdiction," said Doug.

"Oh come on. What do you take me for?"

Like hell this was the end. Like hell Kane would take him from his family.

Suddenly Doug was on top of the desk in one bound. His foot shot out and caught Kane under his chin and he toppled to the floor. In one motion Doug picked up the revolver on the desk.

Near Loren, the blond man's jaw dropped and he stood paralyzed for a moment.

Loren grabbed the huge glass ashtray on a table next to him and brought it down on the blond man's gun arm with all the force he could muster. The weapon clattered to the floor and Loren dived for it and got to it before the blond man gathered his wits. He stood and pointed the weapon at the blond man and tried to look menacing.

Doug stood on the desk pointing the revolver at the blond man, "Good job Loren. Wow. I didn't know scientists could do stuff like that."

They stood silently for a few seconds and then Loren, who was pretty shaky asked, "What do we do now?"

"Call the cops?" Doug said.

"What about that Tom guy?" Loren asked. "What about Novack?"

"One thing at a time." Doug tied the blond man's hands and tied him to a chair with a lamp cord as Kane started to regain consciousness. He went over to Kane, told him to get back in his chair and told Loren to cover him while he tied Kane's hands with more lamp cord.

Doug glanced at his cell phone and frowned. Then, he picked up the phone on the desk.

Loren said, "You're not calling the sheriff, are you? He's in Kane's pocket." They weren't out of the woods yet.

"No. I'm calling the highway patrol." Doug slammed the phone down. "No dial tone."

Kane smiled.

"Apparently there's a cutoff switch," Doug said. "Where is it Kane?

Kane just smiled.

"Use your cell phone," said Loren.

Doug said, "No service."

"If Kane just turned off the landline, doesn't the switch have to be in this room?" Loren asked, approaching the desk. Avoiding Kane, he leaned over the desk.

"Probably," Doug said. "But we don't have time to search for it"

"Yeah," Loren said. "I don't see it."

"Okay," Doug said. "Let's go." He pulled the phone cord from the wall. "If Kane's minions flip the switch, they can't call the sheriff."

"Go where?" Loren asked.

"Into Thompson. Maybe further."

"What about Kane?" Loren said.

"He's going too."

The two men walked down the hall and onto the porch, guns trained on Kane's back.

Tom lounged by the vehicle and his jaw dropped when he saw what was happening.

Doug said, "Drop your gun on the ground or your boss is a goner."

Tom did so without hesitation.

Doug said, "Move away from the vehicle. Loren, keep them covered."

"No problem." Loren shifted to face both men.

"Come on, Loren, you're a scientist, not a gangster," Kane said. "Threatening people with guns isn't your style."

Asshole. "You have no idea what my style is. You threaten me, I threaten you right back."

Doug went and picked up Tom's weapon. "Kane, get in the back seat of the jeep." He bound Kane's feet and tied him to the spare tire on the vehicle's back end so he couldn't move.

Doug asked, "Where's the radio control for the gate?"

Kane just shrugged with a stupid smirk on his face.

Doug searched for it around the dash. "I think this is it."

"Tom, go into the ranch house," Doug said and started walking for the house.

With Loren's gun at his back, Tom walked back inside.

"What're you thinking?" Loren asked quietly outside the front door.

"We've got the boss," Doug said, gesturing at a porch bench. "I doubt the minions are that motivated."

The two men dragged the heavy bench against the front door.

"This won't stop them for long," Loren said.

"It doesn't have to stop them for long. Come on." Doug ran for the jeep and Loren followed.

Doug started the jeep, drove over to the other vehicle parked nearby and shot out all four tires.

"That's not very friendly," Kane said.

Loren didn't dignify that with an answer.

"That should give us enough head start," Doug said. "Keep your gun on Kane."

Doug drove to the gate and pressed the button on the dash. The gate slid open.

Kane started cursing.

Loren was very relieved. If they hadn't been able to get the gate open they would've been in trouble. He smiled at Doug who pulled the vehicle through the gate and accelerated down the road. The darkness seemed a lot less threatening now than it was on the trip to the ranch.

"That was quite a trick jumping on the desk like that. It saved our lives," Loren said.

"I did a lot of high jumping in high school and college," Doug said. "The judo training helped, too."

Loren had developed a great deal of respect for Doug. "That was something."

"You weren't so bad yourself with that ash tray," said Doug.

"That's true." Loren felt a smile stretch his face. "Thanks." If he could foil criminals pointing guns at him, maybe he could solve all his problems.

They drove in silence--except for Kane who was cursing constantly. He promised Doug and Loren that he would get them.

Loren finally had enough. He turned around. "If you

don't shut up, I'm going to shoot you in the arm." This was a bluff but it made Kane shut up.

The three men were quiet most of the way back to Thompson. For his part, Loren's mind was racing. Who killed Wolfy? Why had Wolfy threatened the Martox plant? Where was Ableson? Was he alive? What was Bill up to? Was he all right? Did Gloria love him like he loved her? How extensive was Kane's dumping operation? What was Novack doing there? And on and on.

It was getting cold and Loren was shivering as they approached Thompson.

"You're right," Doug said quietly on the outskirts of town. "I've decided that we're not going to get any help from the sheriff. He's in Kane's pocket. He probably would arrest us and let Kane go, so we're going to keep going."

"Good." Loren felt relieved.

"However, there's a problem. We're going to have to get some gas here in Thompson."

"If we stop, there's a good chance the sheriff will show up with his gun," Loren said.

"I imagine Kane didn't keep a lot of gas in the vehicles so his hands couldn't go far," Doug said. "I noticed a lock on the gas pump at the ranch. We have to get some gas. We can't run out of gas in the middle of nowhere."

Kane smiled but said nothing. It was only slightly less annoying that all the cursing and threatening.

There was only one gas station in the town. Fortunately, it was on this side of town. Hopefully it was open. As they drove up, there was a light on in the station.

Doug pulled into the station.

Loren quickly jumped out of vehicle and entered his credit card. With a sigh of relief he started pumping gas. He filled the tank quickly.

Soon, they roared off again. No sign of the sheriff. Past midnight, the town seemed deserted. "Sheriff's probably in his office drinking bourbon with the postmaster," Doug said.

Loren laughed a little. "Probably." He was surprised how quickly all this seemed like second nature.

Leaving Thompson seemed to agitate Kane. "I demand to know where you're taking me."

"You'll find out soon enough," Doug said.

"I'd like to know, too," Loren said.

Doug spoke quietly to Loren. "There is a state patrol office in Sterling."

The steady hum of the tires on the highway was soothing to Loren who suddenly realized how tired he was. But the cold and his adrenaline level kept him alert.

He kept his eye on Kane. It was hard to believe under the circumstances but he seemed to be asleep.

Doug was pushing the vehicle and the miles melted away. Thank God there was now plenty of gas in the vehicle. A pickup truck pulled up behind them at high speed and Doug and Loren tensed but the pickup passed them and went on.

"I'm still a little jumpy," Loren said.

Doug said, "Yeah. Me too, but only about twenty five miles to go. Actually Kane's men have very little reason to follow us. If I were them I would be on my way out of the state by now."

"Yeah, that's probably true," said Loren, still thinking about his former colleague Novack. He had mixed feelings. If Novack had committed felonies he should be held accountable. But the Novack he remembered was a decent normal guy.

Lights began to appear as they came to the suburbs of Sterling and Loren relaxed. Doug smiled and glanced over at him.

"What now?" Loren asked.

"I made a note of the patrol office when we came through here," Doug said. "I know where it is."

"Always thinking aren't you?"

"Comes from being a policeman."

"You'd make a good researcher."

"Thanks. Coming from a real one, that's a compliment."

Kane said, "You men kidnapped me." He struggled against his bonds. "I'm going to have you both in prison."

"You kidnapped us first," Loren said.

"We'll see who goes to prison," Doug said.

They pulled up in front of the patrol office and Doug jumped out of the Jeep. "Loren, keep an eye on Kane while I go into the building."

That's me, Loren Sharp, chemist and jailer. He turned and stared at Kane, holding up the gun. Hopefully, nothing else would go wrong.

Chapter 19

Doug approached the duty officer sitting at the front desk. He flashed his badge. "I'm a police officer from St. Louis. I have a prisoner tied up in a Jeep outside that I need to get put in a cell and I need help to investigate the prisoner's ranch."

The officer said, "I need to talk to my captain."

Doug nodded. "Please call him."

"I don't want to disturb him at four o'clock in the morning."

"I insist that you call him. It's very important. Take a look outside."

The officer went to the large front window and saw what Doug was saying was true. When he came back to the desk he called his captain. "Sorry for bothering you, sir. There's a guy here who claims to be a St. Louis cop. He's got a guy tied up in a Jeep outside. He wants to talk to you."

The officer gave Doug the phone.

Doug said," I'm Detective Lieutenant Douglas Sanderson of the St. Louis Police Department. I have a prisoner tied up in a vehicle outside the station who I suspect is involved in illegal waste dumping. I need some help holding him and investigating his operation."

The captain said, "This is pretty unusual but I guess I'd better come in. I'll be there as soon as I can." They hung up and Doug handed the phone back to the desk officer.

The station's main room was large, with various desks and workstations. The few officers on duty went about their jobs without taking much note of Doug. He eventually sat down in one of the two old wooden pews set against the front wall on either side of the front doors.

After a quarter hour a large, powerfully built man entered from the back. He reminded Doug of former Russian premier Brezhnev.

"I'm Captain Hugh Delany. What's this all about?"

"Like I said on the phone, I'm Detective Lieutenant Douglas Sanderson of the St. Louis Police." He told him a sanitized version of their adventure, ending with, "If you want to check on me call St. Louis."

Delany walked back to the radio room and talked to the dispatcher through the open doorway. "Is there a unit in the vicinity of Thompson?"

The dispatcher found a car thirty miles south and Delany told the dispatcher to give them directions to the ranch that Doug supplied.

Delany told the dispatcher to tell a local car to come in and then he had the dispatcher call St. Louis police to check on Sanderson. He told the duty officer to go out and bring in Loren and Kane.

Loren seemed a little nervous as he entered the station. There was no sign of the gun. Hopefully, he stashed it under the seat or something. He sat down next to Doug.

Kane, with his wrists still tied, seemed livid. "I'm innocent! I'm a respectable Colorado businessman and will sue everybody involved in this outrage. They kidnapped me. I demand you arrest these men!"

Delany pointed to Kane and said, "We can detain you for twenty-four hours. We're going to hold you until we figure out what's going on here."

The duty officer took Kane, still protesting, back to a holding cell.

The dispatcher called out from the back of the room. "St. Louis said Sanderson is legit."

"Okay, thanks," Delany said. The two officers from local car one-twenty-one came in and wanted to know what was up. Delany told them the story and said they were going up to the ranch to investigate.

Doug had been keeping a close eye on what was going on. "How about taking a helicopter? Those people left at the ranch may be destroying evidence. The quicker we can get up there the better."

"We don't keep one here," Delany said. "And it would take too long to fly one in."

"Vern Newton can fly us up," Doug said.

"Oh yes, Newton. We've used him on occasion." Delany turned to the dispatcher, who'd migrated up to the front of the room. "Get Vern Newton on the phone, Johnson."

The dispatcher went back to the radio room and a few minutes later called out, "Newton is on line one."

Delany picked up the phone." I want to fly up to the ranch that you visited with Sanderson." Doug was a little surprised Delany agreed so readily. His captain was always grousing about the budget.

Delany hung up. "He said to meet him at the regional airport."

Doug, Loren, Captain Delany, a sergeant, and two

uniformed officers from local car one-twenty-one set out for the little airport in two cars. The trip only took ten minutes and Vern arrived about the same time.

Delany said to two of the officers, "Start for the ranch in the patrol car." He said to the sergeant, "Brock, join us in the helicopter."

Vern looked sleepy but cheerfully greeted the men. "Somehow I thought I'd see you boys again. But not so soon. This way." He pointed at his bird, parked on the tarmac.

Delany said, "Cut the chatter. Let's go."

The men climbed into the helicopter, and it soon took off and banked sharply to the northeast.

"Newton, quit showing off," Delany said. "Go at top speed."

He faced Doug. "Tell me more about what's going on here. How come a detective from St. Louis is investigating waste dumping in rural Colorado?"

Doug told Delany about the Reitz murder and the note on Reitz's calendar.

Delany turned to Loren. "And you, how do you fit into all this?"

"I'm a chemist," Loren said. "I worked at Marchem with Reitz and Kane and Ableson. I mean, I still work there. They don't."

"He'll be able to help us with the chemicals in the dump site," Doug said. "It's a good thing you came along, Loren, even though we didn't solve Reitz's murder."

Loren nodded and then tugged on his earlobe.

Some lights were still on at the ranch. "Let's head towards that giant camo net and the cinder block building," Doug said.

"What's the setup here?" Delany asked.

"This building and the ranch house are the biggest structures," Doug said. "If there are people here, most likely they'll be in one of them."

The copter landed and the men started piling out near the building. Even in the dark they could all see the barrels in the pit. It still stunk of chemicals.

Delany started passing out flashlights. "Newton, can you fly officer Brock up to the ranch house to clear it?"

Vern shrugged. "You're the boss."

"Brock, if the house is clear, find the gate control."

Brock said, "Yes, sir."

Delany got out. "Everyone be careful. Some of Kane's men could still be around."

"Yes, sir," Brock said.

Vern took off again once they were clear.

Loren was already shining his flashlight into the pit and muttering.

Doug was watching the captain. Any doubt he might have had about his story must have been rapidly dispelled when he got a good look at the waste dump. He pressed his lips together.

"This is a mess," Loren said. "A dangerous hazardous mess. I don't understand. Weren't they even concerned for their own safety?"

"Guess not," Delany said, shrugging. "Just a minute." He stepped away, got out his radio and started talking into it. Doug only heard, "More men. Kane ranch outside Sterling."

Once he put the radio away, Doug said, "Let's check in here." Doug and Delany drew their guns.

The door to the building was not locked so the men

entered. Inside, it was a fully equipped lab.

"Wow," Loren said. "This is a pilot plant for manufacturing chemicals."

Except for some papers scattered around the desks in the small office area next to the entrance, the place was in good order. It was deserted.

"Looks like whoever worked here left in a hurry," said Doug.

"I figured that would happen," Loren said from the back of the group. "Why should they take the blame for Kane's operation?"

"What're we looking at here?" Delany asked.

Loren stepped forward. He pointed at two long benches in the front. "Every type of chemical glassware you can imagine here. And along the sides, all kinds of instruments. Those glass-fronted cabinets are full of chemicals in all those bottles. They could probably make just about anything in here." He walked closer to them to get a better look.

Doug examined the office area. The three desks didn't have any personal items on top of them. A desktop shredder's basket was full. Damn. He hated to see evidence destroyed.

"Looks like they tried to cover their tracks," said Delany.

Doug put on some plastic gloves, leaned down and picked up some of the papers from the floor. They appeared to be typical memos and invoices.

"We know who one of them was," Loren said, joining them. "Arnold Novack. A man I knew from Marchem."

"They couldn't have gotten far," Delany said. We could put out an APB if we had a description of the vehicle they were using."

"Sorry, we were too busy to look in the garage," Doug said.

"Yeah, avoiding getting shot," Loren muttered.

Delany said, "Don't worry. We'll get them. And, we've got the mastermind, this Kane guy, right? In a minute, I'll call headquarters on the radio and tell them to put out an APB on any car registered to Earl Kane."

"Also Sidney Ableson," said Doug.

"Who's he?" asked Delany.

"I mentioned him before," Doug said. "He was Kane's partner."

"But he doesn't seem to be around," Loren said. "We haven't seen any sign of him." He looked worried.

"We should check out the rest of the place," Doug said.

"Yeah," Delany said.

They went to the back of the building where the large equipment was.

"These three behemoths," Loren pointed, "are impressively big stainless steel reactors with the usual pumps, pipes and gauges. They look to be about five hundred gallons. You could make a lot of chemicals in them."

"I don't like the sound of that," Delany said.

"No." Loren shook his head. "It's not good. There's also equipment for the isolation of solids, two centrifuges and a large filtering funnel. All you need for small scale manufacturing and most of it the top of the line. If you wanted to make drugs, you could make a hell of a lot."

"We're going to have to get our scientific people out here to collect residues and look around," said Delany. "We need evidence they were making illegal drugs."

"There may well be drugs on the premises," Doug said.

They went back outside as the sun started peeking over the horizon.

Delany's radio squawked. He took it out and pressed a button. "The house was clear, Captain," Doug could hear Brock say. The captain took a step away and started talking.

Doug and Loren watched the sun rise. Loren seemed tired. Doug's mind was racing.

The patrol car they'd last seen at the airport pulled up with two officers and Sergeant Brock.

"I see you found the gate control, Brock," Delany said, stowing his radio.

"No problem. It was on the desk in the office. A lot of papers strewn around up there," said Brock.

"I'm surprised they didn't destroy more in the lab and here at the dump," Doug said.

"It's not so easy," Loren said.

Delany frowned. "Looks like this'll be a big cleanup. What's that stink?"

"Chlorinated hydrocarbons," Loren said. "Carcinogenic solvents."

Delany frowned some more. "This is a hell of a mess."

They had seen enough at the pit and lab so they went in the patrol car up to the ranch house. Brock drove and the other two uniformed officers stayed to guard the pit and lab.

"Did you send the message about the APB, Brock?" said Delany.

"Yes, sir," said Brock.

The helicopter was parked outside the ranch house and Vern was leaning on it smoking a small cigar. "I figured you'd be up here soon so I stayed put."

Chapter 20

Loren was having a letdown. He had never been involved in anything like the last twenty- four hours. Thoughts of Bill and Gloria flooded in. He missed them a lot. And he was very, very tired.

"You don't need Vern or I anymore do you?" he asked Delany.

The captain hesitated, but then said, "No I guess not. We have to get a bunch of people up here. We have the one unit and more should be here soon. We may need you at some point, Dr. Sharp, to testify if nothing else."

"You want to go home?" Doug asked.

"You don't?" Loren asked. He had to see his family. And he had to get back to work on the threat against the Martox plant. This had all been a red herring as far as that was concerned.

"No," Doug said. "I want to help wrap this up."

"I'd really like to get going," Loren said. "I know it's an imposition, but could you pick up my bags at the motel and hotel?"

"Doug said, "Sure. You can pick them up from me in St. Louis."

"Thanks," Loren said. "That would be very helpful."

Delany pointed a finger at Doug. "I assume you are staying, Sanderson."

"Yes, but I need some sleep."

Delany chuckled. "I assume Kane has a bed. That would be ironic."

"Will you fly me to the Denver airport, Vern?" Loren asked.

"Sure thing if I'm no longer needed here," Vern said. "Do I send you the bill, Delany?"

Delany grimaced. "I guess so."

Loren and Vern got in and took off and, despite the roar of the helicopter, Loren slept the whole trip.

As soon as Loren got to the Denver terminal he called his home phone number but no one answered. Then he called Gloria.

Gloria answered after one ring. "Loren! I've been frantic. Bill's in the hospital."

Oh no. He'd known something was wrong. "What happened?"

"He's been burned. Some kind of chemistry experiment."

After the affair at the surplus chemical storage room Loren knew what must have happened. Drugs. "How bad is he?"

"He has third degree burns on his arms and chest but only a couple of spots on his face, thank God."

"I'll catch the next plane," he said. "Can you meet me?"

"Yes."

"If I can't get on the next plane I'll call you. If you don't hear from me I'll be on the next American or United plane from Denver."

"Okay, I'll see you then." She paused and took a breath. "I hope you'll tell me what you've been up to."

"I will. See you at the concourse exit and thanks." He hung up, went to the American counter and got a seat on a plane leaving within the hour. He tried to sleep on the flight without much success. He was too worried about Bill.

Gloria was at the concourse exit when he arrived. She hugged him. "Oh, I'm so glad to see you."

It felt wonderful to be in her arms. "Me too. I missed you." They separated.

"Thanks for helping with Bill," he said. "Is he conscious?"

"They had him sedated when I was there. I talked to the doctor, though, and he was cautiously optimistic."

They hurried to the short-term parking. She drove directly to the hospital. Unfortunately, the traffic was bad.

"This is taking too long," he said, leaning forward in his seat. In spite of his son's shortcomings, he loved him very much. "Bill, Bill, what have you done to yourself?"

She glanced at him. "What's wrong? You don't seem yourself."

"Obviously, I'm worried about Bill. And the trip was trying." That was putting it mildly. The last day in Colorado, especially, was very hard on him. He wasn't used to being held at gunpoint, smashing people with ashtrays, holding guns on others, and riding in helicopters. Frankly, he missed his nice, calm lab.

He yawned. "Among other things, lack of sleep is catching up to me."

"Well, try to take it easy," she said. "I'm pretty sure his burns aren't life threatening."

136

"How did you find out about the accident?"

"I went to your house and looked around again, and noticed your old answering machine had the light blinking. I listened to the messages hoping to hear from him. Instead, there was a message from St. John's that he was in the burn unit. I went right over to the hospital."

"I'm glad," Loren said. "I hate to think of him there all alone." She had really come through for him. He was grateful.

She let him out at the hospital entrance and went to park the car.

He went to the desk and was directed to the burn unit on the third floor.

Before his wife Gwen had gotten sick, the few times he'd been in the hospital he'd almost enjoyed it. He didn't like the pain, of course, but the bed rest, reading and tender loving care had appealed to his couch potato side.

Once Gwen got sick that all changed. He'd spent far too much time in medical facilities, watching his wife suffer. The light green walls and antiseptic odor were oppressive. He hated hospitals now.

A nurse at the nursing station directed him to Bill's room.

Loren slowly walked in. His son looked like a mummy. Poor Bill. He'd seemed to be sleeping but when he entered the room Bill tried to sit up.

He waved Bill down and said, "No. Please, don't exert yourself." He walked right up beside the bed. "What the hell happened?" he asked quietly.

"Nick and I were doing a chemistry experiment and the dumb bustard lit up a cigarette. We were using acetone." Oh, Bill, lying to me on top of everything.

He felt himself frown. "What kind of chemical experiment?"

Bill lost eye contact. "One of the experiments in my college chem lab book. I was trying to get a head start if I went back."

"I don't believe you," Loren said, quietly, but forcefully. "You were trying to make speed. I know you stole chemicals the day you visited Marchem. This is that damn Nick's doing. He probably put you up to this."

"Oh, leave me alone. I hurt."

"What happened to Nick?"

"I don't know. It seems like I've been sleeping for days."

"Bill, you need to straighten up your life."

And then it was as if a dam burst. Bill started to sob. "Dad, please help me. I need help."

Loren could never stand to see his kids cry. It broke his heart. "I will but you have to make an effort."

"I promise," Bill said.

A nurse bustled in. "This young man needs his rest."

Loren's voice was gentle. "Get some rest now. We'll talk again tomorrow. I love you."

Bill, still sniffling a little, nodded.

The nurse said, "You're the dad? I'll have his doctor find you."

Loren walked to the third floor lounge and found Gloria sitting there.

"How is he?" she asked.

"He's hurting physically and emotionally. He seems quite vulnerable."

"I'm sorry." She looked down. "I've been talking to the resident. The other boy, the Ciccone boy, didn't make it."

"Nick died?" He sat down heavily in one of the waiting room chairs. "Oh, no. Poor kid. Now I'm sorry I was so hard on him." There but for the grace of God... He struggled to keep hold of his emotions. Finally, he said, "Bill doesn't know about Nick. It'll be hard on him."

"We don't need to tell him now," she said. "We can wait till he's better." She looked into his face. "How about some lunch?"

"Frankly I'm bushed. I think I'll go home and take a nap after I talk to Bill's doctor."

"I'll take you," she said. "But I insist on dinner at my house around seven o'clock."

Loren checked his email when he got home and had a message from his daughter Ann.

Dear Pop,
The interview at Wisconsin went well but they told me they didn't have funds. I guess I'll keep plugging. I don't know why they invited me if they didn't have funds. Anyway what are you up to?
Love, Ann

The cancellation of the Superconducting Supercollider wiped out many opportunities for physicists for years to come and let Europe took the lead in High Energy Physics.

Loren sent back an email.

Dear Ann,
Please come home. Bill has been in an accident. He's okay but needs some cheering up. You know how much he

likes to see you. I have a lot of things to tell you.
   Love, Pop

Ann and Bill had always been close. Maybe Ann could help him.

Loren fell into bed but had a hard time falling asleep. Many things were going through his head. He thought about Bill. The doctor hadn't had any big revelations; Bill's prognosis was good, but he'd have to stay in the burn unit a little longer. He thought about Gloria, and their possible romance. He thought about Doug and his trip to Colorado. He thought about Wolfy's murder and the threat against Martox he'd made. Unfortunately, he wasn't any closer to solving Wolfy's mysteries.

When he finally did drop off he had a wild dream. He was standing behind a barbwire fence and Mona was beckoning him from the other side. Then, he found himself on the other side of the fence but Mona had changed into a smiling Kane. Behind Kane was a huge bottomless pit. Two of Kane's men started dragging him toward the pit. Loren was screaming and sweating when he woke up. It was six pm. When he calmed down he shaved, showered and read some of the newspaper. Thank God there was no news of the Reitz affair or of Bill's ordeal.

He was trying to figure out how he would handle the situation with Bill. He knew what Bill was up to but if no one else knew, perhaps the experiment explanation would fly. Should he be silent and let matters take their course? He knew that silence would not be the honorable course but a drug conviction would ruin Bill's life. Should he tell Gloria? He had to think on it. It was a tough decision and one which could have serious consequences. He decided to wait until six-fifty to leave for Gloria's. He would be late for a change. That would surprise her.

Gloria opened the door when he started up the walk. "Loren you're late. This is a first."

He smiled. "I'm turning over a new leaf."

She smiled back. "I don't know if this is an improvement."

"You can't have it both ways."

They went in. Loren sat down at the kitchen table and Gloria set a gin and tonic before him. He drank it down and Gloria gave him another.

"Good stuff," he said.

"Okay, Loren, what have you been up to? Why did you rush off to Colorado?"

Loren told her the whole story of his trip, leaving out nothing.

"My God, it sounds like a movie thriller. This Sanderson sounds like Superman."

"It was not exactly what I expected when I agreed to go. And yes, Doug is quite a guy."

"I'd like to meet him," she said.

His first reaction was no. Was that fear that he felt? How would he stack up against Doug? He made himself smile. "Maybe someday."

"It was good you were along. Sanderson was lucky to have you. Those chemicals sound very dangerous."

He nodded. "They were dangerous." Come to think of it, he did make a significant contribution. He felt a little better.

"Any news on the Martox process?" she asked.

"No," he said. "I assume Silk Benson is handling it." He hoped so, anyway.

Dinner was filet mignon with Béarnaise sauce, baby carrots, Caesar salad and homemade cheesecake. They drank a nice zinfandel. Coffee and brandy followed.

Loren pushed his chair back from the table. "Wow, Gloria, I knew you could cook if you wanted to but that was outstanding. Thank you for an excellent dinner."

She beamed. "Thank you."

Now that dinner was over he was starting to get a little uneasy. He was remembering the night that Gloria asked him if he knew she was a woman. He'd been mulling that ever since.

"Gloria, I have been thinking about what you said last time about you being a woman."

She became attentive. "I hope I didn't upset you." Somehow, he didn't think she meant that.

"No, I'm glad you said it. I've been thinking about it and analyzing my feelings."

"That's the scientist coming out, I guess." She chuckled. "What's your conclusion?"

"You know I enjoy your company very much. You've become my best friend. I thought you probably just thought about us as friends. I've been and still am afraid that if romance entered the picture you would be put off and we would not see each other anymore." He paused. "But if the moment of truth is here, the fact is I have decided that I do love you very much."

He waited on pins and needles.

She got up, came over and kissed him hard. "That's my answer." Her eyes sparkled.

He laughed. "Good answer."

Smiling, she took him by the hand and led him to her bedroom. She immediately started to take her clothes off.

He'd only seen her in business pants suits and was startled. "Wow, Gloria, you're beautiful."

"Thank you and shut up." She started to help him disrobe and he joined in enthusiastically.

In spite of all the problems he'd been having lately, Loren was a very happy man.

Chapter 21

Doug decided to take Delany's suggestion of getting some sleep in Kane's bed. He wanted to stay around for the investigation but he was beat. He went to the ranch house.

Before he slept he looked around Kane's office. It was a bit chilling because of the close call they'd had in the office when they'd captured Kane, but he wanted to see if there was sufficient information to document what Kane was up to. The papers spread around the floor had to do with running the ranch. Apparently Kane's men had removed or shredded everything having to do with criminal activity.

There was a locked file cabinet in the room and Doug rifled through the desk and found some keys. One of them opened the cabinet. It contained folders with the names of what appeared to be small chemical companies. The employees must not have had access to the cabinet, so nothing had been shredded. There were records of shipments of unnamed materials, probably chemicals. A typical page consisted of a consignment number, a cost number and a number of unknown meaning. Some of the sheets were green and some were pink. It appeared that more than waste was being shipped in and some things were shipped out.

Could it be some kind of barter system? Were the chemical companies giving Kane drug ingredients in exchange for taking their toxic waste? It would be a sweet system since Kane would have trouble getting his chemicals, but shipments to a small chemical company would be innocuous. There were no records of drug shipments but they had to exist. That probably was what was being shipped out. A business as large as Kane's would have to have some accounting. He'd have to look further, but at the moment sleep was becoming a necessity.

He walked down the hall opening doors looking for a bed. In one room, much to his surprise, he found a young, attractive woman cowering on top of a bed. They were supposed to clear the house. Could she be some kind of witness?

Doug said, "Hello. Who are you?"

The woman shook her head and said something in Spanish. She apparently didn't know English so Doug went outside and asked the officer who was guarding the ranch house if any of Delany's men spoke Spanish.

"I know a little," the officer said. "Why?"

"There's a woman inside in one of the bedrooms."

The officer nodded like this was common knowledge.

Doug suppressed a sigh. Why didn't they mention her? "Can you help me ask her a few questions?"

He shrugged. "Okay." It turned out the officer spoke better Spanish than he admitted to. The two had quite a conversation.

The officer said, "She says she's *Señor* Kane's housekeeper. She's very frightened."

Doug said, "Tell her she won't be hurt and that she can stay in the house until things are sorted out." The officer relayed the information.

She relaxed a little. "*Gracias. Gracias.*"

Now it was time for sleep. Doug found Kane's bed and collapsed after setting an alarm. The bed was very comfortable.

When he woke up he felt like a new man. Inside and outside the place was swarming with policemen. Three patrol cars were parked in front of the ranch house. He got a ride down to the pit and found Delany. "Hey, Delany. How's it going?" There were men in the pit in moon suits sampling the drums.

"There you are, Sanderson," Delany said. "We've got technicians here and in the lab taking samples. They say that they can use the on-site equipment to do some preliminary identifications. Kane had quite an operation."

"Good," Doug said. "I wish Loren had stayed. He would've been helpful."

"Our men can handle it," Delany said.

One of the men in moon suits came up to Doug and Delany. Through the face mask, he looked grim. "There were three drums toward the back which were blue instead of black like the others. They were for solids rather than liquids. They had a removable top so we decided to open them right away. We found three bodies."

"My God. We better take a look. Set us up with a moon suit so we can go down," Delany said.

Doug and Delany slipped the protective suits over their clothes and went down in the pit. They found three dead bodies in fairly good condition. Apparently the airtight drum did a good job of preservation. One body was of a middle-aged man in a white shirt and tie, but no coat, with three bullet holes in his chest and a lot of bloodstains. One was of a middle-aged woman, apparently strangled, and the third was a young man in a khaki uniform also with bullet wounds and lots of bloodstains.

Doug's instincts were right: Kane was evil. He'd been a cop a while now and seen some things… But this was bad.

He said, "I'll lay odds that the older man is Sidney Ableson. I saw some pictures of him and his family during my investigation. He and Kane must have had a falling out. The woman could be Ableson's wife. I'd guess the younger man was one of Kane's employees."

"Poor bastards." Delany said, shaking his head. "We'll ship the bodies to the morgue in Sterling. The boys there will identify them, I'm sure." Delany told his men to take plenty of pictures.

Doug and Delany left the pit and took off the moon suits.

"This case is getting more and more complicated," Delany said.

"Yeah. Murder, drugs, toxic chemicals," Doug said. "You know, there's a young woman up at the house who was Kane's housekeeper. She doesn't speak English. We have to do something about her."

"I'll look into it."

"There are also records in Kane's office that seem to describe some of his activities."

"They didn't get shredded? That's a break, at least," Delany said, "We'll investigate everything. From the looks of it, Kane's a dead duck. Probably a lot of the people that did business with him are also in a lot of trouble."

"Yeah," Doug said. "Kane is really an evil man."

Delany nodded. "I agree."

"I knew Kane was a crook, but even I'm a little surprised he's so twisted." Doug had seen enough. "I think I'm going back to Denver. Please keep me informed of developments. You can email me."

"I sure will. You certainly deserve it. You and your chemist friend blew the lid off this whole operation," Delany said. "Don't forget to document everything you've seen. One of my officers back at the station can help you with the paperwork."

Doug suppressed a sigh. "I know the drill."

"And we'll obviously need you back here for the trial. Do you want a ride back to town?"

"No, I have a rental car about a mile down the road. Can get someone to drive me to the car?"

"Done," said Delany.

Chapter 22

Ann's car was in the driveway when Loren arrived home from Gloria's place after a glorious night and a leisurely morning. He hurried into the house. He found her reading the paper and drinking coffee. Hugs and kisses were liberally exchanged. If she wondered where he'd been, she didn't ask.

Loren loved Bill but he adored his daughter Ann Lauren. She was twenty-eight, petite, blonde and pretty. Damn smart, too.

"How was the trip from school?" said Loren. "You made good time."

"The trip was fine." She put down the paper. "What's this about Bill?"

"He was in a fire. He's in the hospital. He has burns on his arms and chest but he'll be all right." He sank down in one of the kitchen chairs. "His friend Nick was killed."

Her hand flew in front of her mouth. "Oh, no. Killed! Does Bill know?"

"He didn't when I saw him. Even so, he's down mentally. That's why I asked you to come home. You could always talk to him."

"How did this happen?"

Loren wrestled with himself about whether to tell Ann the truth. "Bill and Nick were doing a chemistry lab experiment and a solvent caught fire. He said he was getting a head start if he went back to school." He felt terrible about lying.

"A chemistry experiment!" Ann said. "That's pretty lame."

He knew it was lame. Loren just shrugged.

"Well, I guess I'll go right over to the hospital." She stood.

"Yes, that would be good. We'll go out to dinner when you get back." He gave her directions and she left in her Neon. He watched her drive away, happy to have her home.

He sat back down at the kitchen table. The Bill emergency was handled for the moment. Wolfy's murder was still a complete mystery. He could call Ilse Reitz, but the poor widow'd been through enough. Plus, frankly, he found her rather unpleasant.

He debated calling Doug for an update on the whole Kane drugs and dumping thing but decided it could wait until Doug got back to town.

He should check in with Benson though and see if any progress had been made on the Martox threat. Reluctantly, he made the call. "Hi, Silk, Ted. It's Loren."

"Did you find something out about Martox?" Benson demanded.

"No," Loren said. "I was just checking with you. I guess you didn't find out anything, yet?"

Benson exhaled. "Maybe there's nothing to find."

"Maybe." But that wasn't what Loren's intuition was telling him. "Can I help?"

"Not right now," Benson said. "I've got a huge team

going over everything with a fine-toothed comb."

"I'll tell you what," Loren said. "I'll ponder it. When I get a particularly tough problem I put my subconscious to work on it and sometimes the answer comes to me."

"Really? That works?"

"Not every time, but sometimes, yeah."

"Okay, Loren. That would be helpful. Thanks. Stay in touch." They hung up.

He decided to take a nap. His subconscious worked well when he was asleep. And, he hadn't gotten much sleep last night. He smiled.

He slept well until he was awakened by Ann's return.

He got up and went into the family room. When he saw Ann he threw her a kiss and said, "How's Bill?"

"He was sleeping when I got there," she said. "When he woke up he told me about the chemistry experiment gone wrong. Frankly it sounded pretty far-fetched. When I said so he clammed up. I'll tell you more later. I thought I heard dinner promised. I'm starving."

"Sure," he said. "Where do you want to go?"

"How about Ron's?" she said.

He grinned and pretended to groan. "I might have known. Okay, that's fine." Ron's was a neighborhood restaurant that had a lot of nostalgia for the family. They'd been there many times over the years and Ann loved to go there when she was home. It was less than a mile from the house.

The place wasn't full, so they got a table right away and sausage pizza and Sam Adams beers were ordered. It was very casual with lot of pictures of local sports teams on the walls.

"Remember the last time we came here with Mom?"

Ann said, smiling, but somehow still managing to look sad.

Loren grunted. "Yes, when Bill spilled his drink all over the table."

"I really miss Mom," Ann said, tearing up.

"Me, too. I'll always miss her," he said. "But tell me more about your visit with Bill."

"He said he was glad to see me but then he started crying." She dabbed her own eyes with her napkin. "I haven't seen Bill cry since we were little. He says you've been pressuring him. I don't know. He seemed a little off center."

"What do you mean?"

"He wouldn't look me in the eye. He was aloof. Almost like he was guilty of something. He seemed in bad shape mentally."

Loren was a little surprised. "I don't think I have been pressuring him. I don't even see much of him. Maybe he's still mourning his mother."

"Maybe, but it's time to move on," she said. "Even though I miss Mom, I haven't given up. I know she wouldn't want that. Mom wouldn't want to see him like this."

"True. It is time for him to move on. I sometimes think he uses his mother's death as a crutch." The waiter placed beers in front of them and they each took a sip.

"How are you?" she asked. "What are you working on at Marchem?"

He told her about his latest project to develop a new chemical manufacturing process. She seemed interested, asking a lot of questions.

Conversation was interrupted by the arrival of the pizza. They ordered two more beers.

Bad Chemistry

The pizza smelled very good and they both were hungry. Most of the pizza was devoured in a hurry.

"What about you, Ann Lauren?" he asked. "What's going on with you?"

"You know I went to Wisconsin," she said. "They said I was great but that they didn't have any funds. I don't know why they invited me if that was true. Maybe they just wanted to say they interviewed a female. I sent out twenty-three applications. They are a pain to fill out. I only have three unanswered places left." She frowned.

He shook his head. "What a shame. I know how hard you've worked. Eight years of probably the hardest curriculum there is. Maybe if some of the mandarin professors would retire, you could have your chance in academia."

"Yeah," she said. "It would probably help if they would give up their empires of graduate students and post docs."

"Half the post graduate students are foreign," he said. "We train them so they can go back to their countries and compete with us."

"Well, I have mixed feelings about it," she said.

"Or they take places that could be held by Americans," he said. "Much of the time the American taxpayer even pays their way. The only reason is so the big name profs can maintain themselves and their big university programs."

"It's not so black and white," she said. "Pop, you sound like some kind of nineteenth century xenophobe.

"I guess so, but it's true. It's a shame," he said. "Maybe you should consider industry."

"I've never seriously considered that, but maybe

you're right," she said.

He leaned back in his chair, feeling a little sheepish about getting so worked up, and finished his beer. "Oh well, what are we going to do about Bill?"

"For now, support him," she said. "I guess we'll have to wait until he's better to do anything else."

"Will you go and see him tomorrow?" he asked.

"Yes, I will," she said. "I hope he's feeling better."

They left the restaurant and drove to Loren's house. They both were very tired so they watched a little television and turned in early. Before bed, he called Gloria to wish her a good night.

The next morning they were both up early and Loren left for the lab and Ann went to the hospital.

Loren was looking forward to doing some research but, when he got to the lab, Andy said there was a policeman waiting for him in the lobby. What does Doug want now? He walked over.

However, Doug wasn't waiting for him. Instead, there was slovenly dressed, balding fifty-year-old man there. What was this about?

"Hello, Dr. Sharp?"

Loren nodded.

"I'm Sergeant Kelly."

Sergeant Kelly reminded him somewhat of lieutenant Colombo, that old character on television. "Nice to meet you, Sergeant Kelly. What can I do for you?"

"I understand your son was in a rather suspicious fire. There was a fatality so we are investigating. Do you know anything about this?"

Loren felt his face get hot. Sins of omission to Gloria

and Ann were one thing but lying to the police was another. He had to make a quick decision.

"Just what he told me. He and the Ciccone boy were doing a chemistry experiment. He'll be studying chemistry in the fall and was doing some college chemistry experiments to get a head start."

"Does that make sense to you?" Kelly asked.

"Yes. We're interested in chemistry in our family. I guess he wants to emulate his father."

"What was the Ciccone boy doing there?"

"I guess he was just curious," Loren said, sweating a little.

Kelly said, "I guess we'll put it down as an accident then."

Phew. "Yes. I think that's the correct decision. It was good to meet you sergeant. Say hello to lieutenant Sanderson for me."

"You know Sanderson?"

"I met him on a case he was working on."

"Oh, must have been the Reitz murder."

"I assume that Doug is still working on that."

"Yes," Kelly said. "Of course, the case is still very active. Well, goodbye then. It was a pleasure to meet you."

Loren said goodbye and started walking back to his lab. He was depressed. He hoped he'd done the right thing in lying to Kelly. He wasn't used to lying and it made him very uncomfortable. Some choice, his honor or his son. But he needed to do it to save him. Bill could still have a good life if he would straighten out. It was a hard decision. The whole affair so unnerved him that he found it difficult to concentrate. Gloria was practically the only good thing going on his life right now.

When he got back to the lab there was a note to call Barry Smith at engineering. He'd done lots of work with Barry so he knew the number and immediately dialed it.

"Smith speaking," Barry said.

"It's me," Loren said.

"I have good news and bad news. What do you want to hear first?"

"Good."

"Manufacturing management is considering your process."

"That is good news."

"Yeah, but they think there's too much capital. They want us to reduce it by at least six million"

That was upsetting. "Wow. That's going to be tough." Really tough. They'd already reduced it by as much as they could.

"We better have a meeting and probably very soon," Barry said. "I'll set it up."

"Let me know when."

"Will do." They hung up.

And then, Loren tried to focus on his research and actually got a little done.

Still unsettled by everything, he left work at three o'clock.

Ann was at home. "Hi, Pop." Her visit was another good thing in his life.

"Hi." He felt himself grin. He got a kick out of being called that. "How was your day? How's Bill?"

"He's feeling better physically. There is less pain and they have reduced the Demerol but he seems distant. He won't look at me. He asked me what you had said about the fire. Why would he ask that?"

"I don't know." He was getting better at lying. Unfortunately.

"I think you should see him tomorrow," she said.

"I will," he said. "But in the meantime I have to call Gloria." He'd been thinking of her since their night together. "I'd like you to meet her."

She shook her head, "Oh, that's your lawyer friend. I don't want to meet her."

"Why not?"

"Aren't you dating her? It's too soon after Mother's death. No one can take my mother's place." She was getting emotional.

"Ann, it's been a year. It's time to move on. We talked about this," he said. "But you're right. No one can take your mother's place and that's not what I'm suggesting. I like Gloria and I think you would, too."

"No, I don't want to." She was on the verge of tears so he dropped the subject. It wasn't like her to be so emotional. They chatted until Ann went into her room to use her computer.

He called Gloria. "Hi. I have a lot to tell you."

"Hi," she said. "I have a lot to tell you, too." She sounded upset.

"What's wrong?"

"Can you come to dinner?" she asked.

He glanced at the closed guest room door. "Yes." There was no point in trying to get the two women in his life together tonight. They finished making plans.

He knocked on the guest room door and Ann told him to come in. "I'm going to Gloria's for dinner. You can have whatever you find in the kitchen for dinner."

Sitting on the bed with her laptop, Ann nodded.

"Are you okay?" he asked.

"Yeah," she said. "I'm tired. A quiet night sounds good."

"Good. I'll be home early."

He was distracted during his drive to Gloria's. He couldn't figure out what was wrong with Ann. She was usually a level-headed and kind person. He knew she loved her late mother very much, almost everybody did, but he thought she was over her death. It had begun to drizzle which did not help his mood.

Gloria met him at the door and he thought she looked shaky.

He gave her a peck on the cheek and a quick hug. "Hi there."

"Hi, there, yourself," she said. "Come in."

He went in and sat down in her living room office. "What's the matter Gloria? You look frightened."

She sat down next to him. "You remember I told you that I had taken a divorce case?"

"Yes. I remember."

"Well, it turns out that the husband in the case is a real ass," she said. "I've been kind of hard on him and about an hour ago he called me and used some very filthy and abusive language. Then he said I would be sorry and that he would get me."

After seeing the pictures of Wolfy's body, Loren didn't like the sound of that. At all. "Do you take him seriously?"

Gloria seemed angry. "Of course I do! He's a bad guy. His wife has told me stories. He's beaten her severely."

Loren raised his hand. "Okay, okay. You didn't tell me all that. Maybe I can do something about it." Being friendly with a cop had to be good for something.

"What?"

"I have connections at the police department."

She calmed a bit. "Oh, your friend Sanderson."

"Yes. I'll ask him if he can do something."

"Good. I'm sorry to be a worry-wart but he scared me. I appreciate anything you can do." She stood. "Do you want a drink?"

"Sure," he said. "Why don't you let me get them?"

"That would be nice." She sat back down.

He fixed them each a drink and brought them to the living room.

"Thanks." Gloria took a sip of hers. "What have you been up to? You said you had something to tell me?"

Where to start? Loren took a sip of his own drink. "I heard from Barry about my new process. They want me to reduce the capital by five million!"

"Do you think you can reduce the capital?"

"You can always reduce the capital but what doing so does to the process is another matter. The first thing that gets reduced is raw material handling. You probably wind up with a process that costs more in the long run."

She raised her eyebrows. "So, what are you going to do?"

"I don't know yet." He took another sip. "I was questioned today by a sergeant Kelly about Bill's accident."

"Do you believe Bill's story?"

Loren smiled weakly. "I'm trying."

Gloria shook her head. "I have to be honest. It doesn't seem plausible to me."

159

"I don't think I have any choice but to try to believe him. A drug conviction could ruin his life. He deserves another chance."

"Okay. I hope it turns out all right."

She was too upset to cook so he offered to go out and get some Chinese food.

Loren was distracted by everything, Gloria's abusive phone call, Bill's accident, and Ann's attitude, not to mention Wolfy's murder and the threat against the Martox process He wasn't a good dinner companion. He said he was tired and left by eight o'clock.

Ann was in her room when he got home and he did not disturb her. He was rather upset with her.

After watching some TV, he went to bed, still worried about everything.

Chapter 23

The next morning Barry Smith called Loren in his lab and told him that the process meeting was that afternoon. Loren tried to get some research done but his mind was on the meeting. When he showed up in engineering, Barry and several other engineers were gathered in a conference room as he entered and found a seat.

"I guess I'm the chairman of this meeting," Barry said. "We have to find some ways to lower the Out Of Deep Well project capital from eighty million to less than seventy-five and I hope that that is enough."

Sheila Jacoby raised her hand and said, "Maybe we could remove all the safety devices. That would save a couple million." Sheila was blonde and probably the best-looking mechanical engineer he was likely to ever to see.

"How about skipping the waste treatment? That's five million right there," said Ken Dooly, a control instrument specialist. Loren agreed with them; trying to cut five million was crazy. He didn't think they should cut anything.

Barry was exasperated. "Come on, let's be serious. We need to do this or management will kill the project."

Sheila was angry. "You know, Barry, we did the best job we could in designing this plant. Anything we do now is going to be a step backward."

"I know but we have to reduce the capital or the project is dead," he said. "Morgan won't even present it to the board with over seventy-five million capital. He says that the board won't approve anything over seventy-five million. Capital is tight right now." Mel Morgan was the head of manufacturing.

Sheila shook her head. "I suppose the board members have some pet project they are saving money for. They probably want to make an acquisition. Well, I suppose we can knock out the bulk raw material handling machinery. I think that will save a couple million. We can move the stuff manually in bags or drums. Of course that will mean increased manpower, salaries and cost of goods."

"True, but we need to do it. It'll work," Barry said. "That was a good idea. What else?"

This kind of discussion went on for more than an hour and finally the group had found ways to reduce the capital by six million dollars. There were some suggestions about removing some of the safety equipment but Barry quickly pointed out that was strictly against company policy. However, some of the raw material handling equipment was removed. A few other pieces of equipment were also removed including many of the facilities for the operators. They all left the meeting depressed. Loren was afraid it would not be enough.

After the meeting, Loren took Sheila, Ken and Barry aside. "What have you guys heard about the Martox plant?" he asked.

"Rumors," Barry said.

"Yeah, what's up?" Sheila asked.

Loren felt like he was on the verge of an idea, but it hadn't coalesced yet. "I'm going to send you guys everything we have on the plant. Can you take a look at it? We need fresh eyes. My intuition's telling me there might actually be something…"

They all agreed to help out.

On the way out, Ken said, "Did you guys get interviewed yet about Reitz's murder? There's been a Sergeant Bigelow here questioning people the last couple days."

"I wonder why Doug Sanderson isn't doing it?" Loren asked. If Doug was here he could ask him for advice on Gloria's situation.

Barry shrugged. "Too busy?"

That made sense. He had to wrap up all the stuff from Colorado. And he probably had other cases as well.

After the meeting with Barry, things quieted considerably and Loren got back to work. He had some new research ideas he wanted to try out. He was very excited about the research he was doing and disliked being away from working on it. He was working on a new process to make Marhoe, an old cash cow product herbicide which yearly provided Marchem with a tidy profit. The current process produced a large amount of a concentrated salt stream, contaminated with organic chemicals, which was pumped down a deep well.

A deep well was a well drilled about a mile deep in the earth, which actually was a good method of disposing of waste chemicals. It was thought that the heat and pressure so deep in the ground would destroy any organic chemicals. However, it was bad public relations. Environmentalists conjured up all kinds of horror stories about leakage into bodies of water and Marchem's chairman had decreed that the company would get out of deep wells.

His new idea was to purify the salt steam and send it to a nearby plant, which manufactured chlorine and sodium hydroxide. The chloralkalie plant could then convert the salt to chlorine and sodium hydroxide by electrolysis and send it by pipeline back to the Marchem plant that uses these chemicals in the Marhoe manufacturing process. The result would be an essentially closed loop with no waste and no deep well. This had already undergone a preliminary cost study.

He grabbed a sandwich at the lunch cart and wolfed it down in a short break.

After lunch, he was finally making good progress when the phone buzzed. It was Doug.

"Doug, glad to hear from you." Among other things, he wanted to hear what happened in Colorado. He also wondered about progress on Wolfy's murder.

"Let's meet," Doug said. "I have a lot to tell you."

"Good," Loren said. "I'll arrange a small conference room."

Doug arrived right on time, signed in and they went to the room.

"Sergeant Bigelow didn't get much out of your colleagues. Since you know them pretty well maybe you could fill me in on them," Doug said.

Loren didn't like the sound of that. "I'll try. Are they suspects?"

"Anybody who knew Reitz is a suspect."

Loren really didn't like the sound of that. "What do you want to know?"

"Well, first of all, I don't like it that Ferguson didn't show up for his interview with Bigelow," said Doug. "What's his problem?"

That was suspicious. "Who knows?" Loren said. "Maybe he was afraid he looked guilty. He was afraid of Wolfgang because he thought Wolfy could make trouble for him over the Martox patent. The material was actually Wolfgang's idea, you know. Joe rushed to make the chemical and file a patent disclosure. Wolfgang was notoriously slow in submitting disclosures."

"Is he capable of murder?" Doug asked.

"Doubtful. But who knows?" Loren said.

Doug quizzed him some more about his co-workers but finally Loren said, "Enough. What happened in Colorado?"

Doug summarized what happened after Loren left. "Since then I've been in contact with Delany. He said that they had definitely identified the two older bodies as Ableson and his wife. They are still working on the younger man."

How sad. And awful. "I met Ableson's wife once," Loren said. "She seemed to be a charming but outspoken woman. I wondered what had happened to her."

"Maybe she was a little too outspoken," Doug said. "The police scientists have definitely concluded that Kane was making large quantities of methamphetamines in his lab. They also found traces of LSD and opiates. They had a copy of the Viagra patent and had assembled the ingredients. Most ominous of all Kane's men had made a small quantity of Sarin."

That was horrifying. "What in hell did Kane want with a nerve gas?"

"Who knows? For sale to terrorists or maybe to use on

suspicious visitors like us."

"My God, he's really an evil man." Kane's depravity was hard to believe especially in a man he had known, albeit slightly.

"The police have turned over samples of some of the wastes in the pit to the university chemists," Doug said. "It's apparently quite a cocktail. They say it'll take months to sort out what's there. Besides determining how to dispose of the stuff, they hope to determine the origin. They might be able to go after the producers."

Loren nodded. "It would be really nice if we could find out who he was doing business with. What about the young lady you mentioned in Kane's house?"

"Oh, well it's a sad case. She says her father in Mexico sold her to a man who took her to Colorado secretly and apparently sold her to Kane. She broke down under questioning and right now is in a hospital but she probably will be deported when she is well enough. She may know something about Kane's activities, but it's doubtful."

"I think it would be a crime to deport her if she didn't want to go back, after what she's been through." Maybe Kane had mental problems. It certainly seemed like he at least had some kind of personality disorder.

"Delany wants us to come out to Colorado. He needs to go over what happened with us again. Make sure all the t's are crossed and i's are dotted on the reports, I guess. And he said they needed your chemical expertise. Plus, they would like to give us some award. I refused the award, I hope you agree?"

Loren nodded.

"I said we could be out next week. Delany's paying expenses." Doug chuckled, "My boss, Captain O'Brien, refused me the time off but Delany had his chief call our chief and O'Brien was forced to agree to the trip. I've also cleared you're going with your boss."

"I haven't been much of a researcher lately so I may as well go. But I can't be gone long. I have problems to deal with here."

"Delany also wants to know more about the man you recognized who was apparently working in the lab. They want to go after him and the others who worked for Kane."

"Arnold Novack," said Loren.

"Let's plan on going Tuesday. Have your secretary coordinate with mine." Cops have secretaries?

Loren said, "One more thing. My friend, Gloria, has received a very threatening phone call from a client's husband. She's a lawyer handling the wife's divorce. She's already started legal proceedings against him but restraining orders are often violated. Maybe you can do something about it." He might as well get something out of his connection with Doug.

"It's a little out of my line but I'll think about it and talk to some people. Maybe I should talk to her."

"I'd appreciate it."

Doug left and Loren sat in the conference room thinking for some time. He thought about Gloria and about the next Out of Deep Well meeting and about Bill. And the threat against the Martox plant. And, there was a murderer running around somewhere. He hoped for the best but was very worried.

The ODW meeting was scheduled for late afternoon. There were the usual research and engineering types present. Paul Devereaux, assistant director of manufacturing was presiding over the meeting.

"You people did a pretty good job reducing the capital." said Devereaux. "But what I would like to know is why you didn't come up with these reductions the first time around."

Sheila was irate. Her face turned red. "I resent that. We did the best job we could. We tried to design a top notch process."

"All these changes we made will give us a process which is less safe, less convenient, more wasteful and will provide a higher cost of goods," said Loren.

"Capital is tight now. The corporation has a lot of expenses. Also, we calculate that the cost of goods for the proposed process would be eighty-nine cents per pound versus our present cost of eighty-six cents." said Devereaux. "We have decided to cancel the project."

"For three cents we are canning this clean process?" said Barry. "Does management really want to improve waste generation and get out of deep wells?"

"Of course we want to reduce waste but we need to remain competitive," said Devereaux. "This meeting is adjourned."

Loren couldn't believe it. Canceling over a few pennies was imbecilic. It made him wonder what exactly could happen with the Martox plant. What safety procedures had been axed? For the first time he was truly scared. It was definitely possible something could go wrong.

He took Barry and Sheila aside. "Did you find anything out yet about the Martox plant?"

Barry shook his head. "Too soon to tell."

Sheila said, "They cut some capital late in the design process. But we don't know what the consequences are yet."

"Stay on it." Loren felt like they were onto something. And maybe it wasn't surprising Benson and the official investigators hadn't found anything. They were too confident. They couldn't even consider that their penny-pinching might cause problems.

Loren left the lab in a bad mood and went to the hospital.

Bill seemed to be in a better mood. The doctor had told him he could go home in one day. He said," I've learned my lesson and I want to go back to school."

Thank God. Loren said," I hope that's true."

Bill stared at him for a few moments. "It's weird. I haven't heard from Nick."

He tried unsuccessfully to think of a way to break the news gently. Finally, he just came out with it. "I'm afraid Nick didn't make it."

Bill was shocked. "What do you mean?"

"His injuries were fatal."

"How can that be?"

"Perhaps you should talk to the doctors about it." Being unable to help his son made him very uncomfortable. "I don't know the details."

Bill struggled to not break down and became very silent. He was obviously very upset and on the verge of crying. Maybe this whole episode scared some sense into him.

"I guess it's best to leave you alone," Loren said. "Ann will probably come again tomorrow."

Loren was hopeful on the way home. Maybe his son had turned a corner.

Without Bill to worry about so much, the trip to Colorado with Doug sounded like it would be a very interesting trip. He'd developed a strong liking for Doug. He realized this was quite a change both in his attitude toward Doug and a trip to Colorado and laughed at himself a little.

Ann wasn't home when he got home.

He had an idea and called Gloria. She answered and, after greetings, he said, "I'm sorry about Ann's attitude toward you and I have an idea. I've decided to have you and Ann meet unannounced. I think once Ann meets you, she would like you."

"I don't know about that," Gloria said. "Most people don't like surprises."

"Let's try it."

"Okay, but I'm uneasy about it."

When Ann got home, Loren suggested dinner at Ron's again and she was pleased to go. They got a table in the back and ordered drinks, Bud light for Loren and Pete's for Ann. When Gloria showed up, Loren introduced her and Gloria tried to be charming but the blood drained from Ann's face. Although she answered Gloria's greeting, Ann answered questions only with a yes or no. The dinner was quite uncomfortable for all. When Loren and Ann got home, Ann went directly to her room without even saying goodnight.

A swing and a miss. Clearly he couldn't solve all his problems.

He called Gloria." I must apologize for Ann's behavior. It was inexcusable."

"I'm sorry. I did my best to make her like me. I guess we'll have to try again."

"Yes. We'll try again. Also Doug Sanderson has agreed to see you about the abusive phone call. He'll try to set up a meeting for Monday."

"I'll be happy to see him Monday," she said.

"Good. I'll be there too. Goodbye."

Loren and Ann were on eggshells around each other all weekend. When Bill came home from the hospital she helped him get settled back in his room. At least having him home and back on track was a relief. For Bill's part he seemed to be taking Nick's death hard.

Monday morning Loren met with Barry and Sheila and they went over everything in the Martox process with a fine-toothed comb. Benson had passed from desperate to convinced that Wolfy's threat must have been a ruse--at least that's what he said.

Late Monday afternoon Loren met Doug Sanderson at Gloria's house.

She was very cordial. "I'm very happy to meet you lieutenant. Loren tells me you're Superman."

Doug grinned back at her. "Maybe Loren and I are Batman and Robin."

"Which is which?" she asked.

The two men looked at each other for a moment.

"I guess I'm Batman," Doug said. They all laughed.

"Anyway," he said, "what's this about abusive phone calls?"

"I guess Loren has told you I got a filthy and abusive call from a divorce client's husband." She glanced at him and he nodded. "He threatened to get me, whatever that means. I think he was serious and I'm scared."

Loren reached out and squeezed her hand. He'd hate

anything to happen to her.

"I'll get a tap put on your phone in case he calls again," Doug said. "Threatening phone calls are a crime and we could arrest him."

"Good," she said.

"Give me his name and also his address if you have it. I'll check him out. Maybe he has a criminal record. It would help if he has done something like this before. In the meantime keep your doors locked and have people around you."

"How about some protection?" Loren asked.

"The police department doesn't have the resources to provide that unless there has already been an attack."

"Swell," said Gloria.

"Not even for Robin's, ah, girlfriend?" Loren asked. She flashed him a quick smile.

"Well, for Robin's girlfriend, I'll check into getting some private help," Doug said. "I think I know a guy."

Loren was relieved.

Gloria also seemed relieved. "That would be good. Do you guys want to stay to dinner? I made some meatballs and a pot of sauce?"

"I guess I could," Doug said.

"Sure," Loren said. "Let me call the kids and tell them I'm not coming home for dinner."

Dinner was very pleasant. Doug and Gloria hit it off very well. She was in great form. They did a lot of laughing. The repartee was great. And yet, Loren was slightly uncomfortable. Why? Was he jealous of his new friend Doug? Gloria's spaghetti was very good and she had good chianti. The pleasant evening passed quickly and problems were temporarily forgotten.

Loren ended the festivities. "I better get going. The kids will be waiting for me." He looked at Doug to make sure he was going too. It was as if he didn't want Doug to be alone with Gloria but Doug said he would be going too.

Chapter 24

Doug picked up Loren at his house on Tuesday morning and they proceeded to the airport. Traffic was heavy.

"Do you have a siren or something?" Loren said. "We should speed it up."

Civilians thought cops just used the sirens whenever they felt like it. "Don't worry. I know a short cut." He got off the highway and took some side streets and they made it on time. They parked in a lot and took the shuttle to the terminal. The airport was crowded and there was a line at the American counter.

Loren began to worry again, if his fidgeting and ear-tugging was any indication, but the line moved pretty well. The Denver flight gate was at the end of a long concourse and both men arrived slightly out of breath after hurrying along. They were seated next to each other on the plane.

"Here we go again," Loren said. "I hope this trip isn't as eventful as the last one."

"I wouldn't think it would be," Doug said. "I was quite charmed by your friend Gloria. It was a fun time."

"I noticed that you were enjoying yourself." Loren fidgeted some more.

"You're not jealous are you?" Doug said. "I just

enjoyed Gloria's company, that's all. She reminded me of Mona because they're both such good hostesses."

"Okay." Loren sighed. "Did you find Gloria some protection?"

"Yes." Doug nodded. "Relax Loren. You seem a little uptight."

"A lot's been going on," Loren said. "Or did you find Wolfy's murderer and not mention it?"

"Ah. No." Doug shook his head. "The investigation's still on-going." The staff at Marchem had seemed so promising in terms of suspects or at least background info, but nothing was coming of it. And it didn't seem like Kane and his crew had anything to do with it either.

"Our investigation into Wolfy's threat against the Martox plant is still ongoing, as well," Loren said.

The passengers settled down and the plane took off. Loren watched the panorama on the ground as the plane climbed. Most of the passengers seemed to breathe a sigh of relief when the plane reached cruising altitude.

Doug was reading *Sports Illustrated.*

Loren took out his book, *Khrushchev Remembers.*

"That's an old one," Doug said.

"Yeah. I got it at a book fair. It's quite interesting."

Doug put down his magazine. "Oh? How so?"

"Among other things Khrushchev describes Stalin's paranoia. Stalin was so unpredictable that his colleagues were always in fear of their lives."

Doug chuckled. "Wow. And here I thought I had conflicts with my boss."

"Yeah," Loren said. "It puts it in perspective, doesn't it? I read a book that described Mao in similar terms, paranoid. It makes you wonder if absolute power bring on madness?"

"Well, Kane's power sure seemed to make him mad."

"Yeah."

That depressing topic killed the conversation.

The flight attendant came around with a snack. Loren took one.

Doug ignored the snack and ordered a Scotch on the rocks.

Loren looked at his diet coke. "Why didn't I order that? It smells good."

"Too late, the flight attendant's already up the aisle." He paused. "Do you want me to try to flag her down?"

"No, thanks."

"I wonder who's going to hit the most home runs this year," said Doug.

Loren shrugged. "I don't know, but I think the home run is one of the least interesting plays in baseball. Boom and it's all over. I think a squeeze play is more exciting even though they don't happen much anymore. People don't even seem to care who wins the game."

"You may be right," Doug said. Feeling slightly chastised, he went back to his magazine.

Eventually, the Rockies came into foggy view and were as beautiful as ever. The pilot made a smooth landing in a light rain. It seemed like it rains briefly every day in the Denver area.

Doug and Loren got on the airport train and went to the main terminal. Loren seemed to get a kick out of the music on the train. A plainclothes policeman was waiting for the two men in the baggage area. After greetings and pleasantries, the policeman led the way to an unmarked car parked at curbside. It looked like the visitors were going to have the VIP treatment. The trip from the Denver International terminal to the freeway was a long one and the freeway was backed up.

Doug's stomach growled. He didn't remember this trip being so long. "It's getting to be lunch time."

The officer, whose name was Durkee, said, "Lunch is being arranged at headquarters." After some aggravation they arrived at the headquarters building and Delany was waiting for them and took them to his office.

Delany's office was Spartan. The large wooden desk was fitting for the large man. The top of it featured a green desk blotter, a coffee mug filled with pens and pencils, and a picture of a woman and a young man. The right hand wall had several old and new pictures of men and women in police uniforms. A well-worn couch was against the wall. Like most cops, he'd probably slept on it a few times. Several file cabinets lined the walls.

"A nice flight?" asked Delany.

"No problems," Loren said.

"Want some coffee?" Doug was impatient to get down to business, or at least, lunch.

"No thanks," Loren said. "Had a coke on the plane."

"No thanks," Doug said.

"Is that your family?" Loren pointed to the picture on the desk.

"Yes, my wife and my son the lawyer. I feel like those guys on the wall are my family too. My dad and grandfather were policeman and the others are valued colleagues I met along the way. Let's get down to business."

"Fine. Let's do that," Doug said.

Delany opened a folder and read for a few seconds. "We found two more bodies. They were in side-by-side drums. One was a man wearing a uniform top but no pants. His penis was missing."

"What?" Loren exclaimed.

"What do you mean missing?" Doug asked.

Delany looked pained. "Missing as in gone. He'd been emasculated. The other drum contained a woman, probably Hispanic. She had also been mutilated."

Even as a cop, Doug never really got used to this kind of stuff.

"How mutilated?" Loren seemed shocked.

Delany shook his head. "Her breasts were cut off. We think the guy worked for Kane and the girl was Kane's mistress."

"So, what?" Doug asked. "They had some kind of affair? And Kane found out?"

Loren didn't say anything. He looked like he might be sick.

"Yeah," Delany said. "He won't admit anything. But we think he didn't like it so he took revenge."

Doug shifted in his chair. "That kind of extreme mutilation usually means it was personal. Your theory makes a sick kind of sense."

"Kane really turned into a monster," Loren said. "I trust they are going to ask for the death penalty."

Delany sort-of smiled. "Colorado has had a confusing history with capital punishment. First we had the jury decide the punishment for a convicted murderer but they never voted the death penalty. I guess they didn't want a death on their conscience. Then we had a panel of three judges but it turned out that one of the appointed judges was against capital punishment so that didn't work. Now we are back to having the jury decide punishment. Maybe this Kane case will be enough to make a jury decide on a death sentence."

"I hope so," Loren said. "Kane deserves it."

Doug cleared his throat." Anything else new?"

"More of the same chemicals and sludges. No radioactivity yet, thank God. They did find a liquid that they haven't identified yet. Our guys at the University are working on it."

"Can I have a sample?" asked Loren. "I'd like to help."

"Sure, I'll give them a call. We can probably get it out here before you go back."

"I can't take it on the plane. Could you have it shipped to my lab?"

"Sure, we can do that." Delany looked at his notes. "We've been trying to figure out Kane's finances and find out who he was doing business with. There are no names, only initials. There are three payments of five thousand dollars to someone or something with initials WAR. Do you know the middle name of your victim Wolfgang Reitz?"

"I think it was Adolf," Loren said. "Some people kidded him about it. Both the WAR and the Adolf. He didn't like it."

The plot thickens. Reitz was involved with Kane. "Hey, that's very interesting," Doug said. "What would Kane be paying Reitz for?"

"Wolfgang was a world class phosphorus chemist," Loren said. "Maybe it was for consulting. Somebody said Kane was trying to make nerve gas."

Now they all looked like they might be sick.

After a few moments, Delany said, "That's definitely

something we need to check out." "Maybe Reitz was blackmailing Kane?" Doug turned to Loren. "Would you say Reitz needed money?"

Loren nodded. "You saw his fancy lab, didn't you?"

Doug's stomach growled again and the other men looked at it. "Ah," he said. "Nice to be back in Colorado. When's lunch?"

Delany smiled and motioned. "Follow me"

Lunch was catered, a buffet with lots of goodies. The odor of garlic was enough to set mouths watering. Loren selected spaghetti and potato salad and Doug made himself a huge sandwich. There was no beer so they had to make due with iced tea. Delany had a huge plate with some of everything.

The three men joined three others already sitting at the conference table. There were introductions around the table. Present were: Assistant District Attorney Jon Franklin, Delany's assistant Sergeant George Vosquez, and Public Affairs Specialist Henry Hoffman.

"First off, we would like to fill you two in on what more has happened since you left," Delany said. "You heard about the two new bodies. We also found two Hispanic men hiding in the barn. They claimed they were hired to care for the animals and to do general handyman work around the ranch. They also claimed they didn't know about the waste pit. We put them in protective custody. They had green cards although they couldn't speak English very well.

"If they committed crimes, they'll probably be questioned and deported back to Mexico, even if they were coerced," Hoffman said. His frown indicated he didn't think it was good.

Doug got up to make himself another sandwich and get some pasta.

Delany kept talking. "We've had a crew in the pit at Kane's ranch since you left. We've found about twenty-five hundred drums and twenty-five fiber packs filled with waste. We're still sampling them but it's going slowly because we have to be very careful. Like I said, we haven't found any radioactivity yet so that's a break. We have installed two chemists from our forensics lab in Kane's lab and they tell me that there is enough equipment there to at least to do preliminary analyses. We have also contracted with the university in Boulder to do more extensive testing. They have mentioned that you, Loren, might be of help to them."

"I'm willing. That's why I came," Loren said as Doug sat back down.

Franklin said, "The Feds are also getting involved. The experts say that it could take over a year to wind things up. It's a mess."

"Yeah." Hoffman nodded.

"Have you identified anything yet?" asked Loren.

"A mixture of chlorinated hydrocarbons is in a large numbers of the drums," Sergeant Vosquez said. He was a tall, very handsome Latino. He seemed to be very personable.

"We could take you up to Boulder after this meeting Loren. If you're willing," said Delany.

"No," Loren said "I think I'll rent a car and drive out tomorrow." Doug was a little surprised.

"Suit yourself," Delany said. "Vosquez can give you the information."

Delany continued. "We have identified the third body

originally found in the pit. His name was Rob Tillman. He has a record for theft and fraud. He probably was working for Kane and they had a falling out. We are investigating Charles Shapiro, Kane's lawyer, but so far he's clean."

"I think you should investigate Sheriff Swieki too," Doug said. Swieki was definitely crooked.

"You mentioned that before. We'll be doing that," said Delany. "We think he was being paid by Kane. We haven't been able to apprehend Kane's henchmen yet. They apparently got away clean but we are working on it."

"What about Novack?" Loren asked.

"This man Novack, what can you tell us about him?" Vosquez asked.

"He retired from Marchem Company a while ago," Loren said. "He was a chemist. I didn't know him very well. He was a pretty quiet guy. He kept pretty much to himself. You can probably get all the info on him you need by contacting Marchem personnel. I can give you a phone number."

"Good," said Delany.

"Looks like you guys are doing a fine job," Loren said.

"What about the woman I found, Kane's supposed housekeeper?" Doug asked.

"She's calmed down and is being put up at a hotel. She wants to stay in Colorado. We're going to try to find her a job since she was a victim of Kane. Her story's been in the papers. She seems to be a smart girl and has been learning English. It's good PR with the Latin community to try to help her," Hoffmann said. "The public seems to have a lot of sympathy for her according to the letters to the editor."

"I don't blame them. I feel sympathy for her," Doug said. "She seemed terrified when I found her."

"I suppose it would be good PR to help her," Loren said.

Delany agreed. "We're working on it. Vosquez, will you help Hoffmann on this?"

Vosquez smiled and nodded his head. "Sure thing."

Delany continued. "We could use some more evidence against Kane about the killings. I'm sure he killed, or had killed, the dead people in the pit but we would like a more solid case. He's a dead duck as far as the illegal dumping is concerned. It would help a lot if we could get answers out of his employees. I assume they'd know about his activities. Maybe we can offer immunity from prosecution and some incentives if they turn states evidence."

Doug got up and went for some more iced tea and Loren asked about a men's room.

"Down the hall to your left, "said Vosquez.

Loren left for the restroom and the meeting seemed to be about to break up. When he returned Delany said it was time for their depositions.

Franklin led Loren and Doug to a room equipped with a television camera. Inside they could see a microphone sat on a table in front of the camera and there was a straight-back chair. It didn't look very comfortable.

"Who wants to go first?" Franklin asked.

Loren and Doug looked at each other.

"Loren can go first," Doug said.

The three men entered the room.

Franklin set up the TV system. "The camera and mike are controlled by this switch," he said, pointing to a pad on the table. "If you want to stop speaking, just push the button. When you want to resume, push it again. We want a video and a transcript. One of our employees will keep an eye on you in here and prepare the transcript. Doug, you'll have to leave the room. We don't want you to be influenced."

"I know," Doug said. What did he think, he was a rookie?

"Loren, come down to my office when you are done," Franklin said. "It's three-oh-one on the third floor."

"Will do," said Loren.

Doug and Franklin left and went down to Franklin's office. The office was rather lavish for a public servant.

"Coffee, Doug?" Franklin asked.

"Sure." Doug got himself a cup and the two men chatted.

After a while, Loren showed up. "I'm finished."

"Loren, Jon knows Mona!" Doug said. "He's on the art museum board and has purchased some of her work for the museum."

"Small world," Loren said. "How about some of that coffee?"

"Help yourself. It's over there." Franklin pointed.

"Delicious aroma," Loren said. "What's this?"

"Oh, hazelnut, my favorite," said Franklin. "I guess it's your turn Doug. Do you want me to go up with you?"

Again, treating him like a rookie. Doug was starting to get annoyed. "I think I can handle it, Jon."

Doug stood up and walked into the hall.

"How well do you know Mona?" asked Loren. Doug paused to listen.

"Quite well," Franklin said. "We've had some good times together. Do you know her?"

"I've met her. A very attractive lady."

"Indeed she is," agreed Franklin.

Doug was feeling jealous and he was surprised at himself. Mona was his ex. She was supposed to be his past.

"How about those Rockies?" Loren asked. Doug left.

After about forty-five minutes Doug returned to Franklin's office. "I guess that's it. Do you need anything else?"

"I think that will do it," Franklin said.

"We'll be leaving then," Doug said.

Loren and Doug shook hands with Franklin and left his office.

"I should stop by Vosquez's desk and get the contact info at the university," Loren said.

Doug shrugged. "Fine by me."

They did so and then left the building.

"So, to the Radisson?" Doug asked. They had reservations at the Radisson for the night. They were flying out the next day.

"How about going out to Central City for a while as long as we have time to kill," Loren asked.

"No. I don't think so," Doug said. "It doesn't look good for policemen to spend time in casinos. Besides, I have a lot of paperwork to get done. My boss told me if I return without the reports I have outstanding, he'll have me providing security for the Muny Opera."

Loren looked disappointed.

"I have an idea," Doug said. "Mona loves to gamble. I bet she would go with you. She usually is happy to go." Plus, it would probably give him excuse to talk to her or see her. Maybe he could figure out why he was feeling jealous.

Loren seemed skeptical. "Mona?"

"Yes, I'll bet you she would go," said Doug. "Do you want me to call her?"

"I doubt if she'd even remember me. Yeah, how about if you call her?"

"She'd remember you, but I'll call her," said Doug.

A squad car took Doug and Loren to the hotel.

After they checked in, Doug called Mona.

"Hello? Doug? Is that you?" she said.

Doug's pulse quickened. "Yes. I'm back in Colorado with my friend Loren, that Chemist."

"You're back again? So soon?" He could practically hear the smile in her voice.

"He wants to go to Central City and do some gambling," he said. "Are you interested?"

"Are you going gambling?" she asked. "That's a little out of character."

"No," he said. "Just the two of you."

"Aw. It'd be funner if you went," she said. "But, yeah, sure. I'll go. I'll pick him up at the hotel about two." Was he disappointed that Loren and Mona were going to get together?

They hung up. "She says it's a go. She'll be here at two o'clock to pick you up."

There was that jealousy again. What was going on with him? Whatever it was he needed to put it out of his mind.

He was going to work on the Reitz case, go back to the very beginning. He had copies of all the files and reports on his laptop. Hopefully, a change of scenery would help him see everything with fresh eyes.

Chapter 25

Loren was pleased but a little apprehensive. He didn't quite understand his feelings for Mona. He loved Gloria.

He freshened up and changed his plane reservation to indefinite departure. Just before two o'clock he went down to the lobby to wait for Mona. Mona was right on time. She was driving a silver Mercedes convertible. The top was up.

"Nice car." Loren got in. "Art glass must pay pretty well."

Mona laughed. "I do all right." She was dressed in a black denim pants suit with a white blouse with Georgia O'Keefe tulips. Her black hair was done slightly different than it was when Loren met her. She was stunning.

"How are you Loren?" she said.

"I've been pretty busy lately."

"Has Douglas been running you around?"

Loren nodded. "Doug and others."

Mona set out for Central City with a roar. She was not a timid driver. Her car was hot and she took advantage of it. She negotiated the city traffic expertly and soon was on the highway. The road to Central City wound around huge rock formations. There was a fast running creek alongside the road and, except for the dry vegetation, it was a scenic trip but Loren had a hard time taking his eyes off Mona. They passed several gas stations and small businesses.

"When I first came out here there was nothing built on this road," said Loren.

She smiled. "Yes, the gambling has picked up the economy. I was surprised to hear that you are a gambler, Loren."

He liked to gamble and had been out to Central City several times over the years. He was not a big better but he enjoyed it. "Why is that?"

"I thought scientists were very conservative guys that stayed in their laboratories and did experiments in their white coats."

"No," he said. "Scientists and even engineers are among the biggest gamblers around."

Mona smiled her dazzling smile. "What do you mean by that?"

"I'm not unique but I'll use myself as an example. If I have an idea for a new product or process and convince management it is a good one, the company will invest twenty, thirty, a hundred million dollars to build a plant. There are no guarantees. If the plant doesn't operate correctly, the company could be out a lot of money."

"But you wouldn't lose your job would you?"

"Maybe you would, but probably not. But you would lose something a lot more precious."

"What's that?"

"Your reputation. Without a good reputation no one will trust you with any kind of a significant project." Why would Wolfy risk his reputation on an empty threat?

"I see what you mean. But what about engineers?"

"Same deal. If you design a bridge and it falls down-- which has happened--who will want you to design another

188

bridge?" Wolfy wouldn't risk his reputation.

Mona smiled again. "I understand. That's interesting. But what about academics?"

"Every time you publish a journal article you put your reputation on the line. If you make a mistake someone will discover it and probably humiliate you in print. Some scientists can be vicious," he said. "For example, there was the case of the guys who reported that they produced cold fusion. That's the energy that powers the sun and they said they produced it at room temperature. They took a big gamble when they published without enough evidence but I think they were sincere. Their reputations suffered a big blow. Of course some guys actually publish false results. That's a really big gamble. If the results are significant somebody is sure to try to repeat the experiment. If they can't repeat the results they are usually judged to be bogus. The researchers seldom get away with incompetent or faked results and their reputation is totally destroyed." If Wolfy was telling the truth: the Martox plant was doomed.

"I guess all life is a gamble."

He was getting distracted. "I guess so." Why didn't the experiments they'd already repeated show the plant was in danger?

They passed a place where tourists could pan for gold and soon came to the turn for Blackhawk and Central City. Mona seemed to know exactly what she was doing. She drove through town and up to a topped-off mountain and parked. A shuttle brought them back down into town. There were lots of casinos but Mona led Loren to Harrah's.

"We can start here," she said. "I'll meet you by the front entrance in two hours."

Loren knew if he concentrated on his idea about the

Richard Lowell

plant, it would slip away. He needed to distract himself, so he played the slots. He had some wins but after two hours he had lost enough and went looking for Mona. She was waiting.

"Did you win?" he asked.

"I don't discuss winning or losing. I had fun," she said. "Are you ready to quit?"

"If you are," he said.

"I know a good Mexican restaurant in Golden. Are you hungry?"

"Yes, that sounds good."

They caught the shuttle and jumped into Mona's car. The drive to Golden seemed to be quicker than the drive from Denver. They found a parking place on the street and went into The Wheel restaurant. The aromas pervading the restaurant were very pleasant: salsa and tequila. The walls were crowded with all manner of wagon wheels, most of which looked old and authentic. They were shown to a table and ordered margaritas.

"I wonder where they got all those wagon wheels," Loren said.

"I don't know," Mona said. "Quite a collection."

The margaritas disappeared quickly and they ordered two more.

"I suppose you want to fuck me. Most men do," Mona said.

Loren didn't know what to reply. He didn't want to insult her. His face felt like it was turning the color of a very ripe apple. "I don't know what to say to that, Mona. I have a girlfriend."

"I don't do that anymore," she said. "I suppose Doug told you I was promiscuous. I admit that I was unfaithful when I was married to him but that's behind me. He was always gone and I was lonely and depressed. Men kept hitting on me, even some of his friends, and I finally gave in. I wasn't proud of it, but it happened. I always loved Doug. Still do."

"Did you and Doug get together the last time we were here?"

"Yes. We had a good time but he seemed preoccupied."

That explained the morning Doug was still wearing the previous day's clothes. "I thought so. Do you want to get back together with him?"

"With all my heart."

Loren was going to advise her to tell Doug how she felt, when the waitress appeared and asked if they were ready to order dinner.

"Two more margaritas and, when you bring them, we'll order," Mona said.

Loren wasn't sure they needed another margarita but he said nothing.

"Is that why you went out with me? So I could report to Doug that you'd changed?"

"Partly."

The waitress brought the drinks and he ordered tacos and she ordered fajitas. He was digesting the discussion. He was a bit confused.

They made small talk until the food came, they ordered another drink, and they started eating.

"So you're going to the university tomorrow," she said.

"Yes," he said. "I'm going to help with the Kane investigation."

"From what I hear Kane was a real bad guy."

"The baddest," he said. "Hard to believe the things

191

he did. Even multiple murder apparently. He needs to be brought to justice."

She grimaced. "Don't tell me any more. I don't want to know."

They both focused on their dinners for a few moments.

"How do you like the tacos?" she asked.

"They are excellent," he said. "Just the right amount of spice. This is a nice place."

"It's one of my favorites."

"I guess this conversation clears the air," he said. "I suppose you want me to report back to Doug. That's why we're here, right?"

"I also like to gamble and I like you Loren." She smiled gently.

He didn't know whether to be disappointed or relieved. He liked her, too, but didn't like the idea being used as some kind of messaging service.

The waitress asked if they wanted dessert and they declined.

Loren paid the check and got up. "Ready to leave?"

"I'm ready," she said.

He was a little concerned about her driving ability after three margaritas, but all was well. Back at the hotel, he thanked her profusely for going out with him. She said goodnight and kissed him on the cheek.

When Loren got to his room he debated calling Benson to tell him he was sure Wolfy had sabotaged the Martox plant. But he didn't have any hard data, yet, so he decided against it.

There was a message to call Doug. He wanted to meet for a drink and Loren was agreeable. They met in the lobby bar and were the only customers.

Loren ordered a Corona and Doug a Bud Lite.

"How was the evening?" Doug asked.

"It was fun even though I lost a little money. We had dinner at the Wheel restaurant. Do you know it?"

"Yes, I've been there. How was Mona?"

"She was fine. Look Doug, quit beating around the bush. I think you sent me out with Mona to spy on her."

"What do you mean?"

"You wanted to know if she would try to seduce me. Well, she didn't. In fact she spent the evening singing your praises. She loves you, man."

"What did she say?"

"She wants to get back together with you."

Doug looked very pleased. "I'll be damned. I have to think about this. Ready to go up?"

Loren yawned, "Yeah, I'm ready. I'm going out to the university tomorrow."

"Oh yeah, I remember. I'll be meeting with Delany again."

Loren and Doug went up and went to bed.

Budget Car Rental delivered the blue metallic Mustang to the hotel at seven-thirty a.m. and Loren buzzed off at eight. He felt light and airy. It had been a long time since he had a half-day all to himself. The Denver traffic was brutal but he negotiated it like a native. He got onto Highway 36 in a half an hour. He opened a window and, instead of clean mountain air, auto exhaust assaulted his nose. What a pity.

Whole new communities had bloomed along the roadside since he was along this road five years ago. The route to Boulder from Denver had been almost unpopulated when he first traversed the route. It must be twenty-five years or more since he and Gwen enjoyed their first holiday in Colorado. Both of the kids had attended the university in Boulder. After they ogled the campus, they had to attend college there. He dissolved into a web of nostalgia. He and his wife had adored Colorado and he wished she had been able to endure a trip after the terminal cancer diagnosis. It was not to be. She didn't make it.

Loren gulped lots of miles. He turned off at the scenic overlook and got out. The Flatirons were still standing guard over the jewels in Boulder valley. So many good times. So many memories. He wished Gwen was with him. His vision got a bit blurry. The reservoir was glittering in the bright sunlight--maybe that was the reason. But he doubted it. He was very emotional. He and Gwen had a lot of fun in Boulder while their kids had attended the university. He hadn't been back since Gwen died. Eventually he got a handle on his feelings.

First up: lunch.

The drive down to town took only a few minutes but where to park? That was always a problem in Boulder when school was in session but he found a spot. It had been five years but Pearl Street looked the same. Some shops were deceased but there were some new ones. He saw the Artist's Guild Shop. Gwen had always lapsed into frenzies when she went in there. *Look at that! Isn't that beautiful!* He decided not to go in. He didn't think he could take it.

He saw Roderigo's Mexican Restaurant, a family favorite, and went in. It was lunchtime. The crowd looked very young. He sighed. Were he and Gwen were ever that young?

He got a table and ordered tamales and a Corona. He

munched chips while he waited. The tamales were covered with a sauce that he thought was the spiciest he ever tasted, really excellent.

He leaned back, sipping his Corona and blinked back blurriness. You can't go home again. There were just too many memories here. The trip he'd been looking forward to had left him depressed.

It was time for his appointment at the university. Just as well.

Sergeant Vosquez had given him good directions, even where to park. His contact at the university chemistry department was Professor Palmer, a well-known analytical chemist. He found the chemistry building and found the professor's name in the directory in the lobby, and walked up. The office door was open. Journals, books and students homework cluttered the office.

"Professor Palmer?" Loren asked.

"Yes, you must be Dr. Sharp. You don't look like a student. I've been expecting you. I've heard good things about you. Have a seat. You can move those journals."

Loren took a seat and scanned Dr. Palmer. The professor was a thin man and was probably tall, although Loren couldn't tell because of the desk between them. Male-pattern baldness and a short brown beard were evident.

The professor also gave Loren the once over, but didn't indicate his opinion.

"I understand you have been trying to identify the materials from the pit," Loren said.

"That's right. It's quite a mess. I've never seen anything like it."

"What does it look like?"

"Lots of chlorinated hydrocarbons, some drums look like distillation residues and there are some heavy metal-containing sludges. Probably catalysts. We've been trying to identify platinum because it could pay for some of the work. We might have found some. But it may cost too much to recover it. Let's go up to the lab."

"Fine." Loren stood.

They entered a large room filled with lab tables, scientific instruments and several young people looking very busy. At the other end of the lab, the T.A. said, "Today we're going to look at the chemistry of photography. The first light-fast images were created using silver halide photochemistry but included special treatments including mercury vapors and sodium hyposulfite..."

Palmer gestured for Loren to join him in front of some sophisticated equipment.

Loren said, "I'm surprised you let the students use this expensive equipment."

Palmer chuckled. "Oh, no. They're not allowed to touch it."

"So, what techniques are you using?" asked Loren.

Palmer walked him over to a particularly impressive group of instruments. One of them looked like a cannon. "GC, mass spec for the liquids."

"Good. The most important tool no doubt." He was very familiar with these techniques. GC, gas chromatography, used a long coil of metal or glass tubing filled with an absorbent impregnated with a high boiling liquid. The coil was heated and an inert gas was passed through it. The sample was injected into the gas stream and the individual components were absorbed to varying degrees on the packing. This caused the components to exit the coil at intervals and a detector showed a response for each one. The individual components could then be passed into a mass spectrometer. The components were broken down in the mass spec into every possible fragment and the fragments were subjected to a magnetic field. The path of each fragment depended on its weight and the mass of each is recorded. By mentally--or with the aid of a computer--putting the fragments back together, the scientist could determine the chemical structure of the sample's components. "That's certainly the method I would use," Loren said.

"Yes, of course," Palmer said. "We're using column chromatography on the distillation residues."

Loren had also used this method. It was similar to gas chromatography but used solvents rather than gas. He began to wonder why he was here. These people knew what they were doing. A courtesy visit? Delany's idea?

"I suppose you're doing metal analyses on the sludges," he said.

"Yes. We suspect they are some kind of spent catalysts," Palmer said. "We might have some liquids we can't deal with."

"If so, I'd be happy to help. But you're certainly doing the right things. I don't know what I can add."

Professor Palmer smirked. "Yes, of course."

Was he being patronized? Some college people looked down on industrial chemists because they did applied research while pure research was done in academia. He considered some academic research useless, but he decided to let it go.

He was starting to feel uncomfortable, "I guess I'll take

my leave."

"So soon?" Palmer said. He didn't look disappointed.

"Yes, I have to get back to St. Louis."

Palmer smiled. "Some important research?"

Loren hid his feelings. "No my son is ill."

"Sorry to hear it. Goodbye then. It was a pleasure. I guess you can find your way out."

Loren left thinking the visit was a waste of time. His thoughts went back to St. Louis and he thought he had been away too long. Bill was home and Gloria might be in danger. He broke some speed laws getting back to the hotel.

When Loren got back to his hotel room he got on the phone. His first call was to Ann.

"Hello, Ann. How's everything?"

"Pretty good."

"Good. Greet Bill for me. I hope he is doing okay."

"He seems okay." She paused.

"What's wrong?" he asked.

"I'm depressed about my job situation."

"You'll find something," he said. "I hope to catch an early plane so I should be home tomorrow in the early afternoon."

"Good. I will be watching for you. Do you want me to pick you up?"

"That would be good. I'll call when I get in."

"Fine. I'll see you tomorrow. Bye, Dad."

"Goodbye, Ann."

Then he called Gloria.

"Hello, Gloria. It's Loren."

Gloria's voice was not friendly. "Hello, Loren."

"Is something wrong?"

"I got another phone call."

"From the same guy?"

"Yes. He was even nastier than last time. Loren, I'm scared."

"Didn't the police tap your phone line?"

"Yes, I taped the call but I'm sitting here alone and I'm scared. I think this guy means business."

"What about the guy Doug promised?"

"If he's around, I haven't seen him," she said.

"Lock your doors and call the police," he said. "Hang in there. I'll be home tomorrow."

"Okay, Loren. I'm not too happy about the help I'm getting."

"I'll talk to Doug about it."

"Okay, see you tomorrow then." Gloria was not happy. In fact she was terrified.

Loren called American and made a reservation for an eight o'clock flight to St. Louis. He would have to get up at five a.m. but he decided he needed to get home.

Next, he called Doug and told him he was leaving and about Gloria's phone call. He finished with, "I thought you said you had a friend, a P.I., that would watch over her?"

"I do," Doug said. "I did. I'll call him as soon as we hang up and find out what's going on."

Loren felt a little better.

"I have some news about Kane," Doug said. "I've been with Delany and they've been looking into Kane's finances. They've had a couple of experts going through Kane's computer and they've broken his passwords and gotten into his files. One of the experts happened to be a coin collector and he found a file that he says is a list of super valuable coins, probably several million dollars' worth. We've been looking for them in Kane's ranch house but haven't found them. There is a locked cabinet in Kane's bedroom but it was empty. We're thinking that Kane's men took them when they left."

Loren was himself a small time numismatist. "That's very clever. It would be an easy way to transport a fortune. A few coins would be easy to carry if Kane had to leave in a hurry.

"That's what we're thinking. Delany will be going after them. The state wants to confiscate them to help pay for the cleanup of Kane's mess."

"Good idea. So, I'll probably see you back in St. Louis. See what you can do about Gloria's problem."

"I'll get on the phone as soon as you hang up." They hung up.

Then Loren realized he had voice mail from Ann. "Pop, please call me."

Loren quickly dialed and Ann answered on the first ring.

"Hi Pop, thanks for calling back. I wanted to tell you that a friend of mine at school is also having trouble getting an academic job and he told me he was looking into getting a job in industry. For the heck of it I sent my resume to a few places that I thought could use a physicist. Guess what? I just got a phone call from a computer jock at Boeing in St. Louis and they want me to come for an interview. He says they do a lot of computer modeling and my background looks good to him. Isn't that a gas?"

Loren was surprised. "That's very interesting. Are you going?"

"Why not? See you soon."

Chapter 26

Doug decided to call Mona and asked if she was willing to see him. She seemed happy to say yes. They arranged to have dinner at seven at one of Mona's favorite restaurants, an Italian place called Carlo's.

He arrived at Mona's at six-thirty and she had the margaritas and chips ready. She also had obviously spent a lot of time cleaning and arranging which was usually not her strongest suit. She tended to let things slide while she was doing her glass. She had taken some care in what she was wearing, as well. She looked stunning. She had on a red pants suit with a white blouse and a red patterned kerchief.

They were rather quiet for a while, as if they were waiting for the other to start the conversation. Did she know what Loren had told him? What did she want him to say?

Finally Doug said, "Excellent margarita."

"Thanks. I think it's your old recipe."

"I thought it tasted familiar." Doug finished his drink and said, "I think it's time to roll."

"What's the weather like out there?"

"It's a little chilly."

"Let me get a wrap and I'll be right with you." Her

wrap was a short black jacket he had given her several years ago.

He said, "I recognize that wrap." Was it some kind of sign?

"Yes, I'm still wearing it. I like it."

They left and got in her car and she drove. Not much was said during the ride. It was a short trip to the restaurant and it was easy to park. She'd made a reservation so they were shown to a table immediately.

The restaurant was quite elegant with arches and statuary. The predominant color was cream and the kitchen was open to the seating area. The cooks could be seen doing their thing.

"I like a restaurant that honors reservations. Not all of them do nowadays," he said. "This is a nice place. They seem to know you here."

"Yes, I come here as often as I can."

"If you like it you might as well. Who do you come here with?" Was that a tinge of jealousy again?

"Various people," she said. Sometimes alone."

"You must get hit on when you are alone."

"Sometimes but the staff sort of shoos them away."

"That's good." That was very good. He liked the staff here.

A waiter brought menus and asked if they wanted a drink. They said they wanted margaritas and started studying the menu. Doug finally ordered pasta carbonara and Mona ordered the veal marsala.

Once the waiter departed, he asked, "How did you like the outing with Loren?"

"I always like going to the casino and sometimes it's hard to find someone who wants to go," she said. "Loren seemed very interested in going and he was a pleasant companion. I thought he would be rather stuffy but he was actually pretty interesting. He talked a lot about how most life is a gamble, even being a scientist. He wasn't like I thought he was going to be."

"How so?"

"Oh I guess you would say he was more lively than I expected."

"Did you invite him in?" He couldn't stop himself from asking.

Mona seemed a little angry. "No I did not. I don't do that stuff anymore."

Doug smiled. "Glad to hear it." Could it be true? If so, it would be great.

The waiter brought their salads and they concentrated on eating.

But finally he got to the point and said, "Loren said he thought you still loved me and that you might want to get back together. Is that true?"

A tear appeared in her eye and her nose wrinkled up. "Yes. I meant for Loren to tell you that. I'm sorry for the way things turned out. We were too young for marriage then and I was lonely. You were gone so much."

"No need to be sorry. I was every bit as guilty as you. I was too career-oriented. Please don't be upset."

They stared at each other for a few moments. Now what?

The waiter brought the entrees, interrupting them. "This really looks good."

"The food here is excellent," she said. "How was the salad?"

"Excellent."

He was glad that the food came because he didn't know how to proceed with the conversation. He concentrated on eating. They ate in silence for a while.

Eventually he said, "I can see why you come here a lot. It's got great food and atmosphere. The service is just right too. Not too pushy or too slow."

Mona just stared at him, but then said, "I'm glad you like it. I come here often."

They finished their food in silence. The waiter asked if they wanted some dessert and they declined.

She stared at him again and said, "We can have coffee at my place."

Did that mean what he thought it meant? "Great."

They left the restaurant and drove to Mona's. They walked to the door together and she opened the door. She turned off the security as they entered.

She walked to the kitchen and started putting on the coffee, but turned around to face him, still standing in the kitchen's entrance. "You don't really want coffee, do you?" She held out her arms.

"No." He strode to her.

It was a very nice and friendly evening…

Doug's flight back to St. Louis was an hour late. He hadn't gotten much sleep at Mona's and wasn't able to sleep on the plane. There was too much to think about.

When he landed, there was a voicemail from his aunt asking for progress on her friend's case. He felt a little guilty; he'd been neglecting the case. But that ended now.

As soon as he could Doug checked his email. There was a message from Charlie Wong to call about Carlos. Good. Doug dialed up Charlie's cell phone and Charlie answered immediately.

"It's Charlie."

"It's Doug."

"Oh, Doug. Where've you been? I've called several times."

"I've been out of town on another case. Where have you been?" Doug said. "I tried calling you about the Gloria matter. She was threatened again. Have you been watching over her?"

"Ah, sorry," he said. "I asked my nephew to do it."

"What? That wasn't what we agreed to." Doug was annoyed.

"There was nothing going on, the kid can handle it." He paused. "Do you want to hear about Carlos or not?"

"Yeah. What have you found out?"

"Actually your boy is kind of a homebody. He spends quite a bit of time in his apartment. Otherwise, he went out to dinner a couple times with a woman who lives in a house in the city."

"That would be Maria Martinez. I know about her."

"He seemed to be treating her badly," Charlie continued. "She had to walk behind him and she seemed to be crying one of the times."

"Weird. Some kind of machismo? Go on. Did he go anywhere else?"

"By the way, he drives a two year old Corvette. His apartment building is upscale too. He must be doing well."

"Exactly what he does is what I want to know."

"He went several times to the Spanish Club in South County. It's a social club for Spanish speakers. I know a few members. It has a good reputation. Another place he went was Aztec Printing, a printing plant in Ferguson. He carried a briefcase in and out of that place."

"A printing plant. Very interesting."

"If you say so."

"Does it have retail sales?" Doug asked. "A sales office?"

"I believe it does but I'm not sure," Charlie said.

"Find out will you?" Doug said.

"Okay, will do."

"Anything else on Carlos?"

"He's home. That's all for now. Shall I stay on him?" Charlie said.

"Not for now, but maybe later."

"I'll send you a bill."

"I'm sure you will," said Doug. "I need you to check on what's happening with Gloria."

"Okay, will do." They hung up.

Doug decided it was time to talk to Señor Valdez one on one. He dialed the number and got the answering machine again but left a message. "This is Detective Lieutenant Douglas Sanderson. I have some questions you may be able to help me with about the death of Catalina Perez. I would like to meet with you about this at your home. I think you're there. Please pick up."

There was a long pause and finally Carlos Valdez picked up. He had apparently decided that the best policy was to appear cooperative. That would cause the least suspicion. "Yes, Lieutenant, I don't know what I can help you with but by all means come over. I'll help as much as I can."

Doug drove over as fast as he dared. It wouldn't do for him to get a speeding ticket. More ammo for O'Brien. He parked in front of the building. Charlie was right; the building was definitely upscale. Carlos was listed in the lobby on the fourth floor. He decided to walk up. It would do him good.

Carlos opened the door at Doug's first knock. He was about thirty-five and seemed like he worked out. He had a small mustache and dark wavy hair. He probably would be considered handsome except for a rather prominent nose.

After exchanging hurried greetings, they sat down in the living room. The room was decorated with a modern Spanish feel. There was a big television set, a wooden bar, and furniture that appeared expensive. An open door to a bedroom looked like it was used as an office. There were several bull fighting posters on the walls.

Doug looked around and said, "Nice digs."

"Thank you," Carlos said. "What can I do for you, Lieutenant? Would you like some coffee?"

"No thanks. I've had coffee. As I said on the phone, I'm investigating the hit and run death of Catalina Perez."

"I don't know why you think I would know anything about that. I thought it was an accident."

"Some people don't think so."

Carlos shook his head. "Oh, I think it was. She was an old lady, and I heard her eyesight was failing."

Doug decided a little intimidation was in order, "Look Carlos, if you know something about this you better tell me. Not cooperating with the police is serious."

Carlos seemed worried. "I swear I don't know anything about it." He lost eye contact.

Doug was a little surprised Carlos was so easily intimidated. He bored in, pressing his advantage. "Do you know anything about counterfeit auto emission reports?"

The blood drained from Carlos' face. It was obvious

the question hit a nerve. It took him a full minute to reply. He tried to look unconcerned, "No I don't. Why do you ask that?"

"My aunt talked to me about them. It may connect to Ms. Perez's death."

"Your aunt?"

"My aunt was a friend of Ms. Perez."

Carlos had regained his composure. Was his nervousness an act? "I'm sorry, I don't know anything about the death of Ms. Perez. I don't know why you think I would. I hardly knew her."

"Okay. By the way, what is Merchant Services Incorporated?"

"I sell things--not that it's any of your business."

Doug got up to leave. "If you think of anything that could help, please call me."

He gave Carlos his card and left. It would be a cold day in hell before Carlos would call him. Obviously, he knew more than he was telling.

The reason Doug asked Charlie if Aztec printing had retail sales was so he could pose as a customer. He looked up the address and put on his navy jogging suit and a Ram's hat. That was as close to a disguise as he ever used. He drove over and found the place easily. It was in a commercial area of Ferguson and was in a rather large, old but renovated building. The sign in front said: *AZTEC PRINTING*. There was a parking lot at the side of the building and he parked and entered the building.

The sales room was roomy and contained a counter with a young African American woman presiding. Off to a side was a desk with numerous loose-leaf binders piled up that were no doubt catalogues. The back wall had a picture of an Aztec chief in full regalia.

Doug walked up to the counter and smiled at the woman.

The woman smiled back and said, "Can I help you?"

"I'm interested in getting some party invitations printed."

"You've definitely come to the right place. We have a big selection." She pointed to the desk and said, "Check out the catalogues over there. The invitations are in the red one."

He went to the desk and pretended to be interested. After about ten minutes he got up and said, "I can't make up my mind. You have so many nice invitations. I'll have to think about it."

"When you decide, we'll be here."

Doug hesitated at the door and said, "Say, I've always been interested in the printing business. Do you think I could have a tour of the plant?"

"Oh no, sir. Our insurance does not allow non employees in the manufacturing area."

"Okay, bye then."

He went to the parking lot but instead of leaving he checked out the building. There were several windows along the first floor on the side and back and a loading dock and entry door in back. The loading dock had a large pull down type door, and next to it had a permanent ladder installed for climbing up to the top of the deck. There was a large unattached garage backing on an alley at the back of the property. He decided he'd seen enough so he left.

When he got home he called Charlie Wong's cell phone. Charlie answered quickly.

"This is Charlie."

"This is Doug."

"I didn't expect to hear from you so soon. I'm on a stakeout."

"How would you like to make some hazard pay?"

"Legal or illegal?"

"Illegal."

"Oh, that will cost you."

"Double, triple, what?"

"Depends."

Doug explained that he wanted to break into a printing plant. He told Charlie the plant's owners could be counterfeiters and may be implicated in a murder. He said he needed him as a lookout and locksmith.

Charlie said, "Sounds like fun. Triple fees though. I could lose my license. When do we go?"

"I don't want to get caught either. I would lose my job. On the other hand, I've been thinking of going private anyway."

"I hope not. I don't need any more competition.

"I'll let you know when we'll do it."

Chapter 27

Loren was very tired when he got home from Colorado. A gloomy drizzle stained the day. Ann picked him up at the airport in Bill's car.

"Oh Dad, I'm glad you're home," she said, while driving.

"What's the trouble, hon?"

"Everything has been going wrong."

"Let's talk about it when we get home," he said.

At home, the house had a gloomy feel to it. Blinds were drawn and it seemed dark and airless. Loren and Ann sat down in the living room. Loren could hear a television set droning in the back of the house.

"So what's the trouble?" he asked.

"Bill won't talk to me. I've been trying to be upbeat, but he wouldn't answer me when I talked to him. He's acting very funny."

"Okay, I'll talk to him. What else?"

She was on the verge of tears. "You know my interview at Wisconsin wasn't successful. Then, yesterday when I got two blocks from home a tire went flat on your car. I was in my best suit so I drove home on the flat. I'm sure it's ruined. I'm sorry."

Loren suppressed a sigh. "Okay. We'll get a new one,

Ann. We just have to take problems one at a time."

He opened the blinds, cracked a window and changed the tire, which was shredded. They went to a local tire store and got a new one installed.

"Now I have to deal with Bill," he said, shaking his head.

He found his son lying on the couch in the den watching television. He felt badly, seeing his bandages. "How do you feel?"

Bill ignored him.

"What's this I hear about you not talking to Ann?" he asked.

Bill didn't answer.

Loren turned off the television set and said, "Look here, Bill. I know you have been having a rough time but that's no excuse for treating Ann and I like this. We love you."

Again, Bill didn't answer. He turned his face toward the back of the couch.

"Okay," Loren said. "I'll let you think about it for a while." He didn't have the heart to chastise a young man in such obvious physical and mental pain. "But I'm here for you, if you need anything."

Next Loren called Gloria. "Hello, Gloria. I'm home."

"Oh, Loren. Thank God."

"What's the trouble?"

She was a little angry. "Didn't you hear I had another nasty phone call?"

"Yes, I did. You told me. Do you really think this guy is a problem?

"I certainly do."

"Doug said his guy was on it. He promised. I love you.

I wouldn't let anything happen to you."

"Can you come over now?"

"No. I have some things to do at my lab."

"I'm sure my client's husband isn't kidding. I'm trying to put it out of her mind but it's difficult."

"I'm sure it is difficult."

"I have a lot of legal work to do. I'm trying to keep busy. But I'm uneasy."

"You need something to get your mind off it. Put on some dance music."

"All right." He heard some music start up in the background.

"I'll be over later. I promise. He's not going to bother you in broad daylight."

She didn't seem entirely convinced, but they hung up.

On his way into his lab, Loren stopped at Benson's office. He knocked on the open door. "Silk? I mean, Ted?"

Benson looked up from his computer. "What is it? I'm busy Loren."

"I just wanted to check in and see what you've deciphered about the Martox plant."

"Nothing," Benson said. "We've deciphered nothing." He rubbed his forehead. "I guess we're going to start up the plant on schedule."

Oh no. "I have to say that sounds like a bad idea to me," Loren said.

"Why?" Benson leaned towards him. "Did you figure something out?"

"Not yet," Loren said. "But I'm convinced there's something to it." Wolfy wouldn't gamble his whole reputation for nothing.

"So, basically, you know nothing new." He leaned back. "Thanks for stopping by, but like I said, I'm busy."

When Loren got to his lab, there was a UPS package on his desk that had been mailed from Colorado. Inside was a sealed glass ampoule containing a light yellow liquid.

He carefully removed the packaging and tilted the ampoule up and down. The behavior of the liquid indicated that it was an aqueous solution. The package also contained a note that said the liquid was found at the bottom of a metal fifty-five gallon drum and there was only about four inches of the liquid in the drum. The note stated that the material appeared to be an aqueous solution and that CU group was not set up to handle aqueous materials at the present time.

He took the sample to his hood, scored it with a file, broke off the tip and poured the sample into two vials. He tested part of the sample to make sure it was aqueous and he sent one of the vials down to the analytical department along with a request for High Pressure Liquid Chromatographic analysis with Mass Spectral Analysis. It would probably take a while before he heard the results.

He knew his subconscious was on the verge of figuring something out about Martox and he didn't want to push it.

He got back to work on his current project.

Two hours later he got an agitated phone call from the head of the Marchem Analytical Department. "Is this some kind of joke? Why are you sending us a vial of urine? We're too busy for jokes."

"Urine? I had no idea. It was a sample I got from Colorado."

The caller calmed down and said, "Well, that's what it

is. All the usual ingredients of a urine sample."

"I'm sorry. I'll have to look into it. Thanks." They hung up

Loren immediately called Professor Palmer at the University of Colorado.

Palmer answered his phone and Loren said, "How dare you send me a sample of urine. I don't have time for jokes."

Palmer seemed shocked. "I had no idea it was urine. It was an authentic sample from the waste pit. Are you sure? The police sent the sample and I didn't think we had the proper facilities to handle it. I thought it might be biological. I'm sorry."

Loren calmed down. "Okay, I believe you. Yes. It had all the ingredients of a typical sample of urine."

"I'll be darned. Who would have believed it?"

"I'll look into it further. Goodbye." Loren pulled his ear lobe and decided he would try to talk to Kane or his men about it--if they found them. Maybe they could explain the origin of the sample.

He decided to check on things at home and then go to Gloria's place.

Almost as soon as he got home, someone pounded on the front door.

Loren opened the door quickly. "Gloria. What the hell? I was just about to leave for your house."

Gloria just fell inside.

Loren picked her up and carried her to the living room couch. She seemed comatose.

Ann ran out of her room and was shocked. "Shall I call 911?"

"Yes, and hurry up," he said. "Then get a cold towel."

Ann came back with a wet towel. "I called."

He applied it to Gloria's head and she came around.

"What the hell happened?" said Loren.

"Parsons. Joe Parsons. He showed up at my condo. It was horrible." She shuddered. "He tried to..." She couldn't continue.

"Oh, no," Ann said, sinking down on a chair.

"It sounds awful. I'm so sorry, Gloria." Loren wrapped his arms around her.

She couldn't seem to stop crying.

The paramedics arrived with a gurney in a few minutes.

"You better send the cops to Gloria's condo," Loren said. "This Joe Parsons guy, the perp, might still be there." He clenched his fists. He wasn't a violent man but he hated to think what he'd do to the guy if he had the opportunity.

One of the paramedics got on his radio.

The paramedics checked Gloria's vital signs, lifted her onto the gurney and said, "We're taking her to Mercy Hospital. You can ride along if you wish."

"I'll meet you there, Dad," Ann said.

Loren joined the paramedics for the ride to the hospital.

At the hospital, Gloria was immediately wheeled away.

Ann and Loren sat down in a waiting room. After a while a doctor came and told them they had sedated Gloria and she would be sleeping all night, and they wouldn't be allowed to see her. They decided they might as well go home.

Loren knew he would get more action and information

if he called Doug rather than just the police. He thought a little influence would help and he felt he knew Doug well now. He should have returned from Denver by now. He got on the phone.

"Doug? It's Loren."

"Hi..." Doug said slowly. "You sound upset. What's wrong?"

"Gloria was attacked."

"Oh, no. I'll be right over." Doug arrived in fifteen minutes but he looked like hell. It was very unusual for him; he was careful of his appearance.

"Jeez Doug, you look like shit," said Loren.

"I feel like shit. I haven't slept in twenty-four hours. What's happened?"

"The creep. Gloria's client's husband broke into Gloria's condo and attacked her."

"Is she all right?"

"I hope so. She's resting right now, but we have to do something about this."

"This is a little out of my line but let's go over to her condo and see what went on. I'll see what the cops have on the case." Doug got out his cell phone. "I can drive."

Loren said, "Maybe I better drive. You don't look so good."

When they arrived at Gloria's condo the front door was wide open and the front windows were smashed. There was a hell of a mess inside. Papers were spread everywhere and most of the furniture was in splinters. Two uniformed officers were standing around. They nodded at Doug, seeming to recognize him.

"The bastard," Loren said, fists clenching again.

"We'll get him," Doug said. "Goddamn coward. I can't

stand somebody who attacks women."

He stepped over to the officers. "CSI?"

"They've been here and done their thing," one of them said.

"We were just about to leave when we heard you were coming," the other said. "We waited for you."

Doug nodded. "Appreciate it."

"We'll have to get someone to come in and clean up this mess," Loren said. "And we need to get the windows fixed. Gloria can stay at my place till the house is fixed. I don't know what more we can do."

"I guess you're right," Doug said. "I need some sleep. We'll get an arrest order out for this Parsons guy as soon as we can. Has Gloria been interviewed yet?"

Loren shook his head. "She was too upset. She should be okay tomorrow morning. I hope so, anyway."

Chapter 28

After getting some sleep, Doug decided it was time to pay Aztec Printing a night visit. He called Charlie Wong and they decided to use Charlie's old black Ford. It was a car that nobody would pay much attention to. It was neither new nor old, nor in bad shape or good shape; it was the car Charlie used for surveillance. They decided that Charlie would pick up Doug at eleven pm.

Doug was ready to go in his navy running suit and black running shoes.

Charlie picked him up on time. "Hey." He was dressed similarly, all in black.

Doug was angry with Charlie, but was trying to put it behind him, for his Aunt. He got in the car.

"What's wrong?" Charlie asked.

"That woman I told you to keep an eye on, Gloria, was attacked."

"Oh, no." Charlie pulled out into traffic. "What happened?"

"What happened!" Doug said. "You tell me. You were supposed to be watching her." He forced himself to take a deep calming breath. "I don't know yet. What did your nephew say?"

"I'll have to check with him," Charlie said. "Sorry."

Doug focused on calming his breathing. "So what have

you been doing?"

"I visited Aztec," Charlie said. "I got the lay of the land. I even checked the back door. I think I can open it. I brought my locksmith tools. I don't think they have an alarm."

That was Doug's impression, as well. "Good." Something better go right today.

"I don't get it," Charlie said. "If you get the evidence illegally, it's no good for court."

"If I know what the evidence is, it's easier to get a warrant." His creativity was one of the reasons he cleared so many cases.

It was about eleven thirty when they arrived at the Aztec area. They parked a block away and walked to the building via the back alley. It only took Charlie about two minutes to open the back door. Doug and Charlie entered and closed the door behind them.

The only light in the place was a desk lamp on a desk over to the right side but both Doug and Charlie had brought flashlights. There was a glass-enclosed office to the left of the back door and three desks out in the open to the right each with a computer. Along the sides were large shelves packed with printing supplies, paper stock, ink, parts and various other items. The main part of the room was loaded with all kinds of machines of different sorts.

Charlie whispered, "Wow, I don't know much about the printing business but this looks state of the art."

Doug nodded. "I agree. I don't think we need to whisper. There's obviously no one here to hear us. I don't think these machines are all printing presses. It looks like there are binders and laminators and other sophisticated machines. "

Charlie nodded. "Yes, and lots of computers to control them."

In the center of the room was a large glass-topped under lighted table, maybe ten feet by ten feet, that would be very useful for composing and tracing. Up front, in a corner, was a door with a button combination lock."

"What are we looking for?" Charlie asked.

"Evidence of counterfeiting and of hit and run."

"What would that be?"

"I'll know it when I see it."

Charlie pointed to the locked door. "I think the locked room is a place to start."

"Right. Can you do the button combinations?"

"Yes, but it will take time. Lucky it's a three button. Four buttons are a lot harder."

"Go to it. We only have a few hours. I'll be looking through the desks."

Charlie began to methodically punch in a set sequence of numbers with the dexterity of a talented typist.

Doug got to work searching the room, but didn't find anything incriminating.

After about an hour had passed, Doug asked, "How's it going?"

Charlie shook his head and kept punching numbers.

Doug walked towards the front and just as he got there some headlights appeared on a car turning into the plant parking lot.

"Find a place to hide. There's a car turning into the parking lot."

Charlie hid behind a filing cabinet.

The car turned around and left.

Doug said, "It's okay. The car left. It was just turning

around."

Charlie wasn't happy. "How do you expect me to open this door if you keep interrupting me?"

"Sorry, I thought we were getting visitors."

Another hour passed and Doug was getting nervous. "Can you hurry it up?"

"No," Charlie said.

After another half hour Charlie said, "Open Sesame," and the door swung open

Both men entered the room expectantly. On the floor were several large open boxes. There were green card blanks and passport blanks and driver's license blanks.

"Bingo," Doug said. He'd brought his digital camera and began to take flash pictures of the contents of the boxes.

The green card blanks made him think of the two Hispanic men they'd found at Kane's ranch. How do you get a green card if you can't speak English?

"Wow, quite an operation," Charlie said.

There were several closed boxes but Doug didn't want to leave any traces so he left them alone. He thought he had enough.

He did, however, take a green card blank. "I don't think they will miss this."

Charlie said, "It doesn't look like they were doing currency."

"No, I don't think so," Doug said. "The feds get too excited about that. They wouldn't want that kind of problem. I think we have enough so let's get the hell out of here, but I want to take a look in the garage in back."

"Why the garage?" Charlie asked.

"It may hold a murder weapon." Catalina Perez's

murder weapon.

The two men left the building trying not to leave any traces. Charlie got the personnel door to the garage open in two minutes. Inside they found a white van with *AZTEC PRINTING* on the side, a dark blue pickup truck and a dark blue SUV. The SUV did match the description of the vehicle that ran down Ms. Perez.

However, Doug couldn't see any damage or blood on the SUV. "Darn." He took several pictures of the SUV anyway.

"Okay," he finally said. "That'll do it. Let's go."

The two men walked slowly back to the car. They would spark more interest in anyone who was around if they hurried.

While they walked Charlie said, "How do you plan to use this illegally-obtained evidence?"

"I guess it will have to be an anonymous tip. In fact, would you call it in? Somebody could recognize my voice."

"I would need a bonus for that service. Maybe the FBI should be contacted."

"I prefer the local police so I can get involved."

"Okay, just tell me what to say."

They discussed it while Charlie drove Doug home.

Chapter 29

Loren was looking forward to a quiet evening at home after all the drama and worry with Gloria. He'd called around and arranged for her windows to be replaced and a cleaning service to clean up the mess.

He was planning to have a few beers while watching a Cardinals baseball game. After his third beer and the fifth inning of a dull game, he fell asleep. After about an hour of sleep, he was roughly shaken.

When he woke he saw the blurry image of a figure standing over him. "Novack...Arnold... What are you doing here?"

Arnold Novack held a large pistol.

The more awake he became, the more upset he became. "What's the gun for? And how did you get in here?"

"I busted out some glass in your front door and unlocked it. The gun is so you don't call the cops on me."

"I won't call the cops. What do you want?'

"You sicced the cops on me and I want you to call them off."

"I didn't sic the cops on you. Put the gun down and we will discuss it."

Novack thought about it and finally put the gun in his

pocket.

Loren said, "I don't think you have done anything illegal yet so don't start now." He didn't know if that was true but he thought it would calm Novack down. "Where'd you get the gun?"

"It's Kane's."

"I think the police would like to question you about Kane's activities. If you cooperate I think you have nothing to worry about."

"I don't know much. I only worked for Kane for three months. The guys I left with know a lot more than me."

Loren thought it best to try to show he trusted the man. "Look, you go back to wherever you are staying and have a good night's sleep. Come back tomorrow and I'll try to have a policeman friend here. We'll take a statement from you and see what to do next. I don't think you have anything to fear. But I think you should leave the gun here."

Novack looked relived. "Okay Sharp. I guess I have to trust you. It's not like I have a lot of other options. What time?"

"How about nine a.m.?"

"Okay, I'll be here." Novack put the gun down and left.

Loren was a little surprised that had worked. He hoped he had done the right thing. At least he'd disarmed him.

He called Doug to tell him of Novack's visit but got his voicemail. He left a message and asked if Doug could come over at nine a.m. the next day.

Doug arrived the next morning bearing doughnuts. He held the bag up and said, "I've got doughnuts. I hope you've got coffee. There's a guy sitting in a car down the block who seems to be watching the house. I suppose that's Novack."

"Yeah, I guess so. I'm not surprised that he is being cautious. I hope he decided that you looked okay." Loren had made sure his kids were out of the house. Bill had a follow-up appointment at the hospital later and Ann was taking him. Loren convinced them to go a little early and check on Gloria, bringing her some flowers, too, of course.

"I hope so," Doug said.

Suddenly Novack was there. He said, "I see you haven't fixed the glass pane in your door. I'm here to find out what you can do for me." He pointed at Doug," Who's this?"

Loren said, "No, I haven't had time to fix the window. This is detective lieutenant Doug Sanderson. He's very interested to hear about your stay at Kane's ranch."

Doug shook Novack's hand and said, "I'm very happy to meet you. May I call you Arnold?"

Presumably, happy with the cordial greeting, Novack smiled and said yes. Things seemed to be going pretty well so far. Loren decided to let Doug take the lead in the interrogation; he was the expert in this kind of thing.

"I assume that you left Kane's ranch with the other two employees. Is that right?" Doug asked.

"Yes," Novack said. "But we split up here in St. Louis."

Loren didn't like the sound of that. Why had they come to St. Louis?

"I see," Doug said. "What are their names?"

"Warren Wilson and Tom Jerrett." These had to be the men that held them at gun point at Kane's ranch.

"Which is the blond guy?" Doug asked.

"That's Warren."

"I assume you knew about the waste dump," Doug said.

"Yes, but I thought it was legal."

Loren didn't believe that.

From his expression, Doug wasn't buying that either, but let it go. "We've found five bodies in the pit so far. Do you know anything about that?"

"Tom told me something about that," Novack said. He seemed to be getting more nervous. "I think he was trying to scare me into keeping my mouth shut. He said that Kane had killed one of his guards for having an affair with his mistress. I was told he killed the mistress too. I didn't know whether to believe it or not. All this happened before my time. I only worked there three months."

"Do you know where your two companions went?" Doug asked.

"Tom said something about Memphis and Warren said he might visit his sister in New Orleans."

"Okay, that's good information. What else can you tell us?"

"I can't think of anything."

"We have seen some payments by Kane to someone or something noted as WAR. Do you know who that could be?" Doug said.

"No. The only one of us that had any contact with Kane's business dealings was Warren."

"Have you ever heard anyone at the ranch talking about someone named Wolfgang Reitz?" Loren couldn't resist asking.

"I knew Reitz from the lab in St. Louis," Novack said. "Just to say hello to. Not a friend or anything. No, I never heard his name mentioned at the ranch."

"Do you know what happened to Kane's coin collection?

Novack shook his head. "Warren collected a bunch of papers and stuff and put it all in a briefcase when we left. He took it with him. I don't know what all was in it."

"Think. Is there anything further you could tell us about Kane or the two guys?" Doug said.

"No," Novack said. "There's nothing. What happens now?"

"Go back to where you are staying and leave us your phone number," Doug said. "We probably will contact you again. We trust you Arnold. You're best off cooperating with us."

Novack nodded and left.

"You're really just letting him go?" Loren asked. He thought it'd be better to take him into custody.

"Of course not," Doug said. "Your neighborhood is lousy with officers. We're taking him in. I just didn't want to do it inside your house. I didn't want to put you or your kids in danger. You've already had a rough enough time lately.

Doug was a good friend. "Thanks. I appreciate it." Loren stood up. "Do you want the gun?"

"Of course."

Loren stepped towards the kitchen. "I hid it in the clothes washer." He knew the kids wouldn't go in there. He got the gun and handed it over.

"Everything he said about Tom and Warren was hearsay and wouldn't stand up in court," Doug said. "We need to talk to them, or, even better, bring them in. Can you go down to New Orleans with me?"

Loren shook his head. His family needed him. Gloria needed him. "What? Why would I do that? There is no technical issue. No. I'm not going to go."

"You and I are the only people who know what Warren Wilson looks like. You're familiar with New Orleans. Besides, I like your company. I'm sure your boss will let you go."

Speaking of his boss... That reminded Loren that the new Martox plant was in Louisiana. Maybe he could kill two birds with one stone? Get a look at the plant and help Doug?

He'd developed a high regard for Doug and he didn't want to disappoint him. He couldn't believe what he was about to say. "Okay. If Gloria's okay, I'll go. I hope we won't be gone long. When do we leave?"

"Soon."

Chapter 30

When Doug went in to headquarters he was told about the tip they got about a local print shop that was doing some counterfeiting. Charlie must have done a good job calling the tip in about the illicit print shop. He talked about counterfeit emission certificates.

Doug acted surprised and interested.

Captain O'Brien was also interested because he remembered Doug talking about counterfeit emission certificates. He suggested that Doug take lead on the case, including the raid on the print shop. Doug said he was busy but if O'Brien wanted him to go along he would do so. He was chuckling to himself as he went to a judge he knew and obtained a search warrant.

He drove his car and beat the other officers to the printing plant. Sergeant Bigelow and a uniformed officer named Swartz arrived and Doug led them into the printing plant.

The young woman at the counter was too surprised to say anything as the three policemen walked through the front sales office and through the door into the manufacturing area. They laid the search warrant on the counter as they passed.

Bad Chemistry

Three men were working in the plant and they seemed shocked to see the three cops enter. One was working at the light table, one was watching some kind of machine run and one was sitting at one of the desks. All three were wearing khaki coveralls.

Doug displayed his badge. "Who's in charge?"

The man sitting at the desk stood up. "I guess I'm in charge." He was tall and very thin. In fact, he looked like he'd been a POW. "Can I call our manager?"

Doug said, "Sure, you can call."

The man dialed, mumbled into the phone and hung up. "Their manager's coming over."

Were they in for trouble now? So far, this had been going very smoothly.

Doug decided not to wait for the manager. "Who has the combination to the storage room?"

Nobody answered.

"If you don't cooperate, you'll be taken downtown and jailed," Doug said.

The three employees looked at each other. Finally, the tall man said," I have the combination."

Doug got the combination from the tall man. They all moved to the storage room and Doug punched in the numbers and opened the door. The floor of the storage room contained boxes of supplies that had been on shelves in the main room when Charlie and he had been there before. There was no sign of the counterfeit forms that had been there.

Doug felt his jaw drop. Shit. He couldn't believe his eyes.

Somebody must have tipped them off but, since he had found the evidence of counterfeiting illegally, there was nothing he could do. Shit. Who tipped them off?

Bigelow and Swartz didn't hesitate. They rushed into the room and started rooting through the boxes. Doug realized he was acting suspicious and went inside and half-heartedly looked through some boxes.

"I'm not finding anything," Doug said.

"Me neither," Bigelow said.

"Same here," Swartz said.

The employees hadn't entered the room. They stood outside staring at the cops.

After a minute or two Doug said, "Well that's that. I want to have a look in the garage."

The tall man said innocently, "What are you looking for?"

Doug gave him a sharp look. He was acting too innocent. "Never mind. Do you have a key to the garage?"

"It's hanging on a hook by the back door."

They all traipsed out to the garage. With the key it was easy to enter. As Doug suspected, the SUV was gone. In its place was parked a red pickup truck.

He said through gritted teeth, "Let's go. I've seen enough."

The three officers left empty handed.

The list of people who could have tipped off the counterfeiters was very short.

On the drive back to the station Doug decided what to tell O'Brien and landed on: nothing. Since he had entered the printing plant illegally last night he couldn't say much.

Somebody he trusted had sold out. Who? Bigelow had been on the force for many years and his loyalty was unchallengeable. Swartz just found out about the raid before they left. O'Brien? Unthinkable. That left Charlie. Doug was very disappointed but it had to be Charlie. Doug could hardly believe it since he thought of Charlie as an old friend. When he got back to headquarters he parked and sat in his car for a while even though Bigelow and Swartz had already reported in. Finally he went in to face O'Brien.

O'Brien was sitting behind his desk, looking all knowing. "I hear there was nothing to it."

"That's right."

"What happened?"

"Either it was a false report or they were tipped off."

"Who would tip them off?"

Doug had to lie. "I don't know."

"So much for anonymous tips," O'Brien said, smiling.

Doug decided to leave before O'Brien thought of more questions, "Okay. Well, take it easy O'Brien. I'll be seeing you." He was happy he didn't have to say more.

Doug immediately drove over to Charlie's house.

Surprisingly, Charlie was home. Doug rang the bell and Charlie answered the door.

Charlie smiled and said, "Douglas, what's up? Come in."

Doug did not smile. "How much did they pay you?"

"What do you mean?"

"Don't play games with me, Charlie. I know you had to have tipped the print shop that we were coming. It had to be you."

"Okay. I guess there is no point in denying it. The business hasn't been doing well lately. I thought an infusion of cash would buy some advertising and some new equipment and business would pick up. I knew you couldn't turn me in given how we obtained the evidence. I'm sorry. I needed the money."

"I'm pretty disappointed in you Charlie. I won't be able to use you anymore."

Charlie nodded. "I figured that. Do you want to come inside and discuss it?"

Doug said, "There's nothing to discuss. Goodbye, Charlie. I hope it was worth it."

"Bye, Doug. Put some pressure on Carlos. He must know a lot about the printing business." Charlie seemed to be trying to make amends. But too little, too late.

Doug shook his head and left. He was depressed. It started to drizzle when he got back to his car that made him even more depressed. Not only did he lose the chance to break the counterfeiting racket and solve a murder, but also he lost a friend.

But then he thought of Carlos. Maybe all was not lost after all. He smiled. He'd have to visit Carlos again soon.

On the drive home Doug began to wonder if he was over-extended. The Kane case, the Reitz case, O'Brien, Loren, the printing-related murder, Charlie, Mona and all the rest. It was a lot to keep track of. He decided he would get a good night's sleep and try to reorganize things tomorrow.

When he got home he headed right to the shower. He usually spent about two minutes in the shower. Tonight he stayed in for fifteen. He kept the water as hot as he could stand and felt better when he got out.

He had several phone messages and some email but he ignored them and went to bed. He had trouble getting to sleep, because of all the issues troubling him, but once he got to sleep he slept soundly. When he woke up it was already eight a.m.

He discovered he had no food in the house so he got dressed and went out to a restaurant.

Doug didn't realize he was so hungry until he looked at the menu. Eggs, bacon, biscuits and gravy and lots of hot coffee made him feel better.

While drinking his second cup of coffee he decided the thing to do was to give Carlos some grief and see if he could get some useful information from him.

It was turning into a nice day so the drive over to Carlos' building was pleasant. He parked right outside the building and went in. He remembered the elevator code and went up to Carlos' apartment. After ringing the bell and pounding on the door Doug decided he wasn't there or was not receiving visitors.

But it was a bit strange that he was not there since Charlie said he spent a lot of time in his apartment and it was early in the day. Maybe something was wrong.

He decided to see if he could get the superintendent to let him in. He went down to the basement where the super had an office.

The office door was open and a bald, overweight man was working or playing on a desktop computer.

Doug showed him his badge and said," I think there's something wrong in Mr. Valdez's apartment, number three-ten. I'd like you to let me in.

The super seemed a bit flustered but said, "What do you mean something's wrong?

"Valdez is supposed to be home but he doesn't answer the door," Doug said.

"Maybe he's asleep. Do you have an appointment with

him?" Why was this guy being so uncooperative?

Doug lied. "Yes, I do. This is police business. I have to ask you to cooperate."

The super seemed irritated. "Okay, but I will have to accompany you."

The two men took the elevator up to the apartment and, after knocking, the super used a master key to let them in.

Everything seemed to be in order. Everything was neat and in its place.

There was no sign of Carlos until they entered the bedroom. He was in bed under the covers in his pajamas.

The super said, "Oh, sorry to disturb you, sir." But Carlos didn't move.

Doug went over to the bed. "I don't think he can hear you."

Carlos was quite dead.

Something here was not right.

The superintendent was pretty upset. "Nothing like this ever happened in my building before. I run a tight ship. Nobody can get in here who doesn't belong here."

Doug called it in. While he was waiting he snapped on some latex gloves and looked around. Next to Carlos' bed was a bed stand with a syringe, a candle, a spoon and a vial with white powder. It was obviously drug paraphernalia. Accidental overdose? Or murder staged to look like an overdose? His gut said murder. Carlos wasn't a known drug addict and didn't seem the type.

Doug started looking for evidence of Carlos' activities. Nothing was apparent. He started to go through closets and Carlos' desk. He didn't find anything. It was almost certain that Carlos was distributing the print shop's fake documents but there was no evidence in the apartment. The absence of incriminating documents pointed to foul play.

He took a closer look at the desk; it was especially interesting. It appeared to be an antique. It was a large mahogany piece and was somewhat similar to a desk that his father had for years. He knew that this type of old desk usually had one or more secret compartments so he gave the desk a thorough going over. When he removed the top right drawer he saw that the rear of the drawer was thicker than it should be.

He went to the kitchen and got a table knife and pried up the back of the drawer. The secret compartment opened with a click. The only thing inside was a key that looked like a safety deposit key. If Carlos was murdered and his apartment cleaned of evidence the murderer must have missed the key.

Doug was very excited to find what the key was to and what he would find. He couldn't wait to find out.

But he very carefully put the table knife and everything else back the way he'd found it and put the gloves back in his pocket.

The homicide squad arrived on the scene within fifteen minutes. The lead detective, a guy Doug didn't recognize walked right up to him and said, "You Sanderson?"

"Yeah." His fingers brushed the key in his pocket.

"What brings you here?"

'Anonymous tip,' was on the tip of Doug's tongue, but that hadn't worked out so well earlier. "Connection to another case," he finally said.

"Oh? Care to share?"

No. "We got an anonymous tip about possible counterfeiting. There was nothing to it."

"You wanna send me the file?"

"Sure." Doug nodded. Maybe he would, maybe he wouldn't. "Can I look around?"

"Don't touch anything."

Duh. He stalked around the apartment, pretending to look around.

The assistant medical examiner arrived and examined Carlos. "It looks like a drug overdose but we'll need an autopsy to tell for sure. We'll take the body downtown and get back to you."

Numerous pictures were taken.

The assistant medical examiner left with the body.

Doug left soon after.

Even though he was very busy, Doug decided it was time to see what was in Carlos' safety deposit box. It could be some useful evidence. He had the key he found in Carlos' secret desk compartment but he needed to find out the bank name. He got out a city map and marked several banks closest to Carlos' place. He didn't think it would work but he called one of the banks, said it was police business and asked if Carlos Valdez had a safety deposit box at their bank. The bank person said that they did not give out that information. He guessed he would have to visit the banks. It would probably take him all day.

His first stop was the city courts building. He knew a Judge Atkins, a friend of his fathers, so he went to his office. The judge listened to Doug, didn't ask too many questions, and agreed to sign the needed document.

The next stop was a bank close to Carlos' condo. Doug asked to see the manager and showed his ID and court order. The manager cursed as he worked with his desktop computer. "I think I was happier with the old paper records.

Finally he said, "No one with that name has a box here." Doug thanked him and left.

The next bank, even closer to Carlos' place, seemed more promising. A lot of the employees and customers were Hispanic. The bank manager was a well-dressed Latino with well-groomed white hair. His office was done very tastefully in a style that reminded Doug of Frank Lloyd Wright.

When Doug mentioned the name Carlos Valdez the manager said, "Yes, Carlos is a customer here. He's a friend of mine."

Doug said, "I'm sorry to tell you Mr. Valdez was found dead."

"*Madre de Dios*," the manager said. "What happened?"

"We're still investigating. To your knowledge did he ever do drugs?"

"No. That's impossible. Carlos would never take drugs."

"Again, I'm sorry. It's under investigation," Doug said. "Does he have a safety deposit box here?"

The manager said, "I believe Carlos has a safety deposit box here." He consulted his computer and nodded. "Yes, he has a box here."

Doug showed the manager the court order and the key.

The manager personally escorted him down to the vault. He told the female attendant to help him.

Doug had a moment of nostalgia when he looked through the open vault door and remembered when his father took him to his bank and added him to the list of people eligible to open his father's box. Suddenly, it hit him that was a high point in their relationship and he understood then how much his father loved and trusted him.

"Sir?" The attendant asked.

Doug shook off the reverie. "Please proceed." What was up with him? Why was he so emotional?

The attendant took the key and climbed up on a step-stool to get Carlos' box. She had nice legs.

She handed him the box and he took it to one of the private rooms. The box contained ten thousand dollars cash in one hundred dollar bills and some personal papers. He was disappointed. He hoped for some help with the Aztec Printing case. It was not to be. Better luck next time.

Chapter 31

Loren went to visit Gloria at the hospital as soon as he was able.

She seemed much better and smiled when he came in. "I got your flowers." She pointed at the extravagant arrangement of roses. "Thank you so much. And your kids were so nice when they dropped them off." She inhaled. "Even Ann."

Loren was very relieved. Obviously, Gloria's ordeal put things in perspective. "I'm very glad to see you're doing better." He leaned down to kiss her on the cheek. He didn't mention anything about Novack's visits or his possible trip to Louisiana. He didn't want to worry her.

She smiled up at him. "Yes. They're letting me leave soon. Is your offer to stay at your house still good?"

He smiled back. "Of course. I need to pop into work a little while, but Ann will keep you company if that's okay?" He'd already cleared it with her.

"Yes. Good. And they have a great counselor here; we had a helpful session. She stayed with me when the police questioned me. I'm going to keep seeing her for a while."

"That's great."

Loren went into work and met with Benson.

Benson still claimed they were going ahead with the plant opening. Loren told him he was thinking of going to Louisiana to check it out.

Benson loved that idea.

Loren was on the fence.

He went to his lab to make sure the Out of Deep Well project was still on track.

He was lost in his work, when the phone rang.

It was Doug and he was excited. "We got him."

"Parsons?" Thank God.

"Yes. The dumb bastard was sleeping in his own apartment. He was so drunk they had to carry him out to the squad car."

"Are they going to put him away?"

"Oh yes. The phone calls, the assault, attempted rape and murder. He should get at least ten years."

"Great. Gloria will be relieved."

"Where is she?"

"At my house. I'll call her."

Loren called Gloria and told her the good news.

"Thank you," she said. "That's wonderful news. I'm so relieved. In fact..." She paused. "I want to have you and Doug over to my place for dinner to celebrate. We had such a nice time before. I need something positive to focus on. And you know I enjoy cooking. It calms me."

"That sounds nice," Loren said. "I'm in if you're sure you're up to it," he said. "Should I call Doug?"

"Yes." They chatted for a few more minutes before hanging up.

Bad Chemistry

That evening Loren arrived promptly at Gloria's at the appointed hour of six pm. He brought wine as usual.

Doug met him at the front door, also bearing wine. "Hello."

"Hello, yourself." Loren rang the bell.

Gloria opened the door and gave him a hug. "Thanks for all your help, Loren. I can't believe they fixed everything already." Her hug felt great. He was happy she seemed mostly over her ordeal.

Looking around, Loren was impressed the repairs had been done so quickly. "You're welcome."

"Thanks for catching the guy, Doug," she said as she hugged him, too.

They all went inside and she immediately mixed them a drink and poured herself some white wine.

They sat down around her kitchen table. "I like the intimacy of my kitchen." She was jovial. "Well, Batman and Robin, what have you been up to?"

"Nothing much, just the usual murder cases," Doug said.

"Just moving the frontiers of science," Loren said.

She got serious. "I want to thank you both for the help you gave me with the Parsons situation. Loren, for your aid and comfort and Doug, for getting him arrested and probably put away where I won't have to worry about him anymore."

"He'll be an old man by the time he gets out," Doug said.

"Good," Loren said. He thought Doug could have done a little more to prevent the whole thing, but that was water under the bridge.

Gloria smiled. "I'm glad to hear it."

"I wonder why he didn't go after his ex-wife rather than you?" Loren said.

"She left town and he probably couldn't find her," she said. "She warned me he could be violent."

They chatted for a while, enjoying the company and their beverages.

Gloria helped herself to another glass of wine and made another drink for the men.

She took some Romaine lettuce out of the refrigerator and started to portion it into three salad bowls. "I assume you both having salad."

"Yes," the men said together.

She laughed. "So now you guys even talk together?"

"I guess so," said Loren.

After another drink, they settled down to dinner.

She'd pulled out all the stops. She had Caesar salad, French onion soup, tenderloin with Béarnaise sauce and rice Pilaf. All was prepared perfectly. Loren poured his Merlot and Doug his Cabernet during the meal and both were found to be excellent. Dinner conversation ranged over wide areas.

Dessert was mocha cheesecake. Coffee was poured.

"Wonderful. Thank you. I don't know if I can get up I'm so stuffed," said Loren after they finished eating.

"Gee, Gloria, that was impressive. When is your next dinner party?" said Doug.

She ignored him. "Who wants more coffee?"

Both men said, "I'll have some more." They all laughed.

Gloria was pouring more coffee when a phone rang.

"Sorry. I should take this," Doug said.

He stepped into the family room to answer the call.

Bad Chemistry

"Sanderson speaking." Loren could hear him clearly.

"Hello, Douglas. It's Harry. You asked me to call about the autopsy. Mr. Valdez died from an overdose of heroin as we thought. However, the overdose was so extreme that it points to suicide or homicide rather than an accident. In addition, there were not extensive needle marks on the body, which indicates he wasn't an addict. There was also a bruise on his neck indicating there could have been a struggle. All in all, I would say the evidence points to homicide."

Doug said, "Thanks, Harry." and hung up. He returned to the dining room where the others were having a second cup of coffee.

Gloria said, "Not bad news, I hope."

"Sort of," he said. "A key witness of mine has been murdered."

"Oh, no," Loren said.

"Sorry to hear it. What happened?" Gloria asked. She was always curious.

Doug went on to tell about the staged heroin overdose and the bogus print shop that made a lot of different counterfeit documents. Loren was very interested, and Gloria seemed interested, as well.

"What will you do now?" asked Loren.

Doug shook his head. "I'll have to go back to the beginning. I'm sure the murder is connected with the print shop. I'll find the owner of the print shop and see if he has some answers."

"I'm sure there would be information on the owner in the St. Louis business directory," Loren said.

Doug nodded. "Yes, that's where I'll start."

Gloria pointed a finger at Doug. "Producing counterfeit

green cards must be a federal offence. You should contact the FBI. They could be a great deal of help."

Doug chuckled. "You guys seem to think I need help doing my job. But, yes, I'll be contacting the FBI eventually."

"I'm sorry," Loren said. "I know you know what to do. I just like solving problems."

"And as a lawyer I sometimes have trouble resisting giving advice," Gloria said.

"Actually I have one of the counterfeit green card blanks," Doug said. "I won't tell you how I got it but I'm sure the FBI will be interested in its origin."

"Yes. They will have methods to identify it as a counterfeit," Loren said. "I wonder what they would use. Maybe mass spec."

"I'll leave that to them," Doug said.

"Just curious," Loren said.

Gloria changed the subject. "What's happening with the Reitz killing and all that Kane business?"

Good questions. Loren wasn't sure Kane was even involved in Wolfy's death. All they knew was Wolfy had a notation in his calendar about Kane and Kane paid off someone with the initials W.A.R.

"Loren and I are going to New Orleans to try to question a couple of Kane's associates. They may know something about Reitz's death."

Loren winced. He hadn't had a chance to talk to Gloria about it yet. "I'll only go if you're okay with it."

"New Orleans!" she said. "That's Loren's old stomping grounds." She turned to him. "You should go if you can help."

Doug smiled. "That's one of the reasons why I asked

him to go."

Gloria yawned. "I hope you boys are careful. It could be dangerous."

"We're always careful," Loren said, not wanting to worry her. "I guess it's time to say goodnight." They all got up.

She accompanied them to the door. "Goodnight. Drive carefully."

"Good night and thanks," Loren said.

"Me, too," Doug said. He turned and started walking to his car.

Loren hugged her and gave her a peck on the cheek. "Do you want me to stay over?"

"No," she said. "I think I'm all right."

"Are you sure it's okay with you if I go out of town? I can stay if you need me."

"No. I'm okay. Parsons is in jail, right?" She playfully pushed him out the door. "Go catch some more bad guys."

Chapter 32

Loren got picked up by Doug and they drove to the airport. The traffic was light for a change.

"Do we have a plan?" Loren asked.

"I called Delany and he tracked the address of a Jane Wilson in Metarie, Louisiana. He got it from an envelope they found in Wilson's belongings."

"Why doesn't Delany deal with it? Isn't it his jurisdiction?"

"Cops don't have the kind of budgets that let them hare off around the country," Doug said. "We're doing him a favor. Plus, this case has really gotten under my skin." He glanced over at Loren. "Hasn't it for you?"

Five murders, six, if you counted Wolfy, not to mention hundreds of people in danger if the Martox plant went up. But he only said, "Yeah."

Doug parked in long-term parking and the men took the shuttle to the main terminal. A woman with two unruly little kids was also in the shuttle.

They made Loren think of his kids. It seemed like Bill had turned a corner and decided to put his life back together. And Gloria's attack had broken through to Ann, making her act like the good person he knew she was. He sighed. He hoped she would manage to find a job, and happiness like he'd found with Gwen, and now with Gloria. She was pursuing the Boeing lead and had gotten an interview.

"What's up?" Doug asked.

"What?" Loren asked.

"You're smiling."

"Never mind."

After checking in they walked to security. The line at security was not too long. He remembered when there was no security check. That was a long time ago. The terrorists had certainly complicated travel.

He could also remember when people dressed up to fly. Men wore a coat and tie but those days were gone forever. Running suits were popular flying apparel now but people wore almost anything. An obese woman in line even wore a shorts and a halter top.

The two men got through security and walked the long walk to the gate.

They got to the gate with time to spare so they sat down till the flight was called.

When they boarded Loren found that Doug had gotten first class seats. "Wow. Who's paying for this?"

Doug smiled and said, "I'm paying."

"Thanks." Loren settled into the roomy seat and remembered the only other time he flew first class was on the red eye from San Francisco coming home from a conference. He could get used to such treatment.

"That was interesting what you said about the print shop the other night," Loren said. "What got you interested in that case? It seems to be a strange one for a homicide detective."

"As you heard, it didn't turn out to be. There are

potentially two murders. It started with a call from my Aunt Mavis."

"Your Aunt Mavis?"

"Yes. She's quite a lady. You should meet her sometime. She'd told me she didn't need a state inspection on her car, which I usually got for her, because her friend Catalina Perez gave her a filled out form. I told her that was illegal. Later she called me and said Ms. Perez had been killed in a hit and run. I decided to look into the death for my aunt's sake. I interviewed Ms. Perez's son Bobby and looked into some print shops. By the way, the son works at Marchem. Maybe you know him? His name is Roberto Perez."

"Bobby Perez? Yes," Loren said "There's a guy who works at Marchem named Roberto Perez. He worked with Kane at one time."

"Very interesting," Doug said. "I also talked to a man named Carlos Valdez who was connected with the print shop and was the victim of the heroin overdose."

"Interesting. Do you think all these cases are connected?"

"I'm not sure."

"Marchem keeps coming up," Loren said. "On the other hand, it's one of the biggest employers in St. Louis. Maybe it's not surprising." He shifted in his fancy seat. "So what will be our approach in New Orleans?"

"First we try to get the cooperation of the New Orleans police," Doug said. "I had our chief call the New Orleans police chief, who he said he knows, and ask him to cooperate with us."

"That should help," Loren said.

"Then we pay Wilson's sister a visit."

"Sounds good." He picked up the book he was recently reading *Grant Comes East*, a Civil War novel. It was the second in a series of Civil War novels that started with *Gettysburg* and finished with *Never Call Retreat*. He liked the books and was a little surprised that one of the authors was Newt Gingrich. Of course, they weren't very historically accurate which was probably why they were called novels.

The two men read the rest of the flight. Doug read the *Wall Street Journal*.

The flight was smooth and the landing was routine.

As the got up from their seats, Loren said, "This airport used to be Moisant Airport. Now it's Louis Armstrong International."

"I guess that's more appropriate," Doug said.

The men deplaned and, since they only had roll-a-boards, went right to the car rental counters. Doug had reserved a Cadillac.

Loren had made a hotel reservation at the Royal Sonesta.

Doug drove while Loren directed him. Traffic was heavy. There were signs that the city was coming back from the Katrina disaster.

"When were you last in New Orleans?" Loren asked.

"This is only my third time here," Doug said. "Last time I was here for a game between the Rams and the Saints which the Saints won. It knocked the Rams out of the playoffs. I don't remember the year. Jim Haslett was the coach of the Saints. It's ironic that he eventually became the coach of the Rams. He and ex-coach Mike Martz had quite a bitter rivalry."

"Yes. I remember that." Loren looked out the window.

"I'm hoping to have a look at some of the Katrina damage while we are here. You know I have some friends here."

"Yes, I know that," Doug said. "I don't think I'll have time to look around."

"Maybe I should rent a car," Loren said. He was definitely going to make time to look around the Martox plant. He had to see it for himself.

"We'll see what develops," Doug said.

They finally arrived at the hotel after forty-five minutes in traffic and parked in the hotel ramp. They decided to share a room with double beds. By the time they had checked in it was time for lunch so they went across the street and each had a beer and a shrimp po-boy.

After lunch Doug got the Cadillac and they drove to police headquarters. Doug finally found a place to park after driving around for ten minutes.

Inside, Doug told the desk sergeant what he wanted and apparently the sergeant expected them. They were led right to the chief's office. The chief was a tall, handsome man graying at the temples. He wore his hair long and combed back. His office had a cluttered look mostly because he had numerous awards on his walls and desk.

"Hello, Douglas. I hear you're a real hotshot," the chief said.

"I don't know about that," Doug said. "I work at it."

"And this must be Dr. Sharp?" the chief said.

Loren smiled. "Call me Loren."

"I guess you got the email from our chief," Doug said.

"That I did," the chief said. "Jerry and I go back a long way. We worked on a case together about twenty years ago. We were both lieutenants at the time. I like him very much. He seems to hold you in high regard."

"He was a friend of my father's. I hope you can help me with the case we're working on. Loren's consulting."

The chief nodded and said, "Give me the details."

Doug told the chief about their adventure in Colorado and about Kane's waste dump and the murders.

The chief listened intently.

"The waste pit was lethal," Loren said. "Filled with all kinds of chemicals."

"The guys we're looking for were his assistants," Doug said. "We need some more evidence against Kane and hope we can get this guy Wilson to testify against him. Right now the case is pretty much based on circumstantial evidence. Also Wilson may have some information that would help with another case I'm working on."

"This Kane sounds like a lovely guy," the chief said, while shaking his head and frowning.

"Yeah, he's a real menace," Doug said. "We hope we can put him away."

"I'd like to help you, but I can't spare anybody full time to work with you. If you find Wilson we'll help with the arrest and get him shipped back to Colorado. The chief handed Doug his card. "Call me at this number when you need us. It's my private line."

"Thanks," Loren said.

"Thanks very much for your help, Chief," Doug said. "I'll tell our chief how helpful you were."

"Give my regards to old Jerry. Tell him I'll have him down for a Saints- Rams game sometime."

"I'll do that," Doug said.

They left the police station.

"What now?" Loren asked.

"I thought you were going to take a look at the Katrina

damage?"

"I thought you might like to join me."

"I do have a little time. Okay, let's go."

Doug and Loren drove around the city for about an hour. The damage was still extreme in the lower ninth ward but they were expecting that. They were surprised to see the extent of damage in middle class areas, especially near Lake Pontchartrain.

Doug shook his head. "Looks like they have hardly cleaned up let alone rebuilt."

"Yeah, it seems to be going pretty slow. The government seems to be letting the people down."

Doug said, "There seems to be more hurricanes lately than there used to be."

"I think so. It's probably due to global warming."

Doug seemed curious. "Why is that?"

"Hurricanes need heat energy," Loren said. "The ocean is heating up."

"Some of my friends think there is no such thing as global warming," Doug said. "On cold days they ask, *Whatever happened to global warming?*"

"Some of my friends do that, too, but I assume they're kidding. Global warming isn't about major changes in temperature. It's about changes in climate patterns. More droughts and floods, for example."

"I guess you believe it's happening," Doug said.

Loren nodded. "It would be hard to find a scientist that didn't believe it. The evidence is too strong. The temperature increase follows closely the levels of carbon dioxide in the atmosphere. Melting of the polar icecaps is one example of the consequences."

"Is it all bad or are there some benefits?" Doug asked.

Bad Chemistry

"There are a few benefits but not enough to compensate for the bad effects. Some areas will have improved crop yields, for example, but the floods in coastal areas will be disastrous."

"When is all this going to happen?"

"Right now the sea ice is melting," Loren said. "That won't affect ocean levels much since it's already in the ocean but when land based ice starts to melt you will see the sea level rise. Also the ocean expands as it heats up."

"There seems to be some debate whether or not human activities are the cause."

"There are still some doubters. It seems to follow liberal, conservative lines. The liberals are excited and the conservatives are in denial. But the studies have shown it's caused mainly by burning fossil fuels by industry and power plants, or heating and cooling of buildings, with smaller contributions from transportation and agriculture. The carbon dioxide produced has a greenhouse effect that holds the heat in."

Doug grinned. "How come you know so much about it?"

"I read," Loren said.

"How come you scientist types can't find a way to trap carbon dioxide emissions?"

"Actually it's very easy but it is a dilemma. You can trap carbon dioxide by passing the emissions through a lime slurry. The problem is lime is made by roasting limestone which is calcium carbonate. This drives carbon dioxide back into the atmosphere in the same amount as lime's capacity to absorb it. So you've gained nothing. You could use sodium hydroxide, prepared by electrolysis of salt water with electricity from nuclear plants, but what would you do with all the sodium carbonate? There would also be a huge surplus of chlorine. There would also need to be new nuclear power plants, too, but that's inevitable anyway because it's a clean source of power. There've been some other suggestions such as injecting the carbon dioxide into the deep ocean but nothing's being done besides a few weak attempts to limit emissions.

"It's certainly a worry but I guess we won't be alive to see the worst of it," Doug said.

"Probably not."

It was getting toward dinnertime so they started back to the hotel.

"I hope some solutions get going soon," Loren said.

"Yes, I hope so," Doug said.

They went to the room briefly when they got back to the hotel but were too tired to shower. They went to a restaurant across the street and ordered barbequed shrimp and beer for dinner. They sat in the back.

"I guess we are seeing Jane Wilson tomorrow," Loren said.

"Sure, I hope we get something out of her," Doug said.

"Do you think we should call her first?"

"I've been thinking about that. I think we will just drop in on her."

"Okay. If she puts us in touch with Wilson how do we handle him?"

When the food arrived, it was very good and was quickly consumed.

Doug said, "We can offer him immunity if he testifies against Kane."

"Do you think he'll buy that?" Loren said. "I remember him as being a hard guy."

"Well, he doesn't owe Kane anything. We'll see."

They finished dinner and went back to the hotel. They were both rather tired and went up to their room. After watching some television they turned in about ten o'clock.

Loren had a hard time getting to sleep. He kept reviewing his previous trips to New Orleans and how his friends, whom he didn't try to contact this trip, were doing. When he did finally get to sleep he dreamt about explosions and murders.

About seven a.m., Doug puttering around in the bathroom awakened him but he stayed in bed until Doug came out of the bathroom.

"How did you sleep?" Loren asked.

"Like a stone."

"You're lucky. I had a bad night."

"Oh really?" Doug asked. "What's the trouble?"

"I just kept thinking about my other trips to New Orleans and how things have changed."

Loren took his turn in the bathroom and then they went down to the restaurant. They enjoyed a big breakfast, both having fruit, bacon, eggs and fresh, hot biscuits.

When they were finished, Loren said, "It's still too early to visit Jane Wilson."

"We can have more coffee," Doug said.

"Sounds good."

Doug said, "Loren, I know you develop processes for manufacturing complex chemicals, but how do you go about doing that?" He must be trying to pass the time.

"Do you really want to know?" Loren said.

"Sure. I think it would be interesting."

"Well, the first and most important thing you need to find is a good preparative route to the chemical," Loren said. "This is strictly creative puzzle solving using your knowledge and experience with help from some reference books." Maybe talking about this would jog something about the Martox plant.

"Okay," Doug said.

"You may think of several ways to make the stuff," Loren said. "It may be obvious that some conceivable ways to proceed would be too expensive or too difficult. Then you have to consult the literature, especially the patent literature, to make sure no one else has made the material or something similar. Several different periodicals are consulted to find out what suitable raw materials are available at reasonable cost. Then it's time to go to the lab and try out your proposed methods. If a route is successful you celebrate. If not, you go back to the library. Once a chemical route is successful it's time to interact with the chemical engineers to calculate the cost of goods. This is based on a number of things including cost of raw materials, capital costs of manufacturing equipment and staffing. You also have to consult with patent lawyers to try to get your route patented."

"Sounds pretty complicated."

"Well, it can be. For example, the number of steps in the synthesis can be critical. If you have ninety-five percent yields in each of five steps that sounds pretty good. But you really only have a seventy-three-point-five percent yield overall and the other twenty-six- point-five percent becomes waste. That becomes a big disposal problem. A lot of time is spent trying to optimize the yields. Sometimes disposing of waste costs more than manufacturing the product. After all this you spend a lot of time helping the engineers design the plant and doing a lot of related things like testing materials for corrosion." He finished off his coffee. "That's enough of that. I think it's time to get going."

Doug took one last sip. "Okay, I'm ready." He called down to get the car brought around and they left for Metarie.

There wasn't much traffic going west on I-10 so they got to the exit quickly. They found Jane's condo easily and parked on the street.

She answered the door after only two rings of the doorbell but seemed rather bewildered seeing two men at her door. "What can I do for you gentlemen so early in the morning?" She was petite, very blonde, fortyish and quite attractive. She was dressed in shorts and a tee-shirt.

Doug flashed his badge and said, "We are trying to find your brother because he might have some vital information in a murder case. Can we come in?"

Jane shook her head. "I have a policy of not inviting strangers into my condo. I hope Warren hasn't done anything wrong."

Doug said, "No. We just want to talk to him." He must be trying to get her cooperation.

"He was here but he left two days ago," she said. "I don't have enough room in my condo for two. He also put a damper on my love life."

Loren smiled his best smile. "Do you know where he went?"

"No," she said. "He said he would call me but he hasn't."

"Do you have his contact info?" Doug asked.

She shook her head.

Doug gave her his phone number. "If you hear from

him give me a call."

She gave them a big smile. "Sure, I will."

Loren didn't think she was being sincere. "I think it's in Warren's best interest if you do."

"Do you have a photo we could have?" Doug said.

"No I don't."

"It's best if you call," Doug said. "We'll be leaving now."

"Goodbye," she said. "It's been nice to meet you."

Loren was depressed driving back to the hotel. He shook his head. "Even if Warren calls her I doubt she'll call us."

"I'm afraid you're right," Doug said. "We need another approach."

"I have an idea."

"Good. Let's hear it."

"Wilson probably didn't leave Colorado with much cash but we think he took Kane's valuable coins."

"That's right," Doug said.

Loren tugged his earlobe. "I bet at some point he will be trying to sell them."

"You're probably right." Doug grinned.

"Let's look up all the coin dealers in the area and pay them a visit."

"Good idea," Doug said. "For the record, I would have come up with this."

Loren smiled and resisted the urge to say, 'Yeah, but I mentioned it first.'

They went back to the hotel and studied the list of coin dealers in area. There were eleven of them but five seemed to sell mostly doubloons, the aluminum coins that were thrown off the floats during Mardi Gras.

"Shall we split up and visit them singly?" Loren said, in his element.

"No," Doug said. "You provide the coin expertise and I'll play the cop."

"Okay. Let's start here in the quarter."

Doug took the car out and they went off. The first shop was right there in the French Quarter. The owner was very suspicious and uncooperative. He was unimpressed with Doug's police credentials. He denied ever seeing anybody trying to sell expensive coins. Doug and Loren left without any help.

"I hope the rest of them are more cooperative," Doug said.

"Yeah. I hope so, too. What do you make of that last guy?"

"That guy had something to hide," Doug said. "We should keep him on the list and come back if we don't find something else."

The next shop was in Kenner, a little to the west. It was a much more upscale shop with a lot of metal and glass. The owner was a tall, gray haired, distinguished looking man with a white, well-trimmed, beard. "Hello," he said. "Welcome. What can I do for you gentlemen? We have a fine stock of rare coins."

Doug flashed his badge. No one ever seemed to look closely at it.

"Have you had dealings with a blond man lately who wanted to sell very valuable coins?" said Doug.

The man looked surprised. "Why, yes, just two days ago."

"What happened?" Loren asked.

"He had a very nice 1893-S silver dollar. It was a

very nice piece. I figured he wasn't very knowledgeable so I offered him twenty-five-thousand dollars." The man laughed. "It was worth a lot more but business is business. Is it stolen? We get bulletins about stolen coins and it wasn't on the list."

Stolen from Kane. But who knew where Kane got it?

"We don't know," Doug said. "We're more interested in the man than the coin. Did he agree?"

"Yes, but he said he had to have cash," the man said. "Hundred dollar bills, preferably. I agreed but told him it would take me a couple of days before I could raise the cash. He gave me his phone number and said I should call him."

Yes!

Doug and Loren excitedly said in unison, "Would you give us the number?"

The man wrote a phone number on a piece of notepaper and gave it to Doug.

"Thank you very much," Loren said.

Doug shook the man's hand. "Thank you. You've been a great help. I'm afraid the coin buy is probably off."

"Easy come easy go," the coin shop owner said.

Doug and Loren got back in the car.

Doug said, "That was a great idea of yours to follow up with the coins."

"Elementary, my dear Sanderson." Loren smiled. "To the police station?"

"Yeah."

Chapter 33

Doug drove into the lot at police headquarters, and a car was just leaving; they took the spot. He showed the duty officer the chief's card and he called the chief who said the two men should come right in. They told the chief about the coin dealer and the phone number. The chief made a call to one of his detectives and gave him the phone number.

After about five minutes the detective called back and the chief listens for a few moments. "It's for a Super 8 motel in Kenner." He wrote the address on a card and gave it to Doug.

If this Wilson had the balls to steal from an evil guy like Kane, there was no telling what he'd do. "We'll need some backup," Doug said.

"Yeah. I guess we can furnish that," the chief said. He picked up his phone again. "Don, I need you and two uniforms to accompany two friends of mine to bring in a guy from a hotel in midtown. They'll fill you in." He put down the phone. "Sergeant Don Peterson will back you up. His desk is on this floor. Just ask anybody to direct you." All this cooperation was great. Why couldn't O'Brien be this cooperative all the time?

Doug said, "We want to bring Wilson back here to

question him. Okay?"

"No problem," the chief said.

Doug and Loren had no trouble finding Peterson's desk. Sergeant Peterson was short, bald, well dressed and pleasant. The fringe of hair he had left was blond. He was chewing on a toothpick.

"Glad to meet you," he said. "The chief said to cooperate with you so I'm at your service."

"Okay, sergeant, we want to arrest a man at the Super 8 in Kenner," Doug said. "I don't think he has a firearm. But you never know."

"He's associated with five brutal murders in Colorado," Loren added.

"Okay," Peterson said. "No problem."

"The chief said two uniforms," Doug said.

"Yeah," Peterson said. "That should be enough."

Peterson gathered up two uniformed officers who traveled separately in a black and white.

In the meantime, Doug said, "Loren, I don't think you should get involved in this. It could be dangerous. We don't know much about Wilson. There is no reason for you to be involved. You are not a policeman."

Loren seemed a little crestfallen, but he said, "Can I borrow the rental car? I want to do an errand."

"Okay." Doug tossed him the keys.

"Actually, when you question Wilson, ask him about the urine sample I got," Loren said.

"What?" Doug asked with surprise.

"That Professor Palmer in Colorado sent me a liquid sample that ended up being urine."

"Weird. Yeah, I'll ask him."

Doug joined the other three officers. It was a relatively

short drive to the hotel. The two cars arrived at about the same time.

The desk clerk seemed startled to see the two uniformed policemen. "What can I do for you gentlemen?"

Peterson flashed his badge. "We're looking for this man." He flashed a picture of Wilson Delany got from Wilson's drivers license. "Have you seen him?"

"Uh, yes," the clerk stammered. "He's in room three-twelve."

"Give us a key," Doug said.

"Yes, sir." The clerk handed Doug a key.

The four men squeezed into the small elevator and went up to the third floor. Doug cautioned them to be quiet. He hoped to take Wilson by surprise. The four men stopped by room three-twelve and Doug quietly put the key in the lock and opened the door. The Louisiana cops entered the room with guns drawn.

Bringing up the rear, Doug shouted, "Police!"

Wilson was in his underwear sitting on a couch watching television. "What the hell!"

Doug pointed at Wilson and said, "You're under arrest. Put your hands up."

"You again!" Wilson said. "I hoped I had seen the last of you. What are you doing here?"

"We want you to testify against Kane," Doug said. "Put them up."

Wilson reluctantly put up his hands, "I'll have to think about that."

"We're going to take you to police headquarters," Doug said. "We can talk about it down there."

Peterson read him his rights.

After allowing Wilson to put on some clothes, the four

policemen escorted Wilson down and put him in the black and white.

They returned to police headquarters and went in and set up an interrogation room to question Wilson.

Peterson escorted Wilson to the room.

Wilson stared. "What's going on?"

Doug smiled. "Your Mr. Kane is in big trouble. We want to strengthen the case against him so he gets what he deserves. We're hoping you can provide some details."

"What's in it for me?" Wilson said.

"We can probably arrange immunity from prosecution." That was doubtful, but he didn't need to know it.

"What law have I broken?"

"You mean besides holding me and my colleague at gun point, against our will? That's kidnapping," Doug said. "Taking those expensive coins might be one thing. They are valuable enough it would be grand larceny." He frowned. "And maybe you're an accessory to murder."

Wilson shook his head. "I don't know anything about murder and Kane owed me money so I took the coins. I didn't know they were that valuable. I only worked for Kane for two years. You need to talk to Tom."

Doug and Peterson exchanged a look. Criminals always blamed the other guy.

"At any rate I think you would be wise to cooperate," Doug said.

Wilson looked pretty subdued. "Okay. I guess you're right. I'll cooperate. What do I need to do?"

"If you don't fight extradition you will be sent back to Colorado," Doug said. "You will probably be kept in protective custody till Kane's trial."

"Sounds okay," Wilson said.

"Well that's it," Doug said. "What can you tell us about Tom? Does he have a last name?"

"His last name is Jerrett," Wilson said. "He's from the St. Louis area somewhere on the east side. It was something with ville in it. I'll think about it. He came to Colorado with Kane from St. Louis. I think he had worked at the same place as Kane." That all lined up with what Novack had said. Good.

"Another subject," Doug said. "Did you ever hear Kane speak about a man named Wolfgang Reitz?"

Wilson was thoughtful. "Wolfgang, funny name. I never heard Kane talk about him but I used to peek at his calendar occasionally and I think I saw the name there once. I noticed it because I thought it was an odd name.

"We're going to turn you over to the people here until we can arrange for someone from Colorado to come and take you back."

Peterson nodded.

"I can't wait." Wilson was sarcastic

Oh, yeah. Loren had a question. Doug said, "One of the samples from the waste pit turned out to be urine. Do you know anything about that?"

Wilson laughed out loud. "Sure. Things sometime got kind of boring at the ranch so we invented a game with some of the truck drivers. We would sit around drinking beer. We opened the bung-hole and would stand on top of the drum. The guy who missed the hole the most had to buy the beer. After a while we decided Kane wouldn't like us wasting our time so we put the drum in the pit. We didn't want to make Kane angry."

Doug could only shake his head.

He decided they were through with Wilson so he motioned to the guard to take him to a holding cell.

His phone rang. It was Loren. "Hey, Doug. I'm on my way back to pick you up, okay?"

"Sounds good," Doug said. "I'll wait until you get here to talk to the chief. I can brief you when I brief him."

Loren said, "Yeah, and then we can go have some dinner. I'm starving."

"Where would you like to go?" Doug asked.

"How about Galatoires? It's not so hard to get in since the hurricane."

"You've got it. I'm paying," Doug said. "We deserve a celebration."

Doug helped Peterson with his paperwork until Loren arrived.

The chief was in his office and invited Doug and Loren in. "I heard you guys were successful. That was pretty fast."

Doug smiled. "It was mostly because of Loren." He talked about how they had traced Wilson by trailing the coins and what Wilson said in the interrogation room.

"Obviously, it was a group effort," Loren said, smiling.

The chief was impressed. "Do you guys want a job? A lot of our men quit after the hurricane."

Doug shook his head. "No thanks. I assume you were kidding. I've noticed that no one down here calls the hurricane Katrina."

"That's right. We hate the name."

"Yeah," Loren said. "That was my impression."

"We're leaving Wilson in your care until we can get somebody from Colorado out here to bring him back," Doug said.

"Okay, don't worry about it," the chief said. "We'll treat him like a king and send you a bill."

"I'm sure you will," Doug said. "We'll be leaving now. Thanks so much, Chief."

"Thanks," Loren said.

"Bye, give my regards to old Jerry," the chief said.

"I'll do that," Doug said.

Doug and Loren went back to the hotel and Doug called Delany. He told Delany about taking Wilson into custody and that Wilson was willing to come back to Colorado to testify against Kane.

Delany was pleased and said he would send some people to pick Wilson up.

Dinner was jovial and delicious: Martinis, oysters, steak filets and a nice Cabernet.

"What did Wilson say about the urine?" Loren asked.

"It was a joke." Doug relayed the comments and the two men guffawed.

"Wow, I guess they were stir crazy or something out there in the country," Loren said. "I'll have to call Professor Palmer and tell him."

"So what was your mysterious errand?" Doug said.

"I went over to the Martox plant and looked around," Loren said.

"Oh, right," Doug said. "Reitz threatened the plant? What's going on with that?"

"Silk, er, Ted, Benson doesn't know what to do," Loren said. "Millions of dollars are on the line. He says he's checked and rechecked everything about the plant and can't find anything wrong. But…"

"Yeah?" Doug prompted him.

"My researcher's intuition is telling me there is something to Wolfy's threat. He wouldn't make empty promises and risk his reputation."

"It sounds like your researcher's intuition is like my cop gut."

"Could be," Loren said, nodding. "Anyway, the plant is near here, so I thought I better check it out while I was here."

"And?"

"I went over there and met the manager Alan Devers. He said they'd checked everything, even had a bomb-sniffing dog in. I walked all over the plant and didn't find anything either. But…"

"But you're not convinced?"

"No." Loren frowned. "I'm worried."

"Well, if I've learned one thing over the years, it's to follow my gut," Doug said. Maybe his gut had been trying to tell him something lately…

"I suppose we will have to go after this Jerrett character," Loren said.

Doug shook his head. "I see no reason for you to be involved in that. It's not technical or New Orleans. I'll be doing it by myself and you can be pushing back the frontiers of science.

Loren seemed pleased and happy at that news. He drank most of the wine and got a little tipsy. The flight back to St. Louis the next morning was uneventful.

Chapter 34

Back in St. Louis Loren went into the lab and told Benson what he'd found at the plant, namely, nothing.

Benson said, "That tears it. We're starting up as scheduled." He couldn't be dissuaded.

Shaking his head, Loren went into his lab and quickly called Gloria to check in with her. He was glad she seemed to be in pretty good shape.

With most of his problems seemingly solved, he got back to work on the Out of Deep Well project with his assistant Andy.

He was surprised when he got a phone call from his daughter.

Ann was breathless. "Pop, I got an email from Bill!"

"What! From where?" Loren said. As far as he knew, Bill was still at home recuperating from his 'accident.'

"He wants me to send him money to a hotel in Golden, Colorado," she said.

Loren resisted the urge to start cussing. What was that boy up to now? "Colorado? What's he doing there?"

"I don't know," she said. "He says he is in trouble. You know a good friend of his lives in Denver." said Ann.

Trouble? He didn't like the sound of that. "Yes, I remember. The Peters boy. Bill was upset when they moved there," Loren said. "How much money?"

"Five hundred dollars," she said. "He said not to tell you but I decided it would be best to let you know."

"I think you did the right thing. What do you think we should do?"

"I think we should go out there. We can probably help."

At this rate, he should buy a time-share in Colorado. "Okay. When do you want to leave?"

"Tomorrow if we can manage it."

"Go ahead and get airline tickets on line," he said. "Pay whatever it takes."

"Okay."

She was able to get tickets for the next morning. The tickets were very expensive because of the late purchase but haste was called for.

Loren told Andy he'd be out for a few days.

Andy was upset. "Why? You just got back again."

Loren said, "Ann and I have made other plans. It's a family emergency. Bill's in trouble."

Andy said, "It sound like you have to go. Good luck."

The next morning Loren and Ann arose early and drove to the airport. After parking, checking in and walking to the gate they sat down.

Loren said," I guess you have decided to go with Boeing." Loren and Ann had discussed it earlier; Boeing'd made an offer.

"That's the way it's looking right now." Ann smiled. "I'm just glad to finally get a job offer."

"I think you'll enjoy it. It sounds challenging."

"I hope so."

Loren faced Ann and said, "How do you think we

should handle the Bill situation?"

"I think Bill was acting the way he was because he thought you were mad at him and he was ashamed of his behavior," she said. "You better convince him that's not true right away. Then we can figure what to do about his problem, whatever that is."

Loren was always thrilled to see the Rocky Mountains from the air. It was a spectacular view. For some reason as they descended it reminded him of landing in the helicopter on the Kane ranch. That camouflage tarp had hidden all those barrels from view.

The plane was small but on time and the flight was bumpy but otherwise uneventful. Uneventful flights were the best kind. The plane landed smoothly and the passengers disembarked.

They walked to a car rental counter and rented a Ford Taurus. Loren let Ann drive. It was a hectic drive to the Best Western Motel in Golden. After checking in and stowing their luggage in their rooms, they went directly to Bill's room. They could hear the television through the door. Ann rapped on the door. There was no answer.

She rapped again, "Bill, its Ann."

Bill opened the door and was shocked. "Dad, what are you doing here?" Bill was angry. "Ann I told you not to involve him."

Ann smiled. "I thought it was best. You have the wrong idea about him."

Loren raised his hand. "Bill, I'm not mad at you. You made some mistakes and we all make them. We're here to help you and to try and convince you to come home."

Tears came to Bill's eyes. "I want to come home, but

I'm in trouble here and I don't think you can help."

"Can we come in?" Loren asked.

"Oh, sorry. Yes, please come in."

Ann and Loren entered the room. It was a typical one-bed motel room with a small shower-equipped bathroom. There was one stuffed chair and a full-length mirror on the bathroom door. Loren sat on the chair and Ann and Bill sat on the bed.

Loren's voice was calm. "Bill, please tell us about the trouble you're in. Maybe we can help. You know my saying that a problem isn't very big if it can be fixed with money."

"The money I asked Ann for was to sneak out of here and fly home," said Bill.

"Why sneak?" Ann asked.

"It's a long story," Bill said.

Loren raised his hand. "We have lots of time."

"Okay, I'll try. I couldn't face you after the fire, Dad. I was ashamed and felt real bad about Nick's death. I thought you were mad at me and Nick's father called and threatened me. He was very angry with me and said it was my fault his son was dead. I was scared. Nick's father is a tough guy." He shifted on the bed.

"Dicky Peters has been inviting me to come out and stay with him in Colorado for a while and I decided it was a good time to do it. I was able to get a plane ticket with some of my savings and flew out to Colorado."

Loren glanced at Ann, wondering exactly when Bill left home, but didn't want to interrupt.

"I spent the night in the airport after I left and was able to sleep a little on the plane.

"I took a cab to Dicky's house. I had called him on my cell and told him I was coming. He was happy to see me and we had some fun together. He had some classes he had to go to so I decided to take a bus out to Blackhawk and do some gambling. You know I always have liked to play slot machines."

"After I lost most of my money, I went in the bar and had a drink. There was a very pretty waitress in the bar and I started to talk to her. I had several more drinks and got pretty drunk. In order to impress the girl I told her I was a chemist and knew how to make all kinds of drugs."

Loren frowned slightly. Had the kid learned nothing from his latest fiasco?

Bill continued, "The girl disappeared and returned with this guy who said his name was Buzzy B. He looked pretty tough. He wanted to set up a lab for me to make drugs. I was drunk, a little afraid of the guy, and I wanted to impress the girl so I agreed."

Oh no. Loren's heart sank.

"He drove me down to this motel and told me to stay here while he made arrangements for setting up the lab. He told me to stay put. He would have someone watching the motel. When I sobered up the next morning I realized I was in big trouble so I emailed Ann."

Loren shook his head. "That's some story. We'll have to get you out of here."

Bill agreed. "I just want to go home. I've learned my lesson. I think it's time for me to settle down and make something of my life."

"I'm very pleased to hear it," Loren said. "I'm sorry if I scared you away."

"Oh it's not your fault. I was pretty screwed up."

Ann looked anxious. "Do you really think this Buzzy character will try to stop you from leaving?"

"He seemed like he meant business," Bill said. "He appears to be a ruthless guy. I think we have to take him seriously."

"Ugh," Ann said.

Loren pointed a finger, "You know, believe it or not, I have some contacts with the Colorado state police."

"How come?" Bill asked.

"My friend Doug Sanderson and I met several state policemen, including a captain, when we were out here investigating Wolfgang Reitz's murder."

"Do you think they would help us?" Ann asked.

"We can ask," Loren said.

Loren took a card from his wallet. "This guy, Captain Delany, told me to call him if I thought of anything more about the Kane case but I think he will help us. Doug and I were very helpful to him."

He dialed Delany's private number and after three rings Delany picked up. Loren told him the situation with Buzzy B. It turned out that Delany was familiar with Buzzy. He was a man named Buford Broconstein who was under suspicion of distributing drugs but the police could never get enough evidence to arrest him. He got his nickname because when he was excited he talked so rapidly he sounded like a buzzing bee.

Delany's men found references to a 'B.B.' in Kane's documents and Delany suspected that Kane was Buzzy's supplier. Since Kane was now out of business, Buzzy would be looking for a new supplier.

Delany said, "I'll send Sergeant Vosquez over to handle the situation. Vosquez should be there tomorrow morning. It's the least the state of Colorado could do after your help on the Kane case."

Loren said," Thank you very much. I really appreciate this." He hung up.

"Yes they're going to help us," he said. "They know about Buzzy. They're sending down a policeman I know named Vosquez to help. I've met him. He's a good man. He'll be here in the morning. Let's get something to eat."

"I don't think we should be seen together," Bill said. "If Buzzy or a friend of his is watching, he would do something."

"Okay," Loren said. "We can get a pizza."

"Sure, I saw a place across the street," said Ann.

"You two eat it," Bill said. "I better go to the restaurant in case Buzzy is around. He might get suspicious if I don't eat. You guys better stay away from me till the policeman arrives." Bill was trying to protect them. It was a good sign.

Ann left to get a pizza and Loren went back to his room to unpack. He was traveling light so it didn't take long. He removed his shoes and rested on the bed.

She returned to his room with a large sausage pizza. "I remembered this was your favorite."

"Yes, it is. Thanks." He sat up. "And thanks for being such a good daughter." It was a relief not to have to worry about her.

She smiled. "You're welcome." She went to a soda machine and got two diet cokes.

They were hungry and soon polished off the pizza. They decided they would stay away from Bill until Vosquez arrived.

Loren called Bill's room and told him to stay put. He said they'd meet Vosquez when he arrived the next day.

Ann and Loren watched some television and went to bed.

The next morning Loren and Ann were up early, had breakfast in the restaurant and waited for Vosquez in some comfortable chairs in the lobby.

Vosquez arrived with another policeman at nine-thirty. He came directly over to Loren, "Hello, Dr. Sharp. It's nice to see you again."

"Nice to see you, Sergeant Vosquez."

"Call me George," he said

"George." Loren nodded. "I'd like you to meet my daughter Ann."

Vosquez seemed impressed with Ann as they shook hands. "It's a pleasure Miss Sharp. I'd like both of you to meet Sergeant Duncan of the local office."

Loren and Ann greeted the officer.

Duncan shook their hands. "Vosquez thought there should be some local presence on the case." Duncan was tall, red haired and smiled a lot.

Loren suggested that they go to Bill's room, so all four trouped over there. So much for keeping a low profile. Loren rapped on the door.

Bill answered, talking through the door. "Who is it?"

"It's your father, sister and the police," Loren said.

Bill opened the door and they all went into the room.

After introductions Vosquez said, "Bill, I've heard you've been having trouble with Buzzy B."

Bill frowned. "Yes, I've been making a real fool of myself."

"Well, we'll try to straighten things out. Duncan and I will camp in your room with you and surprise Buzzy when he comes to get you. Do you know when he plans to come?"

"He just said he would return when he was done making arrangements. He also said he would have a friend watch me but I think that was a bluff."

"Dr. Sharp, here's a picture of Buzzy," Vosquez said. "Perhaps you and your daughter could sit in the lobby and call us here on the house phone when Buzzy is on his way."

Loren and Ann agreed. As they stepped outside the room, she said, "You know I'm a Dr. Sharp, too."

"Oh, right." He grinned at her.

She said, "Don't say I'll always be your little girl."

"I won't." But they both knew he was thinking it. "Let's take turns sitting in the lobby," he said.

"Okay."

"I'll go first." Loren went to the lobby and Ann went to her room to watch television. They switched roles for meals.

For their part, Vosquez, Duncan and Bill took turns going to the restaurant for meals.

Loren and Ann were both reading in the lobby before dinner when a man strongly resembling the man in Vosquez' picture of Buzzy came in the front door of the hotel.

He passed swiftly right through the lobby.

Ann quickly called Bill's room and Bill answered. She said, "I'm pretty sure he's on his way to the room."

"Okay." They hung up.

Ann and Loren sprinted to Bill's room, but stopped, hanging back, when they saw Buzzy.

Buzzy pounded on the door to Bill's room.

Bill said loudly, "Who is it?"

"It's Buzzy. Open the door."

Vosquez opened the door with his gun drawn. "Hello,

Buzzy. Please put your hands on your head."

Buzzy's jaw dropped. He was speechless but he did as he was told.

Vosquez motioned toward the door. "Let's go for a walk."

Duncan appeared in the doorway. Buzzy was searched for weapons and none were found. Vosquez and Duncan escorted Buzzy down the hall.

Buzzy regained his wits as he walked by Loren and Ann. He said, "I knew I shouldn't have trusted that drunken boy. I haven't done anything wrong."

All three Sharps followed Buzzy and the two cops to the lobby.

The policemen put Buzzy in Duncan's unmarked car and Duncan drove off.

Vosquez went back inside. He smiled. "It's all over."

Loren was happy for a successful end to their trip and getting his son back. "Let's all go out to dinner to celebrate. I know a good Italian place nearby."

"I'm starving," Ann said.

"I'm in. I could use a celebration beer," Bill said. "I'm glad this is all over."

"Isn't that why you got in all this trouble?" Ann asked with a grin.

"Ann," Loren said in his admonishing tone. "Sergeant Vosquez, er, George? Please join us."

"I guess I'm off duty," George said. "Sounds nice. Thanks." He drove to the restaurant.

Dinner was very convivial. They started with drinks-
-except for Vosquez, since he was driving--and wine
was ordered. They ate family style with salad, pasta and

veal dishes. The food was delicious and all four stuffed themselves.

Ann became very animated and told some stories about her graduate school experiences.

Loren told some plant startup stories.

George told about some of his experiences as a policeman.

Bill was quiet but seemed to be enjoying himself.

At the end of the evening, Loren paid and George drove back to the hotel.

After he parked, George said, "Bill, you might have to testify if the case against Buzzy comes to trial."

"I understand," Bill said. "I'm happy to do whatever it takes. I'm turning over a new leaf."

Yeah. Loren avoided cheering out loud.

Then, George said, "Ann, what do you say about getting a drink with me in the hotel bar?"

She looked a little surprised. "Okay. Sounds fun."

Loren said, "Bill, Ann, see you in the morning. We're all going back to St. Louis."

The next morning at breakfast Ann said, "George invited me to stay another day or two to see Denver with him. I'm not working right now, so I agreed."

Loren said, "If that's what you want to do, go ahead."

Bill shrugged. "Have fun."

The flight back to St. Louis was uneventful for Loren and Bill.

After the plane took off Bill said, "You know, Dad, I think I'll go back to school. I'm thinking pre-law."

"Glad to hear it," Loren said. Very glad, indeed.

Richard Lowell

When Loren got home, he went into Marchem. He checked in with Benson who still said the Martox plant was moving forward. He felt like he was closer than ever to deciphering Wolfy's threat to the plant; but it still wasn't quite ready.

Back in his lab, he quickly discovered the reason Andy was upset when he heard that Loren was leaving town. Andy's results review had been scheduled for that day. Results reviews were when the past year's activities were evaluated. The company required them. Subordinates loved them as a time they could have some input into their careers. Supervisors, including Loren, hated them since it became an hour or more of listening to complaints. Having to do them was part of the reason Loren had only one person reporting to him.

Once he realized he'd missed it, Loren rescheduled the review as soon as he got back from Colorado.

Loren and Andy met in a small conference room.

"Andy, I'm very satisfied with your performance," Loren said. "You've shown very good attention to details and your recording and reporting your work has been excellent. I have no major complaints but I think you could do a little better job of coming in on time." Supervisors usually had to have some complaint. It was expected. Otherwise the supervisor was considered too soft. It was also a good idea to put the subordinate on the defensive.

Andy just smiled. "I haven't been feeling too well in the morning. My doctor says I have a thyroid problem."

"Sorry to hear it."

"But that's not what I want to discuss," Andy said.

"What do you want to discuss?" Loren asked.

"I have been with Marchem for eight years now and

I haven't been promoted for four years. I think I deserve a promotion."

Loren tugged his earlobe. "Right now you are a Research Specialist, right?"

Andy nodded. "Yes. For the last four years."

Loren's smile was forced. He was getting uncomfortable. "You know a person with a Bachelor's Degree has to be employed for ten years before they can become Senior Research Specialists."

"I think I'm just as good a chemist as some of the Ph.D.s around here."

"That may be, but rules are rules."

"It's a bad rule. Promotions should be based on merit."

Loren liked and respected Andy and didn't want to argue with him, "Actually I agree with you but Personnel is kind of strict about this stuff."

"Maybe you can talk them into bending the rules."

"I guess I can try." Loren thought Andy was dreaming.

The rest of the review was spent discussing the direction of their research. Loren decided to push for Andy's promotion because he knew that a lot of deserving people didn't get promoted because they had bosses who were too jealous, conservative or lazy to fill out the paperwork.

Loren went back to the lab and tried to do some work but it was hard to keep his mind on it. He kept thinking of the Martox plant, Andy, Ann, Bill and the Kane trial. He wondered if he would be called to testify at the Kane trial.

After puttering for an hour he went home. When he got home there was a message to call Ann's cell phone. Loren kicked off his shoes, opened a beer and called her.

She said, "Pop, I'm going to stay out here for a few

more days. George and I are going out to Estes Park and Rocky Mountain National Park

"Okay, if that's what you want," he said. "When will you be home?"

"I don't know. I'll call you. Say hello to Bill."

"Okay, have fun."

Loren spent a quiet weekend, dividing his time between Bill and Gloria.

Doug called and said things were progressing in the legal case against Kane, but he hadn't found Jerrett yet. They were also taking another look at the Reitz murder from the beginning.

Sunday Ann called Loren from the Denver airport to tell him she was coming home. Loren told her he would pick her up. He decided to invite Gloria over to celebrate the homecoming of Bill and Ann.

When Loren picked up Ann, she was bubbling over, "Oh, I had such a good time. George is a charming guy. We got along really well together." She told him about their dinner at a Mexican restaurant and their trip to a Swiss Inn in Estes Park. They even had a picnic in Rocky Mountain National Park.

"Well, good," Loren said. "I like George, too. This is beginning to sound serious," he joked.

"I invited him to St. Louis," she said.

Huh. Maybe it really was getting serious. "Is he coming?"

"I don't know. We're talking on the phone a lot and texting and emailing."

At the appointed hour of six pm Gloria came and was greeted warmly by all three Sharps. Loren had decided to barbeque and had taken some hamburger patties from the freezer. Ann made some coleslaw and opened a can of brown beans.

Ann sat down next to Gloria. "Gloria, I'm very sorry about the way I treated you when we met," she said. "My only excuse is that I loved my mother very much and I couldn't accept another woman in my father's life. I realize now that was a mistake and that you make my father happy. I haven't seen him so happy since my mother died."

Gloria nodded and said, "I understand Ann. I might have felt the same way in your situation but your father and I have known each other for a long time. I think your mother approved of me. She actually told me that the last time we met. You know we knew each other."

"I didn't know that."

Loren came in from the kitchen. "Who wants a drink?"

"Me," said Ann and Gloria in unison.

"What do you want?" Loren said.

"I want some of that Negra Modelo you bought," Ann said.

"Gin and tonic for me," Gloria said.

"I can help with the drinks," Bill said. He got himself and Ann beers.

Loren made two gin and tonic. "Okay, drink up, everybody. Dinner is almost ready."

Gloria pointed a finger at Ann. "What's this I hear about a new job and a new boyfriend?"

"The job is for sure," Ann said. "I start next week. I don't know about the boyfriend. I invited him to St. Louis. I haven't heard from him but yet. You know he lives in Colorado."

"I hope they both work out for you," Gloria said.

Loren said, "And Bill's thinking about going back to school."

"Yeah," Bill said. "I'm thinking pre-law school."

"Good luck, Bill," Ann said.

Gloria clapped her hands together. "That's great. I'd be happy to help if you needed any advice about classes or anything."

"That would be great," Bill said. "Thank you."

Loren had a moment of happiness looking over the group, and then he had to go check the burgers on the grill.

They all enjoyed the dinner that they ate outside on the deck. The weather was perfect. The food was good and the conversation was good.

"Too bad this guy lives in Colorado, Ann," Gloria said.

"I have an idea about that if things go further," Loren said.

"What do you mean?" Ann asked.

"I have some police connections now," Loren said. "If George comes to St. Louis, maybe something will work out. I don't promise anything."

They finished the meal with some coffee, and coffee ice cream with chocolate sauce.

"Good dinner, Dad," Bill said. "Thanks."

"Yeah, nice job, Pop," Ann said.

"There's nothing like a barbeque on a nice day," Loren said. "Especially with loved ones."

"Yes, it was nice," said Gloria.

All four worked on the dishes and they were done in a few minutes. They went back to the deck and talked till dark. Loren told some of the more pleasant details of his recent trips and Ann gave a blow-by-blow description of her time with George. Gloria told a few new jokes that everyone laughed at.

Later that evening, George Vosquez called Ann and said he wanted to come to St. Louis for a visit.

Chapter 35

Doug and his colleagues had been working hard on the Reitz murder. O'Brien made them re-interview everyone. They even did more canvassing of Reitz's neighborhood.

In addition, Doug had been investigating Carlos Valdez's suspicious death, but he didn't have any fresh leads.

Doug had also been working hard on all the paperwork, dotting the i's and crossing the t's on the Kane case. The only loose thread was Tom Jerrett. He didn't look forward to trying to find him.

When he got home work one day he had a phone message from his Aunt Mavis asking what progress was being made on Catalina Perez's murder. The short answer was: not enough progress was being made. He felt guilty.

He decided Jerrett would have to wait awhile longer.

It was probably time to bring the FBI into the Aztec Printing situation. He needed to be able to prove that the green card blank he had liberated was a fake. He had an acquaintance in the St. Louis office of the FBI but he had not talked to him for years. It took a while but he finally remembered that his name was Bob Davidson. He resolved to go see Bob the next day.

He got good night's sleep and was up early. He went

for a run, took a shower and by nine a.m. he had some breakfast and was off to the FBI office in downtown St. Louis. Not many people knew where the FBI office in St. Louis was but he'd been there before.

There was a parking ramp next to the building and Doug got a parking place easily. He figured he would have to jump through some hoops to get in the building since he had not been there since 9/11. He showed his badge but still had to answer a number of questions and had to go through a metal detector. They made him check his gun.

While all this was going on he was trying to figure out what to tell Davidson about the fake green card blank he wanted examined. He decided to stonewall. After all the security, they decided he was not a terrorist so he was allowed to get on an elevator. The FBI offices were on the third floor. Doug had to wait a long time for the elevator but he didn't mind because an absolutely smashing blonde was also waiting. He wondered if she was an agent. If so, she was the most beautiful one he had ever seen. She reminded him of Mona. He sighed and wondered what Mona was up to.

Upon arriving at the third floor he found a large room divided by partitions. There was a desk opposite the elevator with a formidable middle-aged lady sitting there. He asked her for the location of Bob Davidson. She said third cubicle on the right. He walked over.

Doug waved and said, "Hi, Bob."

A sunny window was behind Doug's shoulder.

Bob squinted from the sunlight and said, "Who the hell are you?"

"Doug Sanderson. We worked together on that south county counterfeiting case about ten years ago."

"Oh yeah," he said. "I remember. How ya doin?"

"I'm fine. I have a problem I hope you can help me with."

"Okay, what is it?"

"I have a blank green card that I suspect is a fake. If possible, I'd like you to do whatever is necessary to prove it's a counterfeit."

"Where did you get it?"

"I can't tell you that right now."

Bob chuckled. "You want me to help you but you won't tell me why? I see you're still up to your old tricks."

He didn't have that many tricks, did he? "Trust me," Doug said. "I'll tell you eventually but right now I have to keep it confidential."

"Okay. I don't like it but I'll go along. Give it to me."

Doug handed Bob the green card blank. "Thanks for helping me. I appreciate it."

"I'll call you when I find out something. Give me your contact info."

Doug handed him his card. "Thanks again. Be seeing you."

Doug figured he could get some help from his friend at the phone company. If Carlos had been working for the illegal aspects of Aztec Printing, at some point he must have called the boss. Doug's friend Helen, an ex-girlfriend, was very cordial and said that furnishing him with Carlos' phone records for the last six months was no problem, and she'd be happy to help him more. He decided to send her some flowers.

When he examined the numbers, he realized the phone records were extensive. There were numbers from several parts of the country. He decided he would look into all of the numbers eventually. He wrote out a separate list of St. Louis numbers. He crossed out numbers to his aunt's phone and to her maid Maria's phone. That left twenty phone calls, five of which were to one number, a landline. Doug called his friend Helen and asked her to get the address where that phone was located. It turned out to be on Conroy Lane, a very ritzy neighborhood.

Counterfeiting must pay well. The phone was registered to a man named Daniel Gallagher. He was expecting a Latino not an Irishman but maybe it was an alias. Doug went for a drive to have a look at the house, but it was gated and he couldn't see it. He decided that Gallagher or whoever owned the house probably didn't do his own dirty work so maybe some surveillance was in order. If he could interview one of Gallagher's employees he might get an idea how to proceed. Too bad he couldn't use Charlie, who would be ideal for the job.

Doug put in a call to Sergeant Bigelow. "Hey, Bigelow. How's it going?"

"Hey, yourself. You got another anonymous tip?" He snickered.

"Ha ha." Would he ever live that down? "No. O'Brien said I could ask you to help me with some surveillance."

"Please tell me it's related to the printing thing," Bigelow said. "I can't believe those guys haven't been busted yet."

"Yes, it is," Doug said. "Let's meet for coffee. That place near the station."

A little while later, Bigelow joined Doug at one of those too-small coffee shop tables. Both men sipped black coffees.

"So, what's the job?" Bigelow asked.

"Keep an eye on this place," Doug said, passing over the address. "Any time a car exits try and follow it and get as much information you can about the car and its occupant. Hopefully, you can get a good picture of the driver."

"And O'Brien's approving all this?"

Doug nodded. "Sure." Doug's gut was telling him this was all connected to the Perez murder. And O'Brien would be happy when it was all said and done.

"I've got a sweet telephoto lens I can use. The subjects won't even know they're being observed. When do you want me to start?"

"Now."

The very next day Bigelow called Doug first thing in the morning. "I got something. Meet me at the station."

At the station, Bigelow had video: a black Lexus exited the estate and Bigelow followed at a discrete distance. The Lexus drove to Stone's gourmet food shop in Clayton. Bigelow parked in the parking lot and, with camera ready, waited for the man to exit the store. The man was carrying a large bag and seemed quite unaware of his surroundings. Bigelow was able to get several close up photos of the man. The pictures revealed a man who had a bald or shaved head and a large mustache.

"Good job, Sergeant," Doug said, surprised he'd gotten something so quickly.

"Is that guy Latino?" Bigelow asked. "I think he looks Latino. But I checked the license plate number and the car's registered to a Daniel C. Gallagher."

Bad Chemistry

"He doesn't look like a Gallagher to me," Doug said. "Maybe he's an employee? You want to run his face through the database?"

"If you've got a case number," Bigelow said.

They got the paperwork sorted and started the facial recognition search.

"Facial rec can take forever," Doug said. "What we need is fingerprints."

Bigelow frowned, but said, "It's possible but it'll take time."

"Give it a try," Doug said. "Did you try looking Gallagher up on the internet?"

"Not yet."

They looked him up together and found a lot of material. Gallagher was a well-known man around St. Louis. He was active in almost any charity you could name and was a member of the well to do society around town. He had won several awards as businessman of the year and community activist. He owned several successful businesses around town.

They got a lot of info about him online. Daniel Gallagher was a Texan. He met his wife, Mary Mitchell, on a cruise to England. She was a very wealthy widow and still young and nice looking. She was the widow of a very wealthy stockbroker who died the year before of a sudden heart attack at his desk. She was lonely and he was handsome and very solicitous of her. She was impressed and they spent a lot of time together. At the end of the voyage she invited Dan, who said he was a widower, to St. Louis and he accepted. She was still living in the house on Conroy that she had shared with her husband. He dazzled her with his good looks, charm and sophisticated tastes.

The visit lasted two months and ended in their marriage.

Gallagher and his wife had been social lions. They gave lavish parties for prominent friends and contributed large sums to local charities. They seemed to be very much in love and happy. But after two years of marriage, one morning in July, Dan found his wife dead, floating face down in their swimming pool. An autopsy found she had a blood alcohol level that would have meant she was legally drunk. No foul play could be proven and Dan inherited the money and the house. After a suitable period of time Dan continued his community service, parties and charitable contributions. He also began to date some of the local beauties.

"Well, I didn't expect all that," Doug said.

"You can find out almost anything nowadays, online." Bigelow smiled and said, "If he's considered a good guy, it kind of complicates things doesn't it?"

"It sure does," Doug said. "His wife's death is suspicious. Didn't they ever suspect him of murder?"

"I guess not," Bigelow said. "But I do."

"Me, too," Doug said. "Keep up the surveillance. And be careful."

Bigelow kept shadowing Gallagher's employee and finally was able to salvage a paper coffee cup that he threw in the trash. They put the prints in the fingerprint database, but there were no hits.

Doug was very frustrated.

At another meeting of the two men, Doug said, "The guy seems to be a Latino, maybe he has a record in Mexico?"

"Oh, I bet he does," Bigelow said.

"Let's send the photo and prints to Mexico City police and see if they find anything," Doug said.

"Will do." Bigelow nodded.

The Mexican authorities got back to them quickly, notifying them that the man was wanted for several murders and various other crimes. His name was Benito Gomez and he was also known as Bruno G.

When Bigelow passed the info along, Doug said, "Bingo."

The two men had another pow-wow and decided on a course of action.

Doug said, "The next time Bruno exits the estate follow him and at a convenient place pull him over and make some excuse. Tell him his license plate doesn't match the car's registration. That's a good one. Be careful, he may be armed and take exception to being stopped. He probably has a fake driver's license so will be sensitive to showing it. You better take some backup with you and watch him carefully. Tell him you have to take him downtown to check on the car registration. At some point you need to pat him down and remove any weapon he may have."

"Gee, thanks for all the advice." Bigelow smiled. "Sounds like a routine shakedown arrest, nothing new."

Doug was sheepish. "Sorry, I know you know your business. I was just thinking out loud. Give me a call on my cell when you get him downtown."

"Will do," Bigelow said.

Later, Doug was having brunch with Helen, his friend from the telephone company, when his cell phone beeped. Bigelow said that Bruno had just left the estate and that they were following. Doug told him to take him to the back conference room when they got to headquarters. Luckily, they were just finishing their coffee so Helen was not offended by his hurried departure. He broke some speeding laws on the way to the station but was not caught.

Bigelow met him at the door.

Doug asked, "Did you get him?"

"Yeah," Bigelow said. "He got pretty indignant when we said he had to go downtown but Hanson put his hand on his gun and Bruno calmed down. He wasn't carrying. We left his car on the side of the road. He's in the back. Hanson is watching him. I don't think he suspects anything more than a traffic charge of some kind. He had a driver's license that looked very real. If it was counterfeit, it was a good one."

Doug went to his office to pick up some papers and then went back to the conference room. The room was windowless and had an oak table with a green plastic top. There were only four chairs.

Bruno looked surprised. "Who the hell are you?" Bruno's English was quite good. Only a trace of an accent.

Doug smiled. "I'm Detective Lieutenant Douglas Sanderson. I'd like to ask you a few questions about a case I'm working on."

"What could I possibly know that could help you?" Bruno asked.

"Actually, it's more about your boss," Doug said. "I assume Dan Gallagher is your boss."

Bruno didn't answer. He was beginning to look uneasy. Beads of sweat appeared on his forehead.

"We have reason to believe that Mr. Gallagher is the actual owner of a printing company called Aztec Printing."

Doug had looked up Aztec Printing in the business directory and something called Aztec Associates owned it. It was not very helpful.

"I don't know anything about that. I'm just the chauffer and cook." If he was the chauffer could he be the one that ran down Ms. Perez?

Doug continued. "We also believe Aztec is involved in counterfeiting."

Bruno was becoming more and more uncomfortable. He was squirming around in his chair. "I don't know anything about that. I told you I'm just the chauffer and cook." He didn't seem cool enough to be a murderer.

Doug laid the papers he had on the table. They were bulletins about Bruno from Mexico where he was wanted for murder and other crimes. Doug put on his most threatening face. "You better start cooperating or you will be on the next plane to Mexico City."

Bruno paled but said nothing.

"Well, what will it be?"

Bruno thought for a minute. Finally, he said, "Okay, I'll answer your questions."

"Does Gallagher own a black SUV?"

"I don't know."

"You're the driver and you don't know? I thought you were cooperating. What cars does he own?"

"Okay." Bruno looked like he swallowed a live frog. "A black Lexus that I drive, an old Mustang convertible and, yes, a black SUV."

"Have there been any recent repairs to the SUV?"

"You mean bodywork?"

"Yes," Doug said.

"No. The thing is a tank. It would take a major

collision with an armored car to dent the thing. Gallagher made me wash it several times lately, though."

"Isn't that rather unusual?" Doug asked.

"Yes, it is." Bruno probably wouldn't admit all that if he'd killed Perez with the SUV.

"Is Gallagher at the house now?"

"Naw, he's in Vegas. He goes there nearly every month."

"Who is there at the house?"

"Just Fritz," Bruno said.

"Who's Fritz?"

"Fritz Mueller. Gallagher's butt boy, his boyfriend."

Interesting. "Will he be armed?"

"Usually, unless he's sleeping or bathing."

"Okay, thanks for your help. We're going to have to keep you here overnight."

"What!" Bruno said. "You can't do that. I want a lawyer."

"We can keep you twenty-four hours on a traffic charge. We'll keep you comfortable."

"I object."

Doug had a uniform take Bruno back to a holding cell.

Doug and Bigelow sat down to discuss their next move.

"So, I assume we're sending him back to Mexico," Bigelow said.

Doug nodded. "There's outstanding warrants, right? We have to."

"Yeah," Bigelow said.

"Let's delay as long as possible," Doug said. "I think we should take Bruno's car back to Gallagher's estate so we can enter without alerting anyone."

Bad Chemistry

Bigelow was a stickler. "Maybe, but we'd need a search warrant."

Doug reluctantly agreed. "Okay, I'll talk to Judge Atkins."

Doug went to the judge's office. But Judge Herbert Atkins was not agreeing readily to issue a search warrant for Dan Gallagher's house. He knew Dan personally and judged him to be a pillar of the community. "You have to be kidding," he said. The judge was a big man with a full head of dark hair flecked with white.

Doug insisted. "Judge, you have to trust me. Gallagher may have knowledge of a counterfeiting ring and maybe even a couple of murders."

Atkins shook his head. "I just can't believe this. I know Dan Gallagher and he seems to be a very trustworthy person. He's contributed lots of money to various causes around town."

"Please trust me, judge," Doug said. "I know he is dirty. I think he ran down a woman in the street. I don't have much time."

The judge fiddled with some items on his desk. He looked lovingly at a photo of his wife and kids. He looked around his chambers. The room was very tastefully done. It had dark wood paneling with nice original paintings. The carpet was a rich burgundy and the furniture was of substantial dark wood. Finally he glared at Doug. "The only reason I'm doing this is because I owe your father a big debt of gratitude. He got me appointed. You know that. It's probably why you brought me this hot potato. So I'm going to issue this warrant. I hope to hell we won't be sorry."

Doug knew very well that Atkins owed his dad.

"Thank you very much judge. You won't be sorry."

He left before the judge could change his mind. The traffic was heavy driving back to the station and he became very frustrated. He tried some side streets but they were no better than the main streets. It was getting late.

He finally made it back and fortunately there was a parking place in the lot. After he entered he stopped by the prisoner's personal effects locker, and then told the dispatcher to send a car to the entrance of the Gallagher estate. He then found Bigelow sitting at his desk eating a doughnut and drinking coffee out of a polyurethane cup.

Doug blew in like a gale. "Let's go, Bigs. I got the warrant. It wasn't easy.

"Can I finish my coffee?"

"No," Doug said. "Let's go."

"What can I say? Doughnuts and coffee are good." He gulped his coffee and they left.

They hurried out to Doug's car and took off. Bigelow had to tell Doug to slow down. The traffic had slowed down but was still heavy.

Bigelow said, "What's the hurry? The house will still be there."

"Okay, Okay, I'll slow it down," Doug said. "But I think we may be able to close this case tonight."

They picked up Bruno's car and left Doug's car in its place. Doug had taken Bruno's car keys from his effects.

Bigelow looked uneasy about this turn of events, but said only, "What's the plan when we get there?"

"Bruno's car should get us through the gate," Doug said. "I think we should just ring the front doorbell and see what happens."

"That's a stupid plan but I can't think of a better one."

Bad Chemistry

It was dusk by the time Doug and Bigelow arrived at the Gallagher house.

When they arrived at the estate the squad-car was waiting outside and the gate was closed. They expected that and that was the reason they were in Bruno's car. Doug pushed the button he decided was for the radio-controlled gate and the gate swung open. He motioned to the other car to follow them in. The house was very imposing.

They parked in the circular drive and went to the front door. The patrol car arrived at the same time and parked. Doug pressed the doorbell and they waited. There was no answer. They waited a few minutes and pressed the bell again. After a few more minutes a man with a blond crew cut angrily jerked the door open. He had the muscles of a body builder and wore a jogging suit.

"Who the hell are you?" he asked. "How did you get through the gate?"

"I'm Lieutenant Doug Sanderson and this is Sergeant Bigelow. We're from the metro police. I guess you're Fritz Mueller."

"Yah, how do you know me and where did you get Bruno's car?" Fritz said, looking in the driveway.

"Bruno is being held downtown on a traffic charge," Doug said. He showed Fritz the search warrant. "We have a warrant to search this house."'

Fritz started to move his hand to the inside of his jacket but Bigelow grabbed his arm. Doug pulled his gun and pointed it at Fritz' chest. "Easy big guy."

Bigelow opened Fritz' jacket and removed his gun. "I'll just hang on to this for you."

Fritz protested. "You can't do this. This is Daniel Gallagher's house. He'll have your jobs."

Doug motioned to the patrol car and an officer came running up, "Put this man in your car."

"Yes sir," said the officer. He led Fritz to the police car and had him enter the back seat.

Fritz was complaining the whole way. "You'll be sorry for this. Mr. Gallagher will raise hell."

Doug and Bigelow entered the house.

The entry hall impressed Doug. "Gallagher has good taste."

"And a lot of money," Bigelow said. "I bet his late wife designed this."

"Probably."

"What are we looking for?"

"Blank green cards and other printing forms, a black SUV and maybe some interesting documents."

"Where do you want to start?" said Bigelow.

"We'll do a quick walk through of the first and second floors and try to find the entrance to the basement. That's where we probably will find storage," Doug said.

"Maybe in the attic," Bigelow said.

"Possibly."

They walked through the first floor and saw nothing of interest. It was the same with the second. In the hall by the kitchen they found a door that turned out to be to the basement. The basement was finished and had a long bar, lots of seating and a large screen television set.

"Very nice," Bigelow said.

"I bet he's had some great parties down here," Doug said.

"No doubt."

In a back corner there was a door that was locked.

"This looks promising," Doug said. "Think you can

open it?"

Bigelow sighed. "I can try." He took out a Swiss Army knife and began to manipulate one of the tools in the door lock. After several minutes, there was a click and Bigelow tried the door. It opened. "I'll be darned. I haven't done that in a long time."

"Good job Bigs," said Doug.

They stepped into the room. "Okay. This is what I hoped we'd find," said Doug said. All the boxes he'd seen at the print shop were there and they proceeded to look in all of them. They had more time than Doug had at the print shop and found fake green cards, driver's licenses, passports and various identity cards and documents.

Bigelow shook his head. "Pretty dumb of Gallagher to keep this stuff in his home."

"It's probably temporary storage. I suppose he didn't know where to put the stuff on short notice. He probably thought his local reputation would protect him. Who would dare to question him?"

"Guess he didn't know about you, Doug"

"I guess not. Okay, let's get a van out here and haul away the evidence."

Doug took out his small digital camera and took numerous pictures. There would be no doubt where the boxes came from.

Bigelow summoned a police van on his cell phone.

"Now let's try and find the black SUV," Doug said.

"Okay," Bigelow said. "The garage is off the kitchen."

Doug and Bigelow went back upstairs.

Doug told Bigelow to tell the officers in the police-car to take Fritz downtown and book him for resisting arrest. "I don't know if it will stick but we need him out of the way for a while. We don't want him in touch with Gallagher."

The garage entrance was indeed off the kitchen and the door was locked from the inside so Doug easily entered. Bigelow soon followed. There were three vehicles in the large garage: A Mustang convertible, an empty spot and a black SUV.

Doug pointed at the SUV. "That could be a murder weapon."

Bigelow called downtown and requested a CSI team.

With nothing to do till the team came, the men went back to the storage room.

Doug had noticed a one drawer file cabinet in the room with the boxes. "I wonder what kind of evidence of criminal activity is in this file?" he said. The file was locked and they had no luck opening it. "Well, we'll just have to have it taken downtown. The boys in the lab can open it I'm sure."

"It should be easy for them," Bigelow said.

When the CSI team and the police van arrived. Doug explained to them what to do. He told the CSI team to go over the black SUV carefully and try and find evidence of a hit and run. The van driver and his helper loaded up the boxes and the file cabinet and took off.

Doug and Bigelow were the last cops on the scene. Doug went into Gallagher's refrigerator and got out a couple of beers. He handed one to Bigelow.

Bigelow hesitated. "You're not serious, are you? That's against protocol."

Doug grinned. "You're objecting now?"

Bigelow took the beer.

Doug opened his beer and took a swig, and then walked over and sat down in Gallagher's den. Bigelow slowly walked after him...

"He'll never miss a couple," Doug said. "I guess we are off duty. It was a good day's work."

When they finished their beers, they left.

At home, Doug called his aunt and told her he thought they had Ms. Perez's killer. She was relieved.

Chapter 36

Loren's life had settled down. There were no more dramatic trips out of town. He got lots of good work done at Marchem.

The Martox plant opening was approaching, but his intuition told him he was on the verge of deciphering Wolfy's mysterious threat. Silk Benson was no longer even worried about it.

Bill was even back to his old self and was applying to colleges.

Since Ann seemed to be warming up to Gloria, he decided to cook a dinner for the two of them. They were both dear to him and he wanted them to be friends. He was going to make his favorite, veal marsala. He would have rice pilaf and he had picked out a nice pinot grigio because he knew that they both liked it.

Ann joined him in the den.

How are you hon?" he said.

"Good, Pop. How are you?"

"I'm good."

"Is Gloria coming?" she asked.

"Yes, she is," he said. "I hope you two get along."

"I think we will. So when I start my new job do you

have any advice for me?"

"Oh, I have lots of advice for what it's worth." He grinned. She didn't always seem to like getting advice from him.

"Okay, I'm listening."

"What do you think you have to do to have a successful career?"

"I need to do a good job," she said.

"Yes, but that's not all," he said. "The most important thing is getting along with people. If your colleagues like you, and especially your boss, you'll do fine. It is a fallacy among young people that, if they do a good job, they will automatically get ahead. No! The most important thing is getting along with people. An especially good idea is to make your boss look good. When he moves on or retires he will recommend you to take his place. Or he will actually recommend you for another job."

"That's kind of depressing, Pop."

"I know, but that's the way it is." He glanced out the window. "That looks like Gloria's car."

A breathless Gloria came in through the unlocked front door. "I just missed having a major accident on the way over."

"I'm glad you didn't have an accident. What happened?" Loren said, reaching out for a hug.

"A guy was changing lanes without looking and missed me by inches."

"That's happened to me, too," Ann said. "It's a shame the way people drive."

"Well, settle down," Loren said. "I'll get us all a drink. Will it be the usual?"

Ann and Gloria nodded yes.

Gloria asked, "Where's Bill tonight?"

Ann grinned. "He has a date, if you can believe it."

"Oh, I believe it," Gloria said.

Loren mixed two gin and tonics for himself and Gloria, and popped open an amber ale for Ann.

"Oh, that's good, Gloria said after taking a sip.

"Did you have a bad day, Glory?" Loren asked.

"Not till that asshole cut me off."

"Well, you can relax now," Loren said.

"Pop was just giving me the secret of getting ahead in business," Ann said.

Gloria laughed. "Why didn't he tell me?"

"You wouldn't have listened," Loren said with a chuckle.

Gloria looked at Ann. "So, what did he tell you?"

"He said that getting along with people was what it was all about, especially your boss."

"That's good advice unless the boss is chasing you around your desk."

"That didn't happen, did it?" Loren said.

Gloria nodded.

Loren shook his head. "In our conservative chemical company?"

"You better believe it."

Ann was frowning. "I'm sorry to hear that."

"Who?" Loren said.

"Oh, I'm not going to name names," Gloria said.

"I can guess."

"Oh, don't bother," Gloria said. "It's water over the dam."

They chatted about more pleasant things.

"Who wants another drink?" Loren asked.

"Me," Gloria said."

"I'm okay," Ann said.

Loren got Gloria and himself another gin and tonic.

"I can't imagine who at Marchem would disrespect you like that," Loren said when he brought back the beverages.

"Let's drop the subject," said Gloria.

"I'm sorry about the way I acted when we were together earlier," said Ann.

"Forget it," said Gloria.

Loren waved an arm and said, "Let's eat." They sat down at the dining room table and he made a big show of opening the wine.

"What are we drinking?" Gloria asked.

"Pinot grigio, the real stuff."

"Good, I like it," Gloria said.

Loren served the veal, rice and some salad. Conversation slacked off as they ate. Finally they finished eating.

"Thanks, Pop," Ann said. "I'm stuffed."

"Loren, I have to say that was delicious," Gloria said. "It must have been a lot of work."

"No, not really," he said. "Good ingredients give good food. Now, who wants coffee?"

Both Ann and Gloria wanted regular coffee.

"Sorry," Loren said. "I don't have any dessert, too many calories."

Gloria and Ann answered in unison, "Good, I don't have room anyway."

"Shall we go back to the family room?" he asked.

Ann shook her head. "First, I'll do the dishes."

"I'll help," Gloria said.

"They'll wait," Loren said.

"No, we'll do them," Ann said.

Gloria and Ann seemed to have a good time doing the dishes just talking and getting to know each other.

Loren was glad he let them be together. He was getting a little bored but the ladies finally came back into the family room. They were giggling.

"So what's so funny?" he asked.

"Oh, never mind," Ann said. "You wouldn't find it funny."

"What's new about the Wolfgang situation?" Gloria asked. "I met him a couple of times over patents and he seemed like a reasonable guy. Why would he do this strange thing?"

Loren grimaced. "He believed he is the real inventor of the Martox manufacturing process and that he deserves some recognition. That's why he wrote the letter to Silk Benson."

"Tell the truth, did he have a case?" asked Gloria-the-lawyer.

"I guess he could have made a case," Loren said. "But a lot of inventors have not gotten credit for their discoveries."

"For example?" Ann asked.

"Well, who invented the steamboat?" Loren asked.

"Fulton," Ann said.

"A man by the name of John Fitch ran a steamboat before Fulton," Loren said. "But Fulton was the first to form a company and haul passengers. People think Morse was the first to use a telegraphic code but a man by the name of Alfred Vail did it before Morse. Morse was the first to actually use it."

"Uh oh," Ann said. "He's starting one of his lectures."

"It's interesting," Gloria said.

He smiled at her. "Have you guys ever heard of Elias Howe?"

"No," Ann said.

"Well, he made a sewing machine before Singer," Loren said.

"How do you know so much about this?" Gloria asked.

"I've done a lot of reading," Loren said.

"Got any more?" Ann asked.

"Sure," he said. "Marconi is credited with inventing radio but men named Lodge in England and Tesla in America showed the principle before Marconi. Marconi formed a commercial company for long distance communication and became famous. Marconi made a bad mistake however. He stubbornly decided to use long wavelengths for long distance communications but short waves work much better. In more recent times, Bill Gates took his operating system from a man named Gary Kildall. I bet you've never heard of Kildall."

"Nope," Gloria said.

"No," Ann said. "I never have."

"I could come up with several more examples," Loren said.

"I guess I saw some shady things when I was practicing patent law," Gloria said. "Did you ever have a problem Loren?"

Loren nodded. "Yes, a few. I was always slow in putting in disclosures. Patents can be very complex. Between incompetent patent lawyers, picky patent examiners, jealous colleagues, complicated patent department rules and deadlines and interferences it can get pretty hairy.

But, then, he smiled. "I remember the time a colleague came into my lab red-faced and shouting, 'How come my name isn't on that patent?' He was really angry. It was about a new method of preparing an intermediate that I had an idea about. I tried it out and it worked so that time I got off my duff and I submitted a patent disclosure. I had a lot of other things going so the optimization and details were assigned to this colleague. He did a nice job but the disclosure was in before he even got to work and the basic idea was not his."

Loren went to the kitchen and came back with the coffee pot. "Any takers?" he said. There were none.

"Most people don't realize that it is the idea that is patentable," Loren said. "It must be reduced to practice but the inventor is the one whose idea it is. Sometimes a really key improvement can allow another inventor's name on a patent but that is rare. I remember once a colleague submitted a patent application with seventeen inventors. I thought, 'How could seventeen people have the same idea?' People don't realize that a patent with the wrong inventor's name on it is an invalid patent. Of course there are some bosses who insist on having their name on every publication even if they hardly know what is in them."

Gloria said, "I hope I wasn't incompetent or lazy as a patent attorney."

"I'm sure you weren't but there are plenty that are," he said. "They take pride in saying they don't know any chemistry."

"At any rate it doesn't seem like Wolfgang should be killed over it," Gloria said.

"We don't know the motive behind his killing," he

said. "There are some other things going on." His brain was buzzing.

Chapter 37

Doug Sanderson was exhausted. He hadn't had a good night's sleep all week. All he wanted to do was take a shower, have a beer, watch some baseball and go to bed early. He had the shower but found he didn't have any beer. Damn.

He did have a bottle of excellent champagne in his fridge that he was saving for a special occasion. "What the hell." He opened the bottle. He poured himself a glass in one of his crystal flutes and settled down to watch some baseball on TV. He just got interested in the game when the phone rang.

It was Bigelow. "I was just talking to the CSI folks and they have some results. Can we meet to discuss them?"

Doug had mixed feelings but knew he had to hear the results, "Why don't you come over here? You know the way. I've got an open bottle of champagne."

"Okay, I'll be right over."

He'd finished another glass of champagne and watched another inning when the doorbell rang.

He opened the door to a smiling Bigelow who was carrying a manila folder. "Come in Bigs. You look like you have good news. Let's sit in the kitchen. Want some champagne?"

"Sure, why not?" Bigelow said. "I'm not on duty. What are we celebrating?"

"Nothing special," Doug said. "A successful day I guess."

His kitchen was left over from his marriage with Mona. It was all white with an island in the middle and a table over to the side. The windows were covered with art glass from Mona's glasswork. The room was actually very beautiful.

Bigelow had seen it before. "Mona sure was talented. Why did you let her get away?"

"Sometimes I ask myself the same question. So what have you found out?"

"Well, the CSI boys have been busy with their wet q-tips. Dried blood is not easy to get rid of. By just rinsing you won't totally remove it. They found some in the crevices of the back of the hood."

"And?" Doug asked.

"They will compare the DNA with tissue samples from Ms. Perez's autopsy. They should be ready shortly. Then we need to know who was driving."

"Maybe the people at Aztec Printing can tell us."

"I hope so," Bigelow said. "I will start interviewing them this week."

"Good. What else?"

"They opened the file drawer that was in the room with the printing forms. There were four file folders in there plus some cash. One folder had various numbers that look like books for a business. We haven't deciphered them yet. One looked like a schedule of some kind. It had some handwritten notations in the margins. They could be in

Carlos' handwriting that would be evidence of Gallagher's involvement in his death. We are looking for samples of his handwriting. They are also trying to get DNA off the paper and fingerprints off the file drawer. One seemed to be a list of counterfeit products and the fourth was a list of customer's names and addresses. I brought copies." He handed Doug the manila folder.

Doug studied the records. When he got to the list of customers he grunted. "Wow, this is a gold mine. Look at this name." My gut was right. I knew it.

"Yeah, Shapiro," Bigelow said. "What about it?"

"I told you about Earl Kane," Doug said. It was all connected.

"Yes."

"Shapiro was Kane's lawyer," Doug said.

"My God," Bigelow said. "It's all meshing together."

"Yes." He smiled and rubbed his hands together. "I guess I'll surprise Mr. Gallagher with a couple of federal agents when he gets off the plane from Las Vegas."

He looked up at Bigelow. "Thanks for all this info."

Bigelow finished his drink and left.

Doug called his contact at the FBI. Bob was accommodating and said they'd keep a look out for Gallagher.

Doug realized that the green cards owned by Kane's Mexicans were probably counterfeit and must have come from Aztec Printing by way of Kane's lawyer Shapiro. Doug phoned Delany and explained the situation.

Delany said, "I'll phone the Denver police with the info. They can search Shapiro's office. It'd be great to bring him down. He's been a thorn in law enforcement's side for a long time."

The next day Doug went into the office to write a report.

Bigelow stopped by his desk. "O'Brien's not happy," he said quietly.

Doug shook his head. "When is he ever happy?"

"There's rumors you're cutting too many corners," Bigelow said.

Doug felt his eyebrows rise. "Those rumors better not be coming from you."

"Of course not!" Bigelow seemed sincere.

"What does O'Brien want from me?" Doug said. "I solve cases."

Bigelow shrugged and walked away.

Doug got a phone call. "Hi, my name is Josh Mitchell. Mary Mitchell was my mom."

Doug knew the name was familiar but he couldn't quite place it.

Mitchell continued, "Mary Mitchell was Dan Gallagher's wife. I heard you guys got him. I've always been suspicious of him. I want to discuss my mother's death."

This could be the motherlode. "Sure, I'll be happy to speak with you. Where are you?"

"I'm in St. Louis on business," Mitchell said. "I'm at the Adam's Mark."

"Good. Take a cab to Police headquarters," Doug said. "The cab driver will know the way. I'll be waiting for you." Even O'Brien would have to quit complaining if he cleared enough cases.

"Okay. I'll be there in half an hour."

Doug continued his writing and in twenty minutes

went to the front door to wait for Mr. Mitchell. The taxi arrived right on time and out stepped a distinguished-looking man. He was average height, stocky, clean-shaven, well dressed and well groomed. His hair was dark and there were a few gray hairs.

Doug put out his hand. "Very happy to meet you, Mr. Mitchell."

Mitchell shook his hand. "And I you."

The men entered the building and Doug showed Mitchell to a small conference room. The room had a table and four chairs and Doug motioned Mitchell to one of the chairs.

Doug said, "You said you wanted to discuss your mother's death?"

Mitchell settled into a chair, loosened his tie and started talking. "I couldn't get along with Gallagher. I thought he was a crass fortune hunter but my mother was infatuated with him. We had several arguments about him. I had a job at the time that often took me to Los Angeles and I decided to relocate there. I started my own business, got very busy, and gradually my contacts with my mother were few and far between. She was very angry with me and our parting was very bitter. She said she never wanted to see me again. I didn't know she had died till a friend of mine sent me the St. Louis paper with the story of her drowning. The whole matter was over, even the inquest, by the time I heard about it."

"So you decided to let it go."

"Yes. I'm not proud of it but, at the time, I felt powerless."

"Go on."

"The same friend sent me a link to the story of

Gallagher's recent arrest. I decided I couldn't avoid telling what I know anymore, so here I am."

"Yes. Go on," said Doug.

"The idea of my mother drowning in the swimming pool is ridiculous," Mitchell said. "The pool was strictly my father's idea. It was kind of a status thing with him. My mother never wanted it and she never swam in it. She was very proud of her hair and went to the hairdresser two or three times a week. At most she might put on a swimsuit and sit by the pool but she never went in it the whole time I was growing up. Her going for a swim at night is ridiculous. Also, my mother was a very light social drinker. The idea of her passing out drunk is just not believable. I'm sure her friends would agree."

"Anything else?" Doug said.

"That's about it."

"Thank you. How often are you in St. Louis?"

"About once every three months," Mitchell said.

"Okay," Doug said. "Thank you. Please leave me your phone number. I will probably have to contact you again." They exchanged cards and Mitchell asked to have a taxi called and left.

Doug decided he had to look into the Mary Mitchell Gallagher death. It couldn't hurt to have more leverage on Gallagher.

He looked at the newspaper article reporting Mrs. Gallagher's death. The article stated that Mr. Gallagher was at his country club, Oak Tree CC, the night she died. The details agreed with what Mitchell had said, drunk, swimming at night, drowned.

He pulled the police file, such as it was. The

investigating officer was Lt. Joseph O'Brien. There was no autopsy. The whole report was pretty short. Uh oh. He wondered if old Joe screwed up or maybe did something more serious. He debated going to ask O'Brien about it, but decided against it for the time being. Accusing his boss of being sloppy, or worse, wouldn't endear him to him.

He'd been to Oak Tree with his dad years ago, and knew some people there. Maybe he could find out a few details. He drove to the Country Club. The club was one of the most prestigious in the area. He parked, entered the club and went right to the general manager's office. There was no secretary and the door was open. Numerous golf themed photographs crowded the walls of the office and a glass cabinet with trophies was in a corner.

Doug rapped on the open door and was motioned into the office. The occupant was a white haired gentleman of somewhat advanced years.

He smiled at Doug and said, "What can I do for you, young man?"

"I'm Lieutenant Douglas Sanderson of the Metro Police. I believe you may have some information that would help with a case I'm working on."

"I think I knew your father," the manager said. "Was he a member here?"

"Yes, he was," Doug said. "You must have been here a long time."

"Forty years next month," said the manager.

"Congratulations," Doug said.

"I'm happy to meet you," the manager said. "Your father was a fine man. I will be happy to help you in any way I can."

Doug smiled. "Do you know a man named Dan

Gallagher?"

The man became upset. "I certainly do. I thought he was a fine man until I read about him in the paper. It's very upsetting." He frowned. "Of course, there was that terrible business with his wife."

"What can you tell me about that terrible business?"

"Nothing," he said. "Just what was in the paper. She drowned. Why?"

Doug ignored his question. "Can you give me the names of his friends here?"

"I don't keep those kinds of records but our pro probably will know who was in his golf foursome. Let's go down to the pro-shop and ask him." The manager got up from his desk.

The two men went down to the lower floor and entered a shop crammed full of golf merchandise.

There was an office in the back and a man--apparently the pro--was sitting at a desk. The pro was a big man with a ruddy complexion and thinning hair. He was dressed in slacks and a golf shirt and said, "Well, hello, John. To what do I owe your visit? And who's your friend?"

"This is Detective Lieutenant Doug Sanderson of the police department."

The pro chuckled. "Goodness, what have I done?"

The manager said, "Douglas, this is our pro, Jack Archer."

Doug said, "Good to meet you Mr. Archer. Maybe you can help me with a case I'm working on."

"I'll help any way I can," Archer said.

The manager said, "I'll leave you two alone now." He left and Doug and Archer retired to Archer's office and sat down.

Archer said, "What can I do for you?"

"Do you know Dan Gallagher?" Doug said.

"Yes, unfortunately I do know who he is," Archer said. "He's a member. He golfs quite a bit. I've been reading about him lately. A policeman, I think his name was O'Brien, was out here a while back inquiring about Gallagher and his golfing buddies. It was about his wife's death, if I recall."

"I would like to talk with the men in his golfing foursome."

"Actually it's a threesome. They pick up a forth each week. They say it makes it more interesting to meet someone new every week."

"So who's the threesome?" Doug asked.

"A man named Sam Murphy, a man named Sean Mallory and, of course, Gallagher. I heard Mallory had a heart attack last week and is in intensive care so you won't be able to talk with him."

Doug wasn't happy. "Do you have an address on Murphy?"

"I can give you that but he was in here earlier," Archer said. "I think he's upstairs having lunch. I can take you up and point him out."

They went up to the dining room and Archer pointed to a man dressed in golf clothes having lunch with another man.

Doug walked over, introduced himself, and asked the man if he would meet him in the bar when he was done with lunch. The man agreed.

Doug waited about fifteen minutes and Sam Murphy came into the bar.

Murphy put out his hand and said, "Hello, I'm Sam

Murphy."

Doug took his hand and said, "Doug Sanderson."

"I believe you are with the police," Murphy said.

"That's correct, I have a few questions to ask you about Dan Gallagher."

"I figured. He's been in the papers lately. Another policeman asked me some questions about Gallagher a while back. I think his name was O'Brien."

"Yes," Doug said. "He's now my boss."

"Oh really?"

"You played golf with Gallagher the day his wife died?" Doug asked.

"Yes, I did," Murphy said.

"What time did you finish?"

"I think it was about five pm."

"What did you do after you finished?" Doug asked.

"I showered and met Sean in the bar," Murphy said. "We had a couple of toddies and went in to dinner."

"Wasn't Gallagher with you?" Doug asked.

"No," Murphy said. "He said he had to talk with somebody. He didn't say who."

"Did you tell O'Brien that?

"No. He didn't ask. I'm a lawyer. I don't usually answer questions that aren't asked."

Doug was surprised and angered. "Thanks for the information. Is there anything else you can tell me about Gallagher?"

"Well, there was one incident that was strange."

"Go on."

"Well, as I said, I'm a lawyer. Some people think some of my clients are shady characters. I don't think so. Anyway, one day, a while back after golf, Dan asked me if

I knew where he could get some GHB, the date rape drug. I guess he thought one of my clients could supply it. I told him no and asked him what he wanted it for. He didn't answer me." Murphy looked Doug in the eyes. "I decided to not withhold the information after reading about Dan's new crimes. He's not the man I thought he was."

Lawyers could be very annoying. But all Doug said was, "That's certainly interesting. Anything else?"

"No, I guess that's it."

"Thank you very much," Doug said. "You've been very helpful."

He knew it. His cop's guy was never wrong. Apparently Catalina Perez wasn't the first woman Gallagher murdered.

Doug left. He called Loren. "What do you know about GHB?"

"The date rape drug?" Loren asked.

"Yes."

"I know that it's gamma hydroxy butyric acid. That's about it."

"I guess you don't know anything about the metabolism?"

"No. Why don't you ask one of your forensic guys?"

"I will but I thought you might know something."

Doug put in a call to the crime lab and talked to a chemist. He asked how fast GHB would be metabolized and he found out it was metabolized pretty fast. However, if the victim died soon after imbibing, it could perhaps be found.

Doug called Josh Mitchell for permission to exhume his mother's body. He agreed.

Doug presented the case to the county prosecutor and permission was given to exhume the body.

Chapter 38

Loren had several new research ideas he wanted to try out. When he got to his lab the next day, however, he found Peter Rose, his young colleague, there. Peter was a very serious and sincere young man who was a little overweight. Loren liked him a lot and was mentoring him.

Peter said, "It seems like you've been gone a lot lately."

"Yes," Loren said. "But that's over now." Until he figured out what was up with the Martox process...

"What's the deal with Ableson and Kane?" Peter asked. "You wouldn't believe the rumors that have been flying."

Loren gave him a brief description of what happened in Colorado.

Peter was shocked. "I just don't understand how a man like Kane can do things like that. He puts all of the chemical industry in a very bad light. The rest of us try our best to develop clean manufacturing processes and he messes everything up. It's disgusting."

"I agree," Loren said. "It's too bad. We just have to keep trying to do our best."

"It would be nice if management was trying to do their best and would allocate more money to waste elimination,"

Peter said.

"Well, business is business," Loren said "They try to compromise. There is a lot of competition out there and waste elimination sometimes costs more than making the product."

"We're in a tough business. Between the government and the activists we get beat on from both sides," Peter said. "What did all that have to do with Reitz?"

Loren said, "Apparently none. It was a washout from that angle."

"Do you believe what Wolfgang said about the Martox process?" Peter asked.

"Like I told Benson, Wolfy was not a kidder."

"But the process has been run hundreds of times in the lab," Peter said.

Loren shrugged. "I know."

"You talked to him just before he died, didn't you?"

"Yes."

"Well, what did he say? Could you get any idea what was up?"

Loren shook his head. "No, he was hostile and told me to leave. When I first got there he seemed glad to see me but, when I asked him to shed some light on the letter he sent to Benson, he became belligerent and told me to get out." Loren froze, mind racing.

Finally, he said, "My God, maybe that's it."

In his peripheral vision, he saw his lab assistant Andy step closer.

"What?" Peter asked. "You look like someone just hit you in the face."

All the events of the past few weeks were finally coalescing in Loren's mind. From Wolfy's comments, to the darkness under the camo tarp, to the photochemistry comments in Professor Palmer's lab, to the plant tour. All of it.

"Light, a light-catalyzed reaction," Loren said, slowly. "The reaction has always been run in glass equipment in the lab. Oh my God. The plant reactors are stainless steel so no light can enter. I saw that when I toured the plant. If all of the chemicals are added and they don't react as they go in, the temperature will go through the roof when they do react." He stared at Peter. "There could well be an explosion."

"Jesus, maybe that's it," said Peter.

"Andy, go to the storeroom and get ten grams of nitromethane and stop at Ollie's lab and get some of the Martox aldehyde," said Loren. "Immediately."

"I'm on my way," said Andy, who had been trying to pretend he was not listening to the conversation.

Loren set up a small, three necked flask in the hood, with a funnel for adding liquids and wrapped the funnel and flask in aluminum foil. He put a thermocouple probe in one of the flask's neck's to measure temperature. The flask was stirred with a magnetic stir bar.

Peter watched everything with great interest.

After about fifteen minutes Andy returned with the chemicals.

Loren weighed out the aldehyde, poured it into the flask and swept the flask with nitrogen. He told Andy to turn out the lights in the lab so the thermocouple readout was the only light and he closed the hood doors. Loren added the nitromethane all at once by reaching around the hood door and then he reclosed the door.

The three men stared intently at the thermocouple

readout.

It stayed steady at twenty-seven degrees centigrade.

"My God, nothing's happening," Peter said. "There should be a heat effect."

Andy whispered, "Shit."

Loren didn't reply.

They let the chemicals stir for about ten minutes and there was no reaction.

After that Loren reached in, removed the aluminum foil and told Andy to turn on the lights.

Nothing happened for about thirty seconds and, then, suddenly the thermocouple readout said one-hundred degrees. Then two-hundred. The mixture started fuming and the temperature reading went off scale.

Even though the reaction was being done on a small scale, the explosion was impressive. The flash and sound were striking.

All three men jerked back.

The hood filled with a brown gas. When the gas cleared, the flask and funnel were gone and the hood shelf was covered with a layer of glass shards. The thermocouple readout was blank.

Loren, Peter and Andy stood silently for almost a minute and then Loren said slowly, "I think we have proven the hypothesis."

"Wow," Peter said.

"Yeah," Andy said.

"I have to talk to Benson right away," Loren said. Should he call? No. In-person was more persuasive.

He left at once and walked very quickly over to Benson's office.

At Benson's office, he told Rose he needed to see

Benson at once.

She said to go in.

Benson was on the phone but with Loren's sudden entry he hung up.

"Loren, what's going on?" he asked.

"Wolfgang's threat is real," Loren said.

"What do you mean?"

Loren told Benson about the hypothesis and experiment that they had done.

The blood drained from Benson's face. "I've told the plant to start up," he said.

Loren was very angry. "How could you do that with Wolfgang's threat unresolved?"

"I decided that Reitz was bluffing. We are losing thousands, maybe millions, every day that plant is idle."

Loren was livid. "You greedy bastard, you may have caused a catastrophe."

Benson seldom took criticism well but this time he seemed to realize Loren was right.

"Did you send down someone from technology?" Loren asked.

"Of course."

"Who?" Loren asked.

"Len Bachman and Debbie Johnson," he said, grudgingly.

"Len and Debbie! My God! They're rookies. They've never been to a plant startup. I doubt if they even know about the Reitz situation."

"I told them about it, but I said it was a bluff. I thought it would be an easy startup and that it was time for them to gain some plant experience."

"You've got to call the control room and tell them

under no circumstances to add chemicals," Loren said. "Hopefully they are still water batching. I've got to get down there."

"Yes, yes, get down there," Benson said. "You can take the Lear. I'll call the airport."

Loren left hurriedly, drove as fast as he dared to the airport and the Lear Jet was waiting for him. He greeted the pilot and they took off. It was the first time he'd had flown in a company plane. He was very tense but he couldn't make the plane go any faster.

"What's wrong, sir?" the flight attendant asked.

Loren was well aware that catastrophic events can occur as a result of chemical manufacture, often due to human error or carelessness. "I'm trying to avert a catastrophe."

"Oh?" she asked. "Tell me about it." Maybe she was trying to calm him down.

"Fine," Loren said. "After World War II the chemical industry expanded a great deal. This led to exciting new products, such as drugs and plastics, but also to a proliferation of chemical accidents. Generally these were caused by human error or carelessness. One of the earliest serious incidents occurred at Seveso, Italy in 1976. A plant making trichlorophenol, an ingredient in the common herbicide 2,4,5T, let the temperature get too high in a distillation vessel. The resulting decomposition released a cloud of decomposition products that contained dioxin, a very toxic and possibly carcinogenic material. The cloud of material was widely dispersed and resulted in the contamination ten square miles of land. More than six-hundred people had to be evacuated and over two-thousand people were treated for possible poisoning." Citing the facts and figures was calming him a little.

He said, "An explosion at a fertilizer plant in Toulouse, France killed thirty people, injured over two-thousand and left more than eleven-thousand homes and public buildings without windows. Again, carelessness was a big factor in this incident. The chemical in question, ammonium nitrate, was stacked in a dump with minimal surveillance and security with extreme negligence."

In the meantime, the flight attendant starting looking more tense.

Loren said, "An even more serious accident occurred at Bhopal, India. During a night in 1984 a large tank of methyl isocyanate, an ingredient in insecticide manufacture, erupted. About twenty-five-hundred people died that night and sixteen-thousand died in subsequent years from effects of the chemical. A very large number of claims were made for injuries and losses. The most probable reason for this incident was claimed to be caused by a disgruntled employee who added several gallons of water to the tank on purpose. The chemical reacted violently with water with the evolution of heat. The heat caused the chemical to boil up over the safety valve, which led to the gas cloud that spread over the city. The Indian government ruled that, even if the disgruntled employee scenario was true, the plant should not have been engineered in such a way that the incident could have happened. The chemical company involved went through very difficult times as a result of this incident and eventually disappeared."

"Oh, dear," she said, gulping.

He continued, "The near catastrophe at Three Mile Island occurred because a small amount of water leaked into a high pressure instrument line causing the instruments to read incorrectly. A courageous operator took a chance that the reactor temperature reading was in error and turned the cooling water back on. This averted an explosion that could have led to the radiation exposure and possible death of forty-thousand people."

She sank down in one of the seats.

"One of the worst disasters occurred in Texas City, Texas in 1947. A French ship, Grand Camp, loaded with about a thousand tons of ammonium nitrate fertilizer blew up in the harbor. A fire had started in the cargo and the ship's captain refused to use water to put it out, thinking water would ruin the cargo. The hold was closed with the hope of smothering the fire. The resulting explosion devastated the town and killed many people. It was not known at that time that ammonium nitrate could detonate. This was the material that was used to destroy the Federal Building in Oklahoma City.

"There have been numerous other lesser incidents of this nature. These occurrences have caused numerous laws to be enacted to protect the public."

"Laws sound good," she said.

Loren was fully aware of the existence of these laws. Such laws made sense and he always insisted on their implementation when he was involved. "Yes. But they apparently can't protect against human stupidity or error."

"I, uh, better go check on the flight crew," the attendant said.

No one else talked to him the rest of the flight down to New Orleans.

Chapter 39

Loren rushed over to the Martox plant as soon as he landed.

Unfortunately, when he arrived at the control room, the supervisor, Alan Devers, said that they'd started a batch of Martox.

Loren quickly told him about the problem.

He was stunned and upset. "What? I thought everyone agreed the whole thing was a hoax. You were even here before and didn't find anything."

"We don't have time to argue," Loren said. "It's a light-catalyzed reaction. You have to evacuate the Martox plant area right away."

But Alan was hesitant. "I don't think I can do that without consulting with the plant manager."

Loren said, "I strongly insist. And you need to do it now. We can square things with the plant manager later. We should move to the administration building and plan strategy."

Alan finally agreed and implemented the evacuation notice over the plant loudspeakers. "Attention please," a robotic-sounding female voice announced. "Please evacuate the building. Proceed to the nearest exit immediately. This is not a drill. Attention please. Please evacuate the building. Proceed to the nearest exit immediately. This is not a drill."

It kept going on a loop.

People started filing out. Thank God.

Loren asked, "Where are Len Bachman and Debbie Johnson?"

Alan said, "Debbie called and said her car wouldn't start, so Len went to get her. Len told me to start without them."

Loren tried to stay calm. "One of them is supposed to be here any time chemicals are being used," he said. "It's standard startup procedure, damn it! I hope you have a nitrogen sweep on the reactor."

"Yes, of course," Alan said.

Barry Smith of Marchem St. Louis engineering joined Loren and Alan in the control room. He said, "What's up?"

Loren knew him; he might be helpful. Loren quickly filled him in.

Barry said, "I've never heard of such a situation."

"You have now," Loren said. He resisted the urge to give his disaster spiel again. They didn't have time now. "Let's move."

Loren, Alan and Barry drove up to the plant gate and told the guard to stop Debbie and Len and tell them to come immediately to the administration building. When the three men arrived at the administration building they went directly to the plant manager's office and walked in. The plant manager seemed startled and upset. He was a tall man with a full head of wavy brown and gray hair.

"This is the plant manager, Stuart Mason," Alan said. "Stuart this is Dr. Loren Sharp."

"Why is the evacuation notice running?" Stuart said. "What do you want? I'm very busy." He looked at Loren and said, "Who are you?" He spoke in a loud voice.

Loren had never met Stuart Mason before but he'd heard the man was an asshole. Looked like the rumors were true.

Loren and Alan sat down and Loren explained who he was and what the situation was. Barry, there being no more chairs, stood.

"You walk in here unannounced and tell me you have shut down my plant and give me some wild story about explosions and I'm supposed to go right along with you?" Stuart said.

Loren saw that he needed some convincing. "We're wasting time. Call Ted Benson in St. Louis and ask him. You know him don't you?"

"Yes, I know Ted. And I think I will call him." Stuart told his secretary to get Ted Benson in St. Louis. After a minute the call came and Stuart told Benson what he wanted.

Loren was fuming. It took all his self-control to remain seated. They needed to act.

"Oh? Oh really? I'll be damned. Thanks Ted," Stuart said as he hung up the phone.

"I guess it's true," Stuart said. "I guess I need to decide what needs to be done."

Soon the phone rang again and Stuart picked up. His jaw dropped. He said," Yes sir. Yes sir. Certainly sir. I will give him my complete cooperation."

He hung up and said, "That was Vincent Samuelson. He said that I should give you my ultimate cooperation."

Alan said, "Jesus, the CEO. This must be really important."

Barry was bouncing on his feet and looked like he was

ready to spring into action.

Loren stood up. "We're wasting time. I need a conference room, the maintenance supervisor and some coffee."

Stuart raised his hands. "Pick any conference room you want. I think they're all empty. Mary, call Geordi Mendez and tell him to get up to the admin building on the double. Also bring some coffee over to Alan and Dr. Sharp."

"Right away," said Mary, Stuart's secretary.

Loren said, "You're going to have to inform the local authorities. The surrounding neighborhoods must be evacuated. We should have done that already."

"I can't do that," Stuart said. "We've never had an emergency here. I don't want one on my record. What danger is there outside the plant area?"

Loren felt his face turning red. "We've found that the explosion is accompanied by a release of nitric oxide--which is toxic. Toxic! Samuelson told you to cooperate. Now do it."

Stuart did it.

Loren picked a conference room that would accommodate about seven people.

Unfortunately, Stuart joined them. Loren hoped he wouldn't be disruptive.

After coffee was poured Geordi Mendez came in. He was a handsome but slightly paunchy Latino.

After introductions were made Loren said, "We are sitting on a bomb and we have to neutralize it. Carefully."

"What can set it off?" said Stuart.

"Air, an increase in temperature, light," Loren said. "Any number of causes."

Geordi crossed himself. "Holy mother of God."

"Jesus," said Alan.

Len and Debbie arrived and took chairs at the table.

"Hi, Dr. Sharp," Len said. "What's up?" Len Bachman was young man who perpetually wore jeans and a tee-shirt. He had been at Marchem for a year and a half and had had a ponytail when he joined the company but that was now gone. His appearance suggested rugged good health and he was always pleasant maybe even obsequious.

"Hi," Debbie said. "Why's the evacuation notice running?"

"Where have you been?" Loren asked.

Len, glancing at the coffee on the conference table said, "Uh, we stopped for coffee."

"You guys are required to me here when chemicals are being used. Required!" He struggled to remain calm. "I'm not happy with you."

"Sorry," Debbie said. She hung her head.

"Yeah, sorry," Len said. "Coffee was my idea."

They appeared sufficiently chastised so Loren moved on and told them what the situation was. They seemed shocked.

"So Reitz's threat was not a hoax," Debbie said.

"No, it's all too real," Loren said. "What we have to do is to get that reaction to go under controlled conditions."

"How do we do that?" Len asked.

"We are going to have to pump the mixture slowly over to a vessel with cooling and light," Loren said. "That's why you are here, Geordi. Let's get the plant piping diagrams."

Alan left and came back quickly with a set of drawings.

"If it's so dangerous why don't we just let it go off?"

Debbie asked. "Property damage is better than loss of life."

"That would be the best course of action but there will be a toxic gas release if it goes off and there could be fatalities," Loren said. "Besides, it could go in the next minute or next year. We can't wait. We have to neutralize it."

"Shit," Debbie said.

"Is there a vessel which we can pipe up to the Martox reactor which has cooling and that we can install lights in?" Loren said.

"There is one in the rework area but it is about fifty feet away and it doesn't have temperature indication," Alan said.

"Anything else?" Loren asked.

Alan said, "Not that I can think of."

Geordi shook his head.

"It will have to do," Loren said. "Could we get lights in it?"

"There is a man-way," Geordi said. "I think it could be done. But it probably would have to be open to the atmosphere."

"I don't see any objections to that," Loren said. "We don't have volatiles."

"We have a supply of floodlights," said Alan.

"Barry, could you get a thermocouple installed in the reactor?" Loren asked.

"I think so," Barry said. "I would have to take a look."

"Good," Loren said. "We'll also need a volunteer pipe fitter."

"I'll do it," Geordi said. "I started out as a pipe fitter and can still do it."

"Great," Loren said. "Let's get going. Alan, see to

installing the lights. Geordi do the repiping. I will assist you." He paused to take a breath. "Len, you can help Alan."

"I'm not going down there," Len said. "I don't get hazard pay."

"I'll do it," Debbie said.

Loren was disgusted with Len. "Fine. Len, you can be in the control room. We need somebody there and it will be safe."

"How about the nitric oxide?" Len asked.

"The control room can be put on internal circulation so no gas can enter," Alan said.

"Debbie, you can help Alan do the lights," Loren said. "Let's go. We're wasting time."

Debbie said, "Loren, won't the pump head heat up when we start pumping out the reactor?"

"She's right," Barry said. "If a temperature increase could set it off, it could travel up the pipes and get to the reactor. We are going to have to cool the pump head."

"Good thinking, Debbie," Loren said. "You can handle icing down the pump. I can help Alan when Geordi doesn't need me. Barry, you set up the temperature indication in the new vessel. Let's go."

"We've got three more guys from engineering down here," Barry said. "Can they help?"

"I think we can do the job without them," Loren said. "We don't want to risk any more lives than necessary."

"Maybe Miss Johnson would rather not be involved," Barry said.

"To hell with that," Debbie just about shouted. "I can pull my weight."

"Okay, okay," Loren said. "Let's get going."

Stuart Mason, who had said almost nothing, left the

room. Apparently he didn't want to be involved.

The group climbed onto three golf carts and set out for the Martox facility.

Loren was very familiar with the Martox facility. The Martox manufacturing area was a four-story unit about fifty yards square with heavy steel mesh floors. The reaction vessels were generally mounted midway between floors. There were many auxiliaries spread around: pumps, safety equipment, controls, control boxes, instruments, solids handling equipment and others. In the center of the unit was a freight elevator that served all four floors. A raised stand, called a pipe chase, ran around the whole area that held a number of pipes and electrical wires.

Off to one side on the first floor was a concrete block building that served as the control room. Inside the control room was a wall of graphics showing the temperature and liquid level of each vessel. The plant ran twenty-four/seven with three shifts of eight hours. It was staffed with one supervisor, generally a chemical engineer, and four operators of varying experience.

Geordi got out at the maintenance building and loaded what he needed for the piping job and the floodlights into a truck and he and Barry joined them at the facility. Barry had gotten the thermocouple setup. There was an eerie quiet in the area that was disrupted by the sound of sirens from the town.

"Well, they've started the evacuation," Loren said. "Good."

Len jumped from the cart and ran into the control room and the rest of the group followed him.

Loren told Len, "Watch the temperature indicators and

radio the group if anything changes."

Each of them took a radio. Perhaps there would be enough time to run if the reaction got started. Doubtful, but maybe.

The ice machine was in a building next door to the control room so Debbie would have to fill several five gallon buckets with ice and take the facility elevator to the third floor to ice down the pump.

Geordi was unloading the pipe and taking it up to the third floor by the elevator.

Loren asked Debbie, "How'd you know about the pump head heating up?"

"I've had a chemical engineering course," she said emphatically as she headed for the ice machine.

Loren and Geordi went to the third floor and started the repiping job.

"Why in hell did they put the pump on the third floor?" Loren asked.

"They told me there wasn't room for maintenance on the lower floors," Geordi said.

"Not the best design," Loren said. "I suppose it saved money. Thank god they put in block valves."

"That's standard design," Geordi said.

Geordi had the first section of the original pipe off when Debbie showed up with the first two buckets of ice. The pump was mounted on a steel grating which would not hold the ice.

"What now?" she asked.

"There are some boards in the room with the ice machine," Geordi said. "Bring two along with the next load of ice."

Loren could hear Alan working with the man-way on

the second floor and went down to see how he was doing. Alan had the man-way cover off and was rigging a support for the floodlights out of aluminum rods and electrical cords.

"Bailing wire and bubble gum, huh?" Loren said.

"Just about, but it will work," Alan said.

Suddenly Debbie shouted from the elevator, "This thing isn't moving. Help!"

"Oh, mother of God," Alan said. "That elevator has been giving us trouble. This is a hell of a time for it to act up."

"What's wrong?" Loren asked.

"I don't know," Alan said. "Sometimes it just quits."

"We have to get her out," Loren said. "We need the ice and if that reactor goes off she's a goner."

The men ran to the elevator shaft and got the exterior doors open. The elevator was stopped between the second and third floors.

"What should I do?" Debbie called to them.

"What do you suggest?" Loren said to Alan. "You know the elevator system."

"There is an emergency door opening switch, but if the car starts moving while she's outside the doors she could be cut in half by the third floor," Alan said.

"Debbie, do you have the boards?" shouted Loren.

"Yes," she said.

Loren said, "Hit the emergency door-opening switch."

She found the switch, pushed it and the interior doors opened. There was about six feet from the elevator floor and the third floor.

Loren said, "Jam the boards between the doors."

She did. "What now?" She looked nervous.

Loren crouched down on the floor and reached down into the elevator car. He was sweating like it was a hundred degrees but was only seventy. "Grab my arms and I'll pull you out," he said. "Alan, hold my legs down."

She grabbed onto him and he pulled. It was good she wasn't a two hundred pound man. He was able to pull her out.

She was shaken but calmed down quickly. "Damn, that was pretty scary," she said. "I guess it's the stairs from now on."

"Looks like everything is under control." Geordi had appeared on the scene.

"Back to work," Loren said. "We're wasting time."

Alan got the lights installed and tested and went to help Geordi who had two ten foot sections of pipe installed.

Debbie arrived with a bucket of ice and two more boards. "Boy, those stairs are a bear."

The boards were installed and she began piling ice on the pump head. She went to get two more buckets of ice for reserve when the first ice melted.

When she got back, Loren told her to go to the control room.

"Is there something else I can do?" she asked. He was impressed.

"No. You've done enough," he said. "We'll make sure that pump head stays cold. You're quite a woman, Debbie."

"You're quite a man, Loren," she said, smiling.

He waved her off. She'd never called him by his first name until today. Perhaps it was another example of how adversity bonds people.

She went to the control room.

With Alan helping, the last sections of pipe were

rapidly connected but connecting to the light catalyzed reactor required a different fitting. Geordi had to return to the maintenance building to get the proper fitting but when he returned they finished the job. Loren told everyone to go to the control room.

Barry met them in the control room and said he had completed the thermocouple installation. "Let's see if this works."

Len was sitting sheepishly in front of the control board, and said, "There hasn't been any change. Anything I can do?"

"No, it's done," Loren said. "It'll work or not. Let's hope it does. Geordi, did you open the block valves?"

"Yes," he said. "It's ready to go."

"Alan, start the pump," Loren said.

Alan pushed a button and the indicator light glowed red. All eyes were on the temperature indicator in the light catalyzed reactor. Half a minute passed and the temperature started up. Alan turned on the reactor cooling. The temperature started back down.

"It works," Loren said. "Thank God."

Shouts of joy went up from everyone. Smiles and backslapping were liberally spread around.

Alan set the reactor to run at fifty degrees centigrade and the pump speed was set.

"We're not out of the woods, yet," Loren said. "I won't relax until the whole batch has reacted."

They all watched the control panel for half an hour and things seemed to be going well but then the lighted reactor temperature started dropping. About one third of the batch had been transferred.

"What's happening?" Len asked.

"The pump must have stopped pumping," Alan said.

"It must have gotten too cold," Loren said. "The fluid probably got too viscous."

"Shall I go up and remove the ice?" Debbie asked.

Loren shook his head. "We don't need to take any more risks. The ice will melt. Alan, stop the pump."

The tension in the group was palpable. How long should they wait? Was the pump damaged? They waited fifteen minutes and restarted the pump. The tension built as they watched the control board. Slowly the temperature in the reactor started up. The group cheered for the second time.

"I better get some more ice—but not too much--and go up there and make sure the pump doesn't get too hot," Debbie said.

"Let me do it," Alan said.

"It's my part of the project and I will do it," she said, forcefully.

"Okay, Debbie," Loren said. "You are our Wiglaf."

She made a questioning face. "What?"

He waved his hand. "Oh, never mind. Go!"

She left the control room with a radio. The temperature of the reactor held at sixty degrees. She called and said that most of the ice had melted and that she would add more as needed.

"God, that girl, ah woman, is probably up there with her hand on the pump head," Loren said. "She's a real hero. I take back everything I ever thought about her."

"She's certainly done her job," Geordi said.

Len looked down at the floor.

After another tense hour the Martox reactor was empty and more cheering erupted.

"Are you going to relax now, Dr. Sharp?" Alan asked.

"Please call me Loren. Relax or collapse." He grinned. Alan said he would finish up.

Loren told to Debbie they were finished and that they were going back to the admin building.

Loren shook hands with Alan and Geordi. "The people in management will certainly hear about how you guys performed."

"You did a helluva job yourself, Dr. Sharp, ah Loren, " Alan said.

Loren, Debbie, Barry and Len rode golf carts back to the administration building and were greeted in the lobby by Stuart Mason.

He said, "Did you save the batch? There are ten thousand dollars' worth of chemicals in that batch."

The chemists were struck dumb. They could not believe where Stuart Mason's priorities were.

About thirty seconds passed Loren said, "Yes. We saved the batch. And also the plant and maybe some lives."

"Yes, of course. I didn't mean that was not important," Stuart said. "You all did a good job. I'll tell management so."

"That's very good of you," Loren said, but he didn't mean it. "Let's go into the conference room for a little debriefing."

First Loren called Ted Benson, told him everything was under control and that he would fill him in when he got back to St. Louis.

There was a little debriefing, very little. It seemed that not much more could be said.

Stuart Mason left and Loren suggested they all go out

for a really good dinner.

"A celebration," Loren said. "Benson will pay."

"That sounds good. Let's ask Alan, Geordi and Barry," Debbie said. "But not Mason." She got on the phone.

Geordi had to go to his daughter's dance recital.

Alan said he would be happy to accompany them, and even said he would drive. He went to get his car.

Barry bowed out, saying that there was too much to do putting the plant back in shape. Hard working guys these engineers.

Alan pulled up to the administration building and everybody piled in.

It was decided that they would go to the French Quarter and Loren, Debbie and Len would stay overnight, since it was on Benson's dime. Alan said his wife was expecting him home after dinner.

The four of them found a place to park after driving around for fifteen minutes and went to the Royal Sonesta. Miraculously, there were some cancellations and they got rooms for the night.

They all walked across the street to Galatoire's, waited in line for half an hour and got a table. The meal was fabulous. Loren had Oysters Florentine, Caesar Salad, steak filet with Béarnaise and cheesecake. The wine was chateau gloria, a very good wine, the name of which appealed to him. They also had some pinot grigio. The others dined very well as well.

Debbie loved her trout.

The conversation was about the day's activities and they were very happy with themselves although Len didn't say much. When they finished their coffee, Alan thanked the others for including him and said he had to leave. After struggling out of their chairs they went over to the hotel.

Loren, still keyed up, suggested a nightcap.

Len said he was tired so he went up to his room. Perhaps he was tired, although it was only eight o'clock. Maybe he thought Loren was going to hit on Debbie and he didn't want to make him any madder at him than he already was. Loren could make things tough on him when they got back to St. Louis.

Loren and Debbie said goodnight to Len and went into the bar. Loren ordered a Metaxa and Debbie a stinger. After complimenting her again on her performance at the plant, he asked her how she got Benson to send her on a startup so early in her career.

"I asked to go. I'm an ambitious girl. I figured it would help my career," she said.

"Yeah? But it's unusual to send someone with so little plant experience."

"Oh well, old Teddy thinks if he's nice to me I'll go to bed with him. Forget that. I don't even like the guy," she said.

He ordered two more drinks. This was getting interesting. "Ted Benson has been hitting on you? I'm surprised. He doesn't seem the type."

"Did I say too much," she said. "He came on pretty strong."

"Tell me more."

"No," she said. "I've probably said too much already."

"At least Ted faced up to our problem. He even called Samuelson."

They finished their drinks in silence, got up to go to their rooms and Debbie said, "Do you want to come up to my room?"

Loren was a little tempted; Debbie was a very appealing woman. But he loved Gloria. He said, "No. I don't think that would be a very good idea."

The next morning they checked out of the hotel and got a taxi. Loren had made a plane reservation for St. Louis and was going to the airport and Len and Debbie were going back to the apartment house where they each had rooms for the duration of the startup.

Loren had taken a shower but still had on the clothes he had on when he left St. Louis. He had a two-day beard. He sat with the driver and Debbie and Len were in back.

"I suppose I'll be taken off the startup," Len said.

Loren turned and smiled at Len." I don't think that will be necessary. Yesterday was a pretty unusual situation. Just do your job the rest of the way. I won't say anything."

Len thanked Loren. The cab dropped Debbie and Len off and Loren continued to the airport. The commercial flight was uneventful

Back in St. Louis, Loren took a taxi to the Marchem campus and went directly to Benson's office. He walked right in.

Benson smiled broadly at Loren and said, "I just got off the phone with Stu Mason. He told me how he organized a task force, formulated a plan and got the situation under control."

"What?" Loren asked. "Did he say he was down at the unit?"

"He implied he was," Benson said. "Didn't really say he was."

"He never left the administration building," Loren said. "His contribution to correcting the situation was zero or less."

"I figured as much," Benson said. "I know Mason pretty well."

Loren told Benson the details of getting the situation at the plant under control and he was very complimentary. "I'm glad no one got hurt. You people really did a job. Saved the company millions. I'm impressed."

The phone rang and Benson picked up.

"Yes, Mr. Samuelson, er, Vincent. All's well. Yes, he's right here. Sure thing."

Benson handed the phone to Loren.

"Dr. Sharp?" Samuelson said."

"Yes, sir."

"I was very impressed with how you handled everything. Please let me take you out to lunch today to thank you."

"Yes. Thank you," Loren said. "Thank you. I would like that." They worked out the logistics.

"Fine," Loren said and handed the phone back to Benson.

To Benson he said, "He invited me to lunch. I've never even met the man."

"Great," Benson said. "I guess it takes something like this situation to get technology appreciated."

"I guess," Loren said.

The lunch with Samuelson was pleasant enough but he asked some probing, barely disguised questions about guilt. He obviously wanted to know who was responsible for the Reitz situation. Loren tried to convince him that no one was to blame, that no one could have foreseen the situation.

Loren brought up the subject of global warming and suggested that Marchem look into doing research on solar energy panels.

Samuelson thanked him for the suggestion and said he would think about it. Loren wasn't holding his breath.

After the lunch with Samuelson, Loren went to his lab and wanted to do some research but everyone in the place kept coming in and asking him about the trip and what happened at the plant.

Loren tried to play it down and not give too many details. Joe Ferguson especially wanted to know details but Loren put him off. He eventually got tired of being interrogated so he went home early.

The next day Ted Benson was transferred to planning. The head of manufacturing--who had absolutely nothing to do with the Reitz situation--was canned outright. There had to be scapegoats, guilty or not.

Chapter 40

Doug didn't like loose ends. Tom Jerrett was a loose end. He figured that the case against Kane was strong enough but his curiosity got the best of him. He really wanted to know what went on at Kane's ranch and it wouldn't hurt to solidify the murder charge against Kane. Warren Wilson, Kane's other employee, said he went to a town near St. Louis with ville in its name. There were several towns on the east side with ville in their name but Belleville seemed to be the best bet. He looked in the Belleville phone directory.

There were six Jerretts. He started calling. The first three never heard of Tom Jerrett. The fourth was answered by someone who sounded like a young girl.

Doug started the same way, he had before. "I'm looking for Tom Jerrett.

"Oh, Uncle Tommy doesn't live here," she said.

"Where does he live?"

"Who is this? I'm not supposed to speak to strangers." She hung up. Well, it was a place to start.

His first stop was Belleville police headquarters where he got the cooperation of the department and a uniformed officer to help him. He thought the presence of a uniformed officer would make the people more cooperative. The officer's name was Jim Jones and he was a very handsome African American. He told Doug that his colleagues often referred to him as Gentleman Jim. Doug filled Jim in on the facts of the case and they left for the house where the girl on the phone lived.

The house was a modest one in a working class area. Doug rang the bell and after a few minutes a disheveled but somewhat attractive blonde woman opened the door. Her surprise was evident when she saw Jim. "What's this? The police, what do you want?"

"We are looking for Tom Jerrett. Do you know him?" Doug asked.

"What's he done?" the woman asked.

"We just want to question him about something that happened in Colorado," Doug said.

"I don't think he wants me to tell anybody where he is," she said. "He likes his privacy."

The Colorado comment didn't faze her so it looked like it was the right Tom Jerrett. That was something. Doug decided to apply some pressure, "If you know his whereabouts and don't tell us, you are breaking the law."

That comment hit home. "I don't want any trouble," she said. "I'm a single mother and can't afford any trouble."

"Then you better tell us where he is," Jim said.

She gave them the address.

The white duplex was in a rundown part of town. Tom Jerrett supposedly lived in the right side unit.

Doug and Jim went to the door and rang the bell.

Tom came to the door after three rings, took one look and tried to slam the door shut. Jim was too fast for him and he was able to block the door open.

Tom took off toward the back but Jim tackled him before he crossed the living room.

"Hey," Tom said. "Get offa me."

"Wow," Doug said, shaking his head. "That was about as fast as I have ever seen a man move. Where'd you learn those moves?"

"I used to play corner for Illinois," Jim said. "We should read him his rights."

Before Doug could reply, Tom was heard from. "What's this all about? I haven't done anything wrong." Then Tom seemed to suddenly remember Doug. "I know you. You were out there in Colorado. I didn't do nuthin'. Kane made me do stuff. I want a lawyer."

Doug held up his hand." You don't need a lawyer. You haven't been accused of anything."

"Well, why are you here?" Tom said.

"Calm down, Tom," Doug said. "We want you to tell us what went on at Kane's ranch. You may have to testify against Kane."

"I don't know. Mr. Kane would be mad. He would kill me."

"Not if he was in jail," Doug said.

"Well, I have a lot to tell," Tom said. "You're sure he couldn't hurt me?"

"Kane will go to jail for the rest of his life if you testify," Doug said. "He can't possibly hurt you."

"What about his men? They could come after me."

"We hope to arrest them and we can protect you," Doug said.

"Okay, I guess I'll have to trust you," Tom said.

"Tom, we want you to come with us down to police headquarters," Doug said.

"Why can't you interview me here?" Tom asked.

"We will have recording equipment downtown and it's more comfortable," Doug said. "We'll drive you."

"Okay."

Jim let Tom up and read him his rights.

The three men piled into Doug's car. Doug drove with Jim in front and Tom, protesting his innocence, in back.

At Belleville police headquarters they found an empty interview room that had a table with a green plastic top and four straight back chairs with no cushions. Doug borrowed a recorder on the way in. He switched the recorder on.

"Tom, this interview is going to be recorded," Doug said.

"Okay by me."

Jim was observing.

"Five bodies were found in drums in the waste pit at Kane's ranch, three men and two women," Doug said. "They have been identified as Mr. And Mrs. Sidney Ableson and three employees of Kane's. What can you tell us about that?"

"Are you sure that Kane can't come after me?" Tom asked. From what Doug remembered of him, Tom was a lot smarter than he was acting. It was probably an act to try to gain sympathy.

"Your testimony will help put him away for the rest of his life," Doug said. What about the bodies?"

"I knew Kane from before he went to Colorado," Tom said. "He used to play golf near Belleville and I caddied for him. He invited me to go with him to Colorado. I was there at the ranch from the start. Ableson came out about a month after me and Kane. I think Kane invited him. "

"Ableson was present for the initial digging of the pit

and he asked Kane if he could invite his wife out. Kane asked if he could trust her and Ableson said sure. Mrs. Ableson came out about a week later with enough baggage to stay a long time." Doug loved it when criminals actually talked.

"After a couple of weeks she found out what was going on at the waste pit and she was upset. She told Kane it was wrong and if he didn't close the pit she would report the pit to the authorities. She kept bugging Kane and I guess he killed her. I wasn't present when he killed her but he told me to get a fiber-pack from the barn and I helped him put the body in it. I put the fiber-pack in the pit. He told me if I ever told anyone about it he would kill me. Since I was a virtual prisoner at the ranch I had to go along."

"What about Sidney?" said Doug.

"When he heard about it, he was, as you might expect, very upset. Again I wasn't present at the shooting but I did the same thing with a fiber pack. Kane warned me again."

"You and Kane put Ableson's body into the pit, right?"

"Yeah," Tom said.

"What about the other three bodies?" Doug asked.

"The girl was Kane's housekeeper and I presume his mistress. One day a man and the girl drove into the ranch. Kane greeted them like he knew they were coming. Kane talked to the man and the man left the girl and drove off. The girl was very pretty. I asked Kane about her and he admitted she was illegal and that he bought her. I decided right then she was something more than a housekeeper. One of the men whose body was in the pit was a hand on the ranch. He was a young guy who provided security and was kind of a gofer and chauffeur for Kane. He was good with guns and I was surprised when Kane called me and told me to bring over a fiber pack." All these guys were going to prison for a long, long time.

"There were two more bodies and a lot of blood. Kane told me that this is what happens to people who cross him. Apparently they had some kind of relationship going that Kane didn't like. He scared the hell out of me. I decided he was not quite sane. Shortly after that he hired Wilson."

"Have you ever heard the name Wolfgang Reitz?" Doug asked.

"No, I would remember that," Tom said. "It's a rather unique name."

"How about Shapiro?"

"Oh sure, he was Kane's lawyer. He was at the ranch several times. He and Kane did a lot of business."

"So Shapiro knew about the waste pit?" Doug asked.

"I would think so but I don't know for sure."

"Well, Tom, we are going to send you on a nice vacation to Colorado," Doug said.

Doug phoned Delany and told him Tom was coming.

Doug had cleared a lot of cases in the last few weeks--but not the Reitz case. It was frustrating. He'd been over the case file backwards and forwards. It was a big file. A lot of people had been interviewed.

He and Loren seemed to make a good team. Maybe he could help him come up with something. He called him. "Loren, I think we should go back out to Reitz's laboratory. Maybe we missed something."

"All right if you think it would help. When do you want to go?"

"How about tomorrow afternoon?"

"Fine."

"I'll pick you up about one o'clock."

"See you then."

The next day the two men drove out to Reitz's lab. The yellow tape had been removed and a new lock was on the door.

"I guess we'll have to get the key from Mrs. Reitz," Doug said.

They went to the back door and knocked. After a long pause, Mrs. Reitz opened the door. "Yah, what is it?"

"Sorry again for your loss," Loren said.

"Yeah. We would like to get into the lab," said Doug.

"I haf had enough of you people poking around here," she said. "I'm sick of your questions. It's about time you leaf me alone." She was as unpleasant as he remembered.

"We won't be long," Doug said. "This may be the last time."

"I suppose I haf to let you in." She got the key and handed it to Loren. "Here. Don't stay long and don't touch anything. The equipment in there is expensive. I'm selling it."

"Fine, fine, we won't be long," Doug said.

Loren and Doug went into the lab. The place had been cleaned and the chalk outline of Reitz's body had been scrubbed away. Otherwise it looked the same.

"Mrs. Reitz shouldn't have passed the police line," Doug said.

"No. I suppose not," Loren said. "You tell her. She's not a very pleasant lady. Where do we start?"

"Why don't you imagine you are doing a cyanide experiment and go through the motions? See if you can find any inconsistencies. I'm going to go through Reitz's papers and books."

Loren looked around. "I can't find any lab coats. I understand the body didn't have a lab coat on. We talked about that before. It's a major inconsistency. Wolfgang always wore a lab coat in the lab."

"Huh," Doug said. "I'm getting déjà vu."

Loren looked around some more. "There is no butyl nitrite. We talked about that last time."

"Yes, I remember. The antidote."

"Wolfgang always had some present when he worked with cyanide," Loren said.

"We can check the pictures of the crime scene. And see if there is an ampoule on the bench top," Doug said.

Loren began examining the two fume hoods in the lab.

Doug was absorbed in one of the books. He waved the book at Loren. "Here's something."

Loren came over and looked at the book. It appeared to be the German equivalent of a college yearbook.

Doug pointed to a picture of a young woman. The text said: *Ilse Mueller, Doktor of Philosophie, Organische Chemie. Thesis title: "Reaction of Hydrogen Cyanide with some Unsaturated Ketones."*

"Yes," Loren said. "And an expert on cyanide. Is Wolfgang in the book? Maybe they were classmates."

Doug turned a few pages. "Here he is. They must have met as students. Do you suppose she's involved in the death of her husband?"

Loren tugged his earlobe. "I suppose it's possible. She apparently had the knowledge and opportunity. But what would be the motive?"

"Who knows?" Doug said. "Husbands and wives often don't get along. Usually, the spouse is the number one suspect in murder. In this case, we didn't think she had the chemical expertise. I think we should question her again."

"Yes, I think we better." Loren pointed to a box on the desk. "What's that red light?"

Doug stared. "Looks like an intercom. Do you suppose she's listening?"

There was a noise at the door like a lock closing.

Doug ran to the door. He tried opening it. It wouldn't open. He shook it. "Looks like we're locked in."

"I don't like this," Loren said.

The heating system began to blow air into the lab even though the temperature seemed just right.

"Some people can't smell cyanide," Loren said.

"We don't have time for one of your lectures, Loren," Doug said.

"Listen! I tested myself once and found I can smell one part per million, well below the lethal dose. I smell it now."

"What?"

"Cyanide! Doug, jump up into the hood!" Loren yelled, and pointed at one of the hoods.

Loren turned on hood, opened the hood door and grabbed a piece of clear plastic tubing off the bench top.

Doug was hesitating at the front of the hood.

Loren quickly opened the hood doors and pushed Doug. "Get in! Get in. Hurry up!"

Doug jumped up into the hood and Loren quickly followed, shutting the hood doors behind them.

Both men had room to sit down with their legs under them. It was dark inside. Doug was scared in a way he'd never been when dodging bullets.

"It's a full size hood," Loren said. "It has attachments for tubing that can deliver nitrogen, air or natural gas." He took out his pocket knife and cut the tubing in half. "Thank God Ann gave me the knife for Father's Day a year ago. I only carry it as a reminder of her and seldom use it."

"What are you talking about?" Doug asked. What are you doing?"

Loren gave him half of the tubing. He pointed to an orange banded air spigot. "Attach the tubing there and stick the other end up your nose. Close your mouth tightly and hold your other nostril shut. Regulate the gas flow so you can breathe easily."

Doug did as he was told and Loren followed suit.

Doug whispered. "How long?" He was sweating profusely

Loren shook his head and put a finger to his lips.

Loren began to squirm around like he had a leg cramp.

Doug was scared. He didn't know what was going to happen.

Loren looked at his watch.

Doug looked at his watch. Five minutes had gone by. A strange thought entered his mind. How long did the Nazis take to exhaust the gas? Another five minutes passed. The men were becoming very uncomfortable but they were still alive. He remembered about cyanide poisoning that if you are alive you are okay because it is a very fast acting poison. Five more minutes passed.

Doug heard the furnace fan start up.

"Ilse must be trying to exhaust the gas," Loren whispered.

Five more minutes passed and the rear door of the lab opened.

Doug peeked through the hood opening.

Ilse Reitz entered the lab and looked around the

quizzically. She didn't see anyone. She took a few steps into the lab. Bitch!

Doug came out of the hood like a rocket. Before she could gather her wits, he had her pinned to the floor.

"Ow! Stop!" she yelled, becoming more and more upset.

"Loren give me that tubing," he said.

Loren stumbled out of the hood and could hardly stand but he handed Doug a piece of tubing.

Doug pulled her arms behind her back and tied the tubing securely around her wrists.

She was hysterical. "He wouldn't let me work! He said he would beat me if I tried to get a job. Most of his ideas were really mine. He was very cruel to me. I hated him!"

Loren was shaking his head.

"Well, there's a motive," Doug said. "Why did you try to kill us? We hadn't done anything to you."

Ilse began to cry. "You were going to arrest me. I don't want to go to jail."

Doug made a call and a patrol car came out and took her away, CSI was on its way.

"I feel kind of sorry for her," Loren said.

Doug shook his head. "I don't. She's a murderer."

Doug and Loren went back to the shed that housed the lab's heating unit. On the heat duct was a fitting for the injection of gas. On the floor was a small steel cylinder used for gas transfer.

Loren pointed at the cylinder by the valve. "I bet we'll find her fingerprints on this."

"I wouldn't be surprised," said Doug.

They went to wait for CSI. "Thanks for saving me, Loren," Doug said. "How'd you know all that stuff?"

"Chemistry." He smiled. "You know all this really puts things in perspective."

"Somebody trying to kill us again?"

Loren nodded.

"I totally agree," Doug said. He wanted to talk to Mona. He wanted to hug Mona. He wanted to do other things with Mona...

A search of the house yielded a box of butyl nitrite ampoules tucked away in a drawer.

"I guess she wanted to make sure Wolfgang couldn't give himself the antidote," Loren said.

"Funny she didn't just throw them away," Doug said.

"I guess she's a saver," said Loren.

The drive back to the Marchem lab was pleasant. The men were quite pleased with their day's work. When they arrived back at the lab both men got out of the car.

Loren waved a hand at Doug. "So long pal. I think I'm off to ask a lady to marry me."

Doug grinned. Great minds thought alike. "Really?" He waved back. "I think I'll do the same."

"Come here." He gave Loren a hug.

Loren seemed a little embarrassed, but he hugged him back. Then he said, "Later, we should have a dinner party..."

Doug laughed and, after a moment, Loren laughed, too.

Epilogue

The judge told Earl Kane that he was the most despicable, deranged defendant whose trial he had ever presided over. Kane had been charged with five counts of first-degree murder plus one count of illegal dumping of toxic chemicals. He was convicted on all counts. The testimony of Tom Jerrett, Warren Wilson and Alfred Novack were big factors in his conviction. They were given immunity. It took two years to completely empty and fill in his waste pit. Kane's maid was given a job as a maid in a Denver hotel. The police were attempting to contact her parents. The valuable coins in Wilson's possession were confiscated and, along with another hoard found in Kane's ranch house, partially paid for the cleanup.

Charles Shapiro, Kane's lawyer, was convicted of selling counterfeit documents, was sentenced to five years in prison and disbarred. His partner turned out to be fictitious. Shapiro thought that a fake partner could come in handy and added class.

Sheriff Swieki was forced to retire. Buzzy B. couldn't be charged with anything since Bill's actions were voluntary and no drug manufacture was actually done.

Joe Parsons, who attacked Gloria, was charged with attempted rape and sentenced to five years in prison. He had to register as a sex offender.

The men at Aztec Printing testified that Fritz took the SUV the day that Catalina Perez was killed. Dan Gallagher and Fritz Mueller were convicted of conspiracy to murder and each was sentenced to twenty years in prison without the possibility of parole. Bruno Gomez was extradited back to Mexico City where he was promptly incarcerated in a maximum security prison.

The murder of Carlos Valdez was never officially solved. Although it was probable that Mueller was involved and under Gallagher's orders, the prosecutor decided there was not enough evidence. Roberto Perez was fired from Marchem because of his association with Aztec Printing.

In a separate trial, Gallagher was convicted of first-degree murder of his wife. For this crime, he was sentenced to life in prison. Josh Mitchell and several of Mary Mitchell's friends testified. On a hunch, Doug sent a picture of Gallagher and his fingerprints to the Texas State Police. After a week's delay they replied that the man was actually a man named Stanley Toliver who was wanted in Texas for swindling several wealthy widows, and some not so wealthy, out of large sums of money. He wasn't even Irish. Doug knew it! Police Captain O'Brien was reprimanded for shoddy police work in the Mary Gallagher case.

A public defender represented Ilse Reitz. No one else would take the job. A plea bargain was arranged: Second degree murder. Ilse was sentenced to twenty years and eventually became the prison librarian.

Charles "Charlie Chan" Wong had to close his private detective business because it became widely known that he was less than honest. Wong eventually lost his license. When last heard of, he was running a Chinese restaurant in Hawaii.

Captain Delany eventually became Chief of Police mostly because of his handling of the Kane case. Vern Newton re-upped and was sent to Iraq. The ranch was taken over by the state and used as an experimental farm run by the University. The farm studied bovine diseases and made some progress. Thus, some good came out of a bad situation.

Loren married Gloria and they had many happy years together. Loren stayed at Marchem the rest of his career and was sorely missed when he finally retired. Gloria had a successful law career.

Doug moved to Colorado and remarried Mona. The second time was the charm for them. He started his own private investigation firm; it was very lucrative. Mona's art became even more famous.

The two couples became good friends and often spent skiing vacations together in Colorado and canoeing trips in Missouri.

Ann and George got married. They were very happy. George took a job with the St. Louis police and eventually made captain. Ann worked at Boeing for several years. She had a big input in the design of several airplanes and enjoyed it immensely. She and George had two children: one boy and one girl.

Bill straightened out and, after some speed bumps, graduated from law school. He married a bridesmaid he met at Ann's wedding and, eventually, was appointed to a judgeship. Gloria and Doug helped him along the way.

Mavis Gage was very pleased to have her friend's murderers brought to justice. When she passed away she left her considerable fortune to Doug--not that he needed it. He gave most of it to charity.

Sergeant. Bigelow was promoted to lieutenant and for a while he was George Vosquez's boss. Richard "Andy" Anderson finally got his promotion. Ted Benson made a name for himself in Marchem planning. Debbie Johnson finally had enough of harassment and lack of opportunities and quit Marchem. She became a travel agent and married a rich client. Barry Smith was promoted to Senior Engineer and retired early from Marchem.

Many dinner parties were enjoyed by all.

Made in the USA
Columbia, SC
31 July 2021

42603543R00202